Not Very Lucky

By

Alan Craig

This is a work of fiction. Any references to real people, living or dead, real events, businesses, organisations, and localities are intended only to give the fiction a sense of reality and authenticity. All names, characters, places, and incidents are either the product of the author's imagination or are used fictitiously, and their resemblance, if any, to real life counterparts is entirely coincidental.

Published by Alan Craig

Copyright Alan Craig 2020

ISBN 979-8-6416-3334-3

Chapter 1

'Are you really sure you want to do this?' he said, resting his left hand on the inside of her bare thigh. 'You can change your mind if you want, you know.'

'Of course, I don't want to change my mind, Darius.' and she placed her warm hand on top of his. She glanced out of the open car window at the moonlight reflecting off the inky water of the flooded Mossbank Quarry. 'But you could have chosen a more romantic spot,' and she punched him playfully on the leg.

It was ten o'clock on a warm July night when Darius had driven them down the farm track. He had parked his shiny white Audi A3 facing the edge of the old quarry, and conscious of the long drop down to the water's surface, he had double checked the handbrake was on before switching off the engine. 'But we always come here before I drop you off at your place when your flatmate's home.' he complained. Leaning towards her, Darius lifted his left arm up and over her head, pulling her closer. 'Besides, I wanted to tell you about the good news I got today.'

She looked up at him sharply, her temper rising just enough to make her cheeks colour. 'What good news? I can't believe you've waited till now to tell me. This better be good, Darius.'

He caught the tone in her voice and answered quickly, 'The solicitor called. We can get the keys to the new house on Monday next week. The builder has just a few bits to finish off, probably by tomorrow.

So in just a few days we'll own our first home together.'

'Darius, that's brilliant! Why didn't you tell me earlier? We could have gone around that way to see how it looks.'

'But you only saw it two days ago, remember. If you go every day then you'll never see any difference. Wait till Monday, it'll look great then, and we can picture where all the furniture is going to be.' He wrapped both arms around her and leaned down to kiss her.

Pushing him off, she looked up at him and smiled, 'So, I've got till Monday to change my mind? Then we'll own a house. I suppose it'll be too late then to cancel the wedding. I can't believe it's all fallen into place so well. Monday, the new house. Next month, the wedding, then our honeymoon to see your family in Egypt, and the pyramids and stuff. As long as there's a beach!' she laughed.

'What do you mean, 'the pyramids and stuff', that's part of my heritage, a wonder of the world, one of man's greatest architectural feats.'

'Shut up, you sound like an analyst! I said as long as there is a beach, it'll be fine.'

'Of course there's a beach, what do you think all that sandy stuff is beside the pyramids? No donkeys though, only camel rides. And remember, I *am* an analyst, I know stuff like that.' and they both laughed this time.

The night was still warm as they sat in the car looking out over the rugged slopes of the old slate quarry, hugging and kissing. Darius was hoping for more than just a cuddle, but she was having none of it. 'It's getting late and we've got work in the morning. It's time I was getting home,' and she shrugged her way out of his embrace, sitting up in the passenger seat.

'Just a few more minutes,' and Darius pulled her towards him again. She gave in and lay down across the centre console, looking up as he kissed her again.

'Heather, get the fuck out of that car! I've told you before, you're not seeing that foreign prick anymore. Get out now.'

Darius and Heather sat bolt upright, the suddenness of the loud angry voice had them both looking around to see who had shouted, and from where. But Heather knew who it was, confirmed a moment later as her brother Adam jumped into the back seat behind the startled Darius.

'I told you Heather, he's not one of us. I told you not to see him again. Clearly you haven't been listening. Well now I'm going to make sure he doesn't see you again!'

'What's going on Adam? Leave him alone, we're getting married, and there's nothing you can do to change that.'

'Oh really, little sis. Well we'll see about that in a minute. Just get out of the fucking car.'

Darius had only seen Adam Watson a few times, each time he had been high, or drunk, or both. He wasn't really worried about him, he could handle himself, but he was at a disadvantage sitting behind the steering wheel. He just wanted to protect Heather and get her home safely.

'Come on Adam, you know we're getting married soon. Just get out of the car and we can talk about this.' Darius was trying to diffuse the situation, trying to avoid a confrontation, trying to avoid having to break Adam's arm, or nose, or worse. He knew he could handle him, he just had to get some room to work with.

'Fuck you, mate. Think because your Mum and Dad have money, buy you a fancy car, send you to a posh school, that you're good enough for my wee sister. Well think again, you pyramid fucker, fucking sand dancer shitebag. No way are you laying your greasy paws on my sister again. I'm going to slice your moombar, cut off your shagging kebab, so no woman will ever want you again. Got it?' and Watson pulled a knife and a piece of rope from his pocket. He slung the rope around the seat in front of him, pulling Darius' neck tight against the head restraint of the driver's seat then held the knife to his throat.

'Come on, Adam, leave him alone.' shrieked Heather, 'Just get out and leave him alone.'

But Heather's pleas went unheeded as one of Adam's friends pulled open the passenger door and dragged her from the car. Darius could only watch as she was pushed across the open ground and bundled into the rear of another car parked nearby. He struggled to free the rope from around his neck, but Watson held the knife to his throat and Darius found himself unable to get free. He was beginning to feel light-headed and dizzy, and his vision was blurred, but he tried to fight his way out of the stranglehold. He turned the key in the ignition, starting the engine, thinking he could jerk the car forward, or reverse and brake sharply to shake off his attacker, but Watson just tightened his grip on the rope.

Another man leaned in the open front door of the Audi and grinned at Watson in the back. 'I take it he's not been listening. Want me to torch him then?'

'Yeah, light him up!'

As Watson held tight to the rope, he made another loop around Darius' chest, tying a knot in the rope at the back, securing Darius to the front seat. The other man pulled a can of lighter fuel from inside his sweatshirt, opened the top and poured the fluid over Darius, over the front car seats and liberally soaked his feet and legs.

'Ready?'

Watson stepped from the car, closed the door then banged on the roof. 'Ready.'

With a box of matches already in his hand, the other man lit one, touched it to the others still in the box, and casually tossed it into the front passenger footwell, where Darius would be unable to reach it. Stepping back, he closed the door, and walked away towards the rear of the car, banging the car roof again as he went. 'Done.'

Watson changed places with the man in the other car and shoved him over towards the rear of the Audi. 'Right you two, push. Come on, get it over the edge.'

The interior of the car was well alight by now, and screams were flying out of the open windows. Watson watched from the front seat of his own car as the other two men pushed on the boot lid of the car, heaving to overcome the parking brake. Gradually the car began to roll towards the edge of the quarry, towards the drop into the water below, but it was going too slowly. They would never get it over the edge before the fuel tank went up.

Watson saw the problem right away and waved wildly to the two men pushing on the boot lid of the Audi. With a short blast on the horn, he started the car, an old Vauxhall Astra, and drove it slowly towards the rear of the Audi as the two men moved aside. With a grinding crash the Audi, with flames shooting from the windows, was slowly shunted towards the sharp edge, until gravity took over and it fell like a white fireball, plunging the thirty feet towards the wet blackness. The only light now was from the moon, and they could see the car nosedive into the water, raising a splash almost back up to the edge where Watson now stood watching. He watched and waited for the car to disappear under the water, but it came to rest with a few feet of the rear end still clear of the surface.

'That'll have to do. Fucker's not coming out of there any time soon.'

The Astra drove out of the quarry site and back onto the farm track leading out to the main road. Heather had been pushed down onto the floor in front of the rear seats, Watson now sat in front beside the driver, and the other man sat in the back with his feet pressing down on Heather, keeping her out of sight. She had seen Darius' car being set alight, and then being pushed over the edge into the flooded quarry, but she had no idea what had happened to Darius himself. She could only believe that he was still in the car, burnt to death, or drowned. She wailed and screamed at the men in the car, but only got a kick in the ribs as comfort. She knew her brother was evil, and unpredictable when he was using drugs, but never imagined he could kill anyone. Now he had killed her fiancé, and God only knew what was going to happen to her.

The car drew up outside a terraced block on Parkside Crescent, a wholly forgettable street in a housing estate in Cowdenbeath, and the men got out. Heather was pulled to her feet from the car floor, bundled in the door of an end terraced house in the block, then up a flight of stairs. She knew exactly where she was, even though she had not been there for many years. It was her parents' house, both dead now, and the place where Adam lived, along with all his junkie friends and hangers on. She was pushed roughly into the main bedroom at the top of the stairs, where she came face to face with her flatmate Rachel.

Rachel was sitting on the double bed, hands tied behind her back, legs tied at the ankles, a scarf knotted in her mouth then tied behind her neck, and a fierce look on her face. 'Rachel, oh Rachel, what have they done to you?' and Heather ran to her side, sat on the bed, and put her arms around her best friend.

'Nothing's happened to her, not yet anyway.' said Adam Watson, following through the door behind Heather. 'But we might keep her here a while, you know, just to have a bit of fun with her. Nice looking girl like Rachel, well, we don't get many girls like her coming round for a visit, do we lads?'

The other two men had crowded into the bedroom and laughed, 'Not like her anyway, nice for a change.'

'That's enough for now, lads. Heather, here's how this is going to work.' began Watson. 'I told you and told you that 'gyppo was not for you. Why would you take up with some Egyptian when there's plenty of local boys here? But you wouldn't listen. I promised Mum and Dad I would look out for you, and this is why we can't have you marrying some fucking foreigner.'

Heather burst into tears again and began screaming at the top of her voice. 'You killed him. You set him on fire. You're evil, sick, a murderer. I don't want you to come near me, I just want to go home. I have to tell Darius' parents.'

'Keep the noise down, Heather. Just shut up. We've got neighbours here, and if you keep shouting off, then we'll have the Police round next. You wouldn't want that now, would you?'

'That's exactly what we need,' shouted Heather, 'Help! Help! call the Police. Anyone! Call the Police.'

Watson leaned over her and slapped her hard. 'Shut up and listen to me for a minute. If you carry on like that, then Rachel here is going to suffer.'

'You wouldn't dare touch her. She's got nothing to do with this. Let her go and call the Police. You're going to prison for this, all of you, and you need to call the Police while you can maybe still make a deal, for some of you at least.' Heather collapsed on the bed, sobbing, clutching at Rachel.

'Heather, you need to shut up and listen to how this is going to work. You are not going to say anything to anyone. Not that prick's parents, not at your work, not to the Police, no-one. You are not leaving here until we are crystal clear on that one fact. You try anything and Rachel here will pay the price.'

'No,' cried Heather again, 'you killed him, I saw you. You have to call someone.' She began to shout again, louder this time, 'You fucking killed him, you evil bastard, you sick weirdo. Help! Help! Somebody help me.'

Watson stepped forward and slapped her hard again, then backhanded her on the return swing. 'Enough, Heather. I'm about to show you why you are going to keep quiet. Lads, take Rachel into the other room, it's time for a bit of fun. And turn on the PlayStation when you go past, I'll shoot some bad guys till it's my turn with her.'

Heather was left crying on the floor and put up no struggle as Adam bound her wrists and ankles, then gagged her with a scarf. She could clearly hear the sounds from the bedroom next door as his brother and his mates raped her best friend.

Chapter 2

'Did you hear that, Mum? That sounded like someone shouting for help.'

'Are you sure? I didn't hear anything, son. There's always noise coming from them next door. I don't really notice it anymore.' Mrs Jackson pointed the remote at the TV and turned up the volume, 'Will you look at that, it's going to rain tomorrow, some summer this is turning out to be.'

Baz Jackson reached over and took the remote control from his mother's hand, pressing the mute button. 'Just listen for a minute, will you. Something's not right next door.' Baz listened carefully for a second or two but could only hear the sounds of gunfire from a video game, and some excited shouting from the players. 'Does that noise go on every night?' he asked his mother, you need to call the Police, or at least the council about that lot next door.'

'What's the point, son. It's been like that since the parents died and the young lad Adam took over the lease. He's a bad lot, and I don't want any trouble. There's always a crowd of them in next door, and lots of comings and goings. I've given up trying to see what's going on, I just keep myself to myself these days.'

'But Mum, they're dealing drugs, having parties all night, and it sounds like they've got a girl in there. I'm sure I heard a scream just a minute ago.'

Baz was planning to stay with his mother for a week or two, he was between jobs now, and he had nothing to keep him occupied at his own home in Colchester. He had served 24 years in the Army, finishing up as a Captain in the Parachute Regiment, and at the age of 44 he was still single, owned his own home and car, and was looking for a suitable second career. Offers of security jobs and consultancies had come along, but he had yet to find the opportunity he was looking for. Short term contracts as a security driver for bank deliveries had tided him over but now he was taking time out to visit his home town of Cowdenbeath while he considered his future.

Just then a thud on the wall made them both look up. 'That sounded like it came from upstairs, Mum. I'm going up for a look.'

'Just leave it Baz, it's them next door, probably fighting again in the front bedroom.'

The thud was repeated several times, as though someone was trying to attract attention. Then a muffled scream could be heard before it all went silent again.

'Will you turn up the volume again, son, I want to hear this programme.'

Baz threw the remote control onto the empty seat on the couch next to his mother. 'I'm going to have a word, there's no need for that kind of noise at this time of night,' and he stepped towards the front door.

Once out in the front garden all Baz could hear was muted gunfire and explosions from the video game; no screaming, no banging, nothing other than the soundtrack from the typical shoot-em up arcade style game. Undeterred, he walked up the path leading to the door of the house next door, pausing at the foot of the short flight of steps. He held his breath and listened carefully, and hearing no new sounds, he banged loudly on the door.

Adam Watson eventually opened the door and looked out, and seeing the man on his doorstep simply said 'Yeah, and what do you want?'

'I'm visiting my mum, next door, and the noise from your house is too loud, she's an old woman, and deserves a bit of peace and quiet from you lot in here. All we can hear is your bloody video game!'

Watson stepped out of the house, closing the door behind him. He leaned towards the man two steps below him, breathing rancid fumes in his direction. 'We're not doing anything wrong, it's just a game on the PlayStation. Tell your mum to turn her volume up a bit if she can't hear her telly. Now, sod off back next door and leave us alone.'

Baz Jackson was not the kind of man to take abuse from anyone, he had met all manner of tough guys in his Army career, and he was not about to back down. 'Just keep the noise down. I'm here for a visit and don't want to hear any more of your racket. Got it? If there's anymore, you'll be the first one I come looking for.' Jackson faked a swing at Watson's chin, and he instantly pulled back, banging his head on the door behind him. Losing his balance, Watson stumbled forward again, missed his footing on the top step and fell towards Jackson. Grabbing him by the front of his shirt, Jackson lifted and spun, setting Watson down on the garden path, blocking his way to the door. Patting him lightly on the head he said 'You should be more careful, mate, you nearly fell there. Next time I might not be so gentle. Now get back in there and turn the fucking volume down!'

Watson brushed past him with a mutter and disappeared in the front door without as much as a backward glance. Jackson, however, stood quietly for a moment, listening. The sounds of gunfire and screams continued for a bit before the volume reduced. It was only then that he strode up the garden path, out the gate, and back to his mother's door. Listening again, he was satisfied that his message had got through, and at least tonight his mother might get some undisturbed sleep.

Heather still lay bound and gagged on the bed, but thankfully the noises from the room next door had stopped when someone knocked at the front door. Listening carefully, she could just make out the conversation between her brother and the visitor. She recognised the caller's voice and realised it was the son from next door who had gone off to the army when Heather was just a baby. She had seen him often enough when he had come home on leave to stay with his parents, but he had been a lot older than her and she had hardly paid him any attention. But she recognised the voice and wondered how she could attract his attention without her brother finding out. Maybe he could get help for her and Rachel, so she lay and thought about how to contact him.

Her thoughts were interrupted abruptly when the bedroom door opened, and Rachel was pushed onto the bed beside her. Two of her brother's friends came in behind her, then her brother himself. 'Now listen up you two. This is how it's going to be. Heather, that shitbag sand dancer boyfriend of yours is gone for good, dead, never to be seen again. Not unless you go swimming in the quarry that is.' The two friends burst out laughing at Watson's attempt at humour.

'Yeah, nobody goes swimming in there, at least nobody that's ever come out alive anyway.' said one of them.

'Right,' continued Watson. 'And we have to make sure that none of you two girls is going to go running off to the Police. So, Heather. We have you here, we have Rachel here, and that's how it's going to stay, until I'm satisfied that you understand what I'm saying. No Police! Rachel is going to be performing a few favours for me and the boys here, for the next few days. Just to make sure you know what I mean.'

Heather and Rachel looked at each other, eyes wide with terror. Rachel's eyes were red with crying, her mascara was running down her cheeks, and a red weal was forming on her left jaw. What looked like a painful graze marked her forehead, and both her arms showed bruising above the elbows where she had been held down. Heather did not need to imagine what had happened to her best friend; she had heard it all through the flimsy bedroom wall.

'If you can convince me over the next few days that you won't go to the Police, then I will let you both go. But Heather, even after I let you go, if I ever think that you will grass us up, then we will all take turns with your friend Rachel. We know where she lives, even if you move, then we'll find her, and fuck her until she's no use to anyone else, ever.'

Heather struggled against her bonds, desperate to get free. She tried to speak through the gag, but only vague squeals came out. Her eyes pleaded with her brother, then with Rachel, but receiving only stony glares in response she lowered them to the ground in submission.

'Good. I see that reality is starting to sink in. Much like what happened to sand boy. That must have been some sinking feeling eh lads? Blaze of glory and all that.' Turning back to his followers, Watson nodded at Rachel. 'Time for some more fun then. Just to make sure Heather knows the score. And this time, I'm first!

Heather lay on the bed and sobbed as Rachel was dragged to the bedroom next door, where the rape began all over again. One man remained with her, leering at her, pulling at the front of his trousers, and Heather was terrified that he would attack her while she lay helpless and bound on the bed. She thought of what she could do to escape or get help. Banging on the wall was an option, the guy next door looked well-built and powerful the last time she had seen him. But if her brother thought she was trying to escape, then he would only make it worse for Rachel. Then for her as well probably. What choice did she have? All she could do was lie there, listening to her best friend being repeatedly raped and beaten in the room next door. She would have to go along with this madness, until she could find a way to protect her and Rachel. Once they were safe, out of this house, and hidden away somewhere, maybe then they could go to the Police. That is if the Police didn't come looking for them first. Surely she would be missed at work, so would Darius, and Rachel? Someone might see Darius' car in the flooded quarry, his parents would worry when he didn't come home. Or would they just think he was staying over with Heather, like he did sometimes.

It was all very well to think of her options, but all she could really do right now was try to block out the sounds from the bedroom next door as her brother and his mates repeatedly raped her best friend.

Chapter 3

Darius' mother, Doctor Neith Bakhoum, had got up at her usual early time of six-thirty, showered, dressed, and eaten a quick breakfast before getting ready to drive off to begin her long day. As a Consultant in the specialist burns unit at St John's Hospital in Livingston she worked with burns patients daily, consulting, treating, and monitoring her patients, as well as leading a skilled team during surgical operations. Her daily journey to the hospital took her anywhere from 40 minutes to an hour, depending on traffic, and her only practical route was over the Queensferry Crossing and along the M8. Luckily, the bulk of the morning traffic headed east towards Edinburgh on leaving the new road bridge, leaving her a relatively quiet few miles to drive west to Livingston. She tried not to complain about the journey, the length of time it took, the traffic, the stress of motorway driving, or the headache she always had when she arrived home at the end of her day. After all, she and her husband had left Egypt nearly 20 years ago in search of a better future, and their careers had rocketed once they completed the GMC registration requirements.

They had already both completed their medical degrees in Egypt and undertaken their training to give them the qualifications required to be a doctor there. Moving to the UK had not been an easy decision, especially with Darius only being 5 years old. But both Neith and her husband Amun had received offers of doctor positions in Fife and had travelled there in high hopes of beginning a new and prosperous life in Scotland. Neith had gradually begun to specialise in burns and plastic surgery and had moved from her first job in Dunfermline to take up a post in a specialist hospital. When that hospital had closed she had moved with her unit to a new hospital in nearby Livingston, St Johns.

Amun, however, was still working in Dunfermline, and continued in his career as an ENT consultant. Keeping mainly office hours, he still scheduled a few surgeries in the evenings, but was home for dinner on most nights. Their current home in Dunfermline was close to the hospital, which was handy for Amun, and close to a motorway junction which was helpful for Neith. Now neither wished to move, having transformed it from a dingy bungalow into a modern and welcoming home for them and Darius.

Amun wandered sleepily into the kitchen as Neith was pulling on her coat, ready to leave for work. 'No sign of Darius this morning, he'll be late for work.' observed Amun as he switched on the kettle.

'I just passed his room, looks like he didn't come home last night. Did he call after I went to bed?' asked Neith, picking up her briefcase and handbag from the kitchen table. She looked around for her car keys, patted her coat pocket and sighed with relief as she heard the jingle telling her the keys were there. 'He usually phones if he's spending the night at Heather's.'

'No call last night though. I know it's not like him, but they have a lot to organise with the wedding just around the corner. Maybe it got late, and he didn't want to call in case it woke us. I'm sure he'll be fine and apologise tonight when he gets home. Now get going or you'll hit the queues at the bridge.'

'Ok, ok, I'm going. See you tonight. I'll call Darius from the car on the way to the hospital.' and Neith left for another routine day in her hospital burns unit.

The Credit Card Customer Services Manager looked out over the rows of call centre workstations in the bank head office. It was almost time for the phone lines to switch over to the manual operators after having been on an automated message service overnight. He spotted a few empty chairs here and there, but nothing that was unusual during the summer months. 'Ok, everyone, lines open in a few minutes, so please can we have some big smiles for our customers. Special offers are on your screens, so ask everyone where the offer pops up automatically.'

Walking up and down the lines first thing in the morning was a routine for the day shift manager, checking the screens, identifying the missing staff, and confirming their names against the holiday list on his clipboard. He would spend most of the day monitoring calls, doing remedial training with some of the advisers, or handling complaints passed up the line to 'the manager'. Stopping at one unoccupied workstation he pressed a button to bring the screen to life and noted the name of the adviser who had not yet logged in.

'Has anyone seen Heather this morning?' he asked the girls either side of the empty station. Both were on calls but were well used to listening to two conversations at once. Both shook their head in answer and went back to the call in progress. Continuing his stroll around the office, the manager noted other absentees, ticked them off on his holiday list and headed to the coffee machine in the breakout area. Once seated comfortably in his glass enclosed office, with his coffee to hand and his clipboard discarded for the moment, the manager picked up his desk phone and called the HR Department. It was quite common for staff to pull a sickie on a Friday or be hungover from being out at a cheap student night somewhere. But he could not think of any event, a concert, a staff night out or anything else that might have taken place the night before. He confirmed that Heather Watson had not called in sick that morning, nor had she arranged any leave at short notice. The manager knew Heather was very conscientious about her job with the bank, and had been progressing steadily towards promotion, so there had to be an exceptionally good reason for her no-show this morning. After getting her contact numbers from HR, he sat back and finished his coffee. He would give her the benefit of the doubt if she turned up in the next half hour. Traffic into Edinburgh from Fife was notoriously difficult at peak times, and he decided to wait a while before he tried to call her.

In the Investment Department a similar situation was apparent. One of the junior Investment Analysts had not arrived for work at his usual time, and the analyst team had begun their morning meeting without him. After discussing the overnight reports from the Far East markets, and reviewing the early movements in the UK, the team dispersed to take care of their usual responsibilities. The UK mid-caps desk supervisor looked around at his team, but he was still one member short. 'Has Darius been in contact with anyone this morning, maybe been held up in a traffic accident or something?' Receiving no answer, he walked over to the window without thinking, and looked out over the staff car park at the rear of the head office building. There were hundreds of cars there, although he knew Darius drove a white Audi. It looked as though every second car in the car park was white, and he gave up looking, turning instead to his team again. 'Anyone seen him in the building, or heard from him at all?' The responses were all in the negative, so he returned to his desk to look up Darius' phone number.

Neither Heather nor Darius answered their cell phones, Darius' phone was underwater, and Heather's bound hands prevented her reaching her mobile. But neither manager was aware of that, and neither of them pursued the matter further.

Chapter 4

Heather woke from a restless sleep and it took her a few moments to figure out why she couldn't move very easily. She was lying on her side facing a wall, her hands were still tied behind her back and her legs were tied together at the ankles. She remembered exactly where she was then, and what her brother had done to her fiancé the night before. The dirty scarf tied round her mouth stopped her from calling out, but she felt like she was about to vomit, and struggled hard to regain control of her stomach before she choked to death. Just as she was about to start kicking the wall in front of her to get some attention, she heard muffled sobs coming from somewhere behind her. With a struggle she managed to turn herself around to face into the room, only to be met with the terrifying sight of her friend Rachel lying on the floor at the side of the bed. Rachel was naked from the waist down, and she too was tied and gagged. But it was the blood covering her thighs and buttocks that freaked Heather out, and she began to scream against the gag in her mouth, but only a pitiful wail made it past the cloth barrier. Rachel was sobbing quietly, facing away from Heather, and Heather tried to get her attention by mumbling through the gag, but without success. Rolling herself towards the edge of the dirty single bed, Heather wriggled her body until she fell over the edge, landing as softly as she could on top of Rachel, propelling herself over her friend to lie face to face on the floor.

Rachel's face was a mess. Her eyes were black from the mascara that had run from her tears. Her nose was bent and crusted with blood. Her lips and chin were also covered in dried blood and a thin line of yellow bile ran from the side of her mouth. Heather contorted herself around again, to get her back to Rachel and her bound hands as close as she could to Rachel's face. Trying to make soothing sounds through her own gag, Heather wriggled up and down until her hands could feel the gag in Rachel's mouth. With fingers she could barely feel, Heather pulled at Rachel's gag until she pulled it free, leaving it loose around her neck. Trying to comfort her, Heather stroked Rachel's face with her fingers, emitting strange sounds through the gag, hoping she would stay quiet and not bring her brother running to check on his captives. It took another minute for Heather to turn around again, this time to face Rachel, and she rubbed her cheek against Rachel's trying to comfort her. With a series of grunts and nudges Heather hoped to convey that Rachel should try to loosen Heather's gag, and Rachel replied with a very quiet 'OK.' Another two minutes passed before they were lying facing each other again, this time able to speak to each other. Rachel continued to sob quietly, but suddenly she opened her mouth wide and looked ready to scream. Heather pushed her head into Rachel's face, whispering urgently.

'No, Rachel. Keep quiet. We can't make a sound until we figure out how we're going to get out of this. If they come back in here, we might never get out of this house alive.'

Rachel closed her mouth and nodded. 'We'll get out of here, don't worry about that. And when we do, I'm going to kill those bastards. All three of them. You've no idea what they did to me last night. They raped me, over and over again, everywhere, all of them. Your brother did this to me, and I'm never going to be able to forget it. The smell of his breath on me, the punches, the kicks, the way he forced himself into me while those two other bastards held me down.' Her voice was getting louder as she got angrier, but Heather shushed her.

'Rachel, I'm so sorry I got you into this. I had no idea they had you here until they brought me back here from the quarry. You know what they did to Darius, don't you?'

'Yeah, they told me in great detail. Especially about what would happen to me if either of us went to the Police. Heather, I can't go through that again, I just can't. We have to keep quiet about this, at least until we get out of this house and we can think about it for a bit.'

'We have to go to the Police, Rachel. They killed Darius. They set fire to him and pushed his car over the cliff into the water. What am I supposed to tell his Mum and Dad?'

'If we go to the Police they'll come after us both. They said if I told anyone they would kidnap me again, rape me again, then kill me. If I tell, they'll do the same to you as well. Trust me, that's the last thing you want to happen. We have to figure out what to do.'

'What about that neighbour that came to the door last night about the noise. If we bang on the wall he might hear and come back again. He was in the Army; he looks like he could help us. What do you think?'

'I think that's a bad idea Heather. There's your brother and his two mates in the house. That's three of them to just one neighbour. And they're high most of the time, there's no way of knowing what they might do if someone comes to the door. We could wait till it's all quiet, hope they've passed out or something, and try to get away then.'

'I think it's quiet enough now. If we bang on the wall surely the neighbour will come to find out what the noise is about.'

'Look Heather. I told you what they said they would do if we told anyone. You can´t do it! You might fancy a cock up your arse, but I certainly don't want to go through that again!'

The three men were lounging on the scruffy sofas in the sitting room. Watson was trying to watch a TV show while his two mates Bugsy and Gasser were counting a pile of banknotes. Clear plastic bags lay at their feet on the floor, some empty, some filled with a dirty brown powder, and empty tins of baby milk formula littered the carpet.

'Stock's getting low, Watty, we've plenty of cash to buy more. We need to stock up for the weekend customers. When are you meeting your man again to get more gear?'

'Never you mind Bugsy, your job right now is to watch those two girls upstairs. I'll sort out our stock shortage. You better stay off the stuff while we've got them here, ok? You got that too, Gasser?'

'Right Watty,' they replied in unison. 'You get the stock; we watch the girls.' replied Gasser.

'Well, one of you better go and see if they're awake yet. It's time we had another chat with them.'

Gasser clumped his way up the stairs and into the back bedroom. He'd enjoyed fucking the dark haired one last night and was hoping Watty might let them do it again this morning. Maybe they might even get to play with Watty's sister, although he wasn't too hopeful. As soon as he entered the room Gasser knew there was a problem. The girls were both lying on the floor, face to face, and both had somehow managed to loosen their gags, which now hung around their necks. 'Watty, you better get up here, quick.' he shouted. 'We might have a problem.'

When Watty ran into the bedroom he could tell there was more than just one problem. A foul stench hung in the air just inside the door. 'Gasser, was that you again?' demanded Watty, 'That's fucking stinking, man.'

'Aw come on Watty, you know I always do that when I'm nervous. I can't help it.' and he farted loudly again, releasing more noxious fumes into the room. Watty pushed the door back and forth to clear the air until it was breathable again, keeping his mouth and nose covered with his other hand.

Sitting on the edge of the single bed, Watty looked down at Rachel and Heather, still huddled on the floor. 'Glad to see you got the message then, ladies. But just to be clear, for Heather's benefit, let me tell you again. If either one of you talks about any part of what happened last night, then Rachel will party with me and the boys again. Heather, I'm sure she's already told you about the fun we had last night. The boys are raring to go again, so make sure you both behave, and I'll keep them away from you.'

Rachel sobbed out loud and looked at Heather, imploring her to stay quiet, to lie still and wait for it all to be over. Heather couldn't stay quiet though, 'You can't keep us here for ever. People will be looking for us, our work will be trying to contact us when we don't turn up this morning. '

'You won't be here for ever, Heather. Just till I'm sure that you'll behave and not tell a soul about any of this.'

Rachel continued to sob quietly; her gag still undone. Heather spoke for both of them. 'We promise, we won't say a word. Rachel has had enough; can't you see that. Let us go and we won't tell anyone. Promise.'

'I think it's still a bit early for me to be sure about that. I might let you go in a day or two, but not just yet. You need to believe what will happen to you if you don't stay silent. Rachel had her turn with the boys, but Heather, I know they want to party with you too. Behave for the next few days and you'll go free. But if you try to attract attention, or try to escape, then I might just let the boys have their fun with both of you.'

'You wouldn't do that to me. I'm your sister for Christ sake! What kind of pervert are you that you'd let those two junkies anywhere near me?' shouted Heather.

Watty leaned forward and punched his sister in the face, splitting her lip and causing bright red blood to gush out and run down her chin as she lay stunned on the floor.

'Take that as a warning. I only just told you about attracting attention. Gasser, gag them tighter this time, and you or Bugsy check on them every half hour. I have to go out for a while. Maybe when I get back we can have another party.'

Half an hour later, as instructed, Bugsy climbed the stairs to check on the two girls in the bedroom. Both had their gags firmly in place, their wrists were still tied behind their backs, and their ankles were strapped tightly together. With one of them on the floor, and one on the single bed, they both lay quietly, watching him. The dark haired one on the bed, Rachel, was still naked below the waist, and he eyed up her pale backside. The blood stains did not put him off, and he stared at her with his eyes almost popping out of his head. He hated being called Bugsy, but he couldn't help the way his eyes stuck out. They had always been that way, just like the way Gasser always farted when he was nervous. Reaching over to the girl Bugsy fondled her breasts through her thin cotton top, squeezing hard and making her squirm. He had never had a proper girlfriend, they all just made fun of him. But he knew what women wanted, he had seen it often enough on the internet, and he was going to take full advantage of her. With Watty out sorting out a drug buy, he could have some fun with one of the girls at least.

Bugsy grabbed Rachel by the hair with one hand and hauled her up into a kneeling position. With his other hand he struggled to undo his jeans before pushing her head down into the bed covers. He was fully aroused already and shuffled behind her, still using his hold on her long hair to force her head down. He thrust at her and missed the first time, but quickly readjusted and entered her, forcing his way deep into her. Rachel bucked and moaned, thrashing her arms backwards trying to push him away, but with no success. Bugsy just pulled harder on her hair and continued to violate his bound victim.

Heather lay helpless on the floor, watching Bugsy rape her friend, and fought her bonds to get into a sitting position, her hands still held behind her. She kicked at Bugsy's legs over and over, trying to unbalance him, but he just drew back his foot and kicked her in the head. Undeterred, Heather tried again, using both feet to launch blows at his legs, but she could not get him to stop. Instead, she began to thump her feet, still tied together, into the floor, trying to make as much noise as possible. She would either get the attention of Gasser downstairs, who might stop Bugsy raping Rachel, or maybe the neighbour would hear and come to the door again to complain.

Bugsy had other plans. He pushed Rachel away from him and stood over Heather, his trousers still hanging loose around his knees. He reached down for Heather's hair, plunging his fist into her long blonde curls, and pulled her towards him. Heather kept on banging her feet on the floor, while wriggling backwards as hard as she could. She could hear feet pounding on the stairs, but she also heard the crash of breaking glass. Rachel had managed to roll onto her back and had kicked at the window above the bed until the glass gave way with a frightening crack. Gasser burst into the bedroom and tripped over the struggling figures of Bugsy and Heather, landing on top of them on the floor. His surprised cry did not cover the loud banging on the front door, or the voice of the burly neighbour.

'What the fuck's all the noise about in there.'

Bugsy and Gasser quickly recovered their senses, and both rushed to the broken window. Looking down they could see the big guy from next door getting ready to pound on the door again. 'Got fuck all to do with you, you nosy prick.' shouted Gasser through the broken window. 'Just fuck off back to your mummy's before I come down there and sort you out.'

'Get down here now, arsehole. It's you that needs sorting out. There's something going on in there, and I'm not having any more shit from you. Now get down here now!'

Bugsy and Gasser looked at each other for a moment.

'Shit. We need to get rid of him before Watty gets back.' said Gasser, starting for the stairs. 'Come on, we can take him, there's two of us.'

Bugsy followed Gasser down the stairs and got to the front door just as Gasser hauled it open. Bugsy ran straight through the opening and headbutted the surprised neighbour before he could react. Gasser followed up with a barrage of kicks as the neighbour fell to the ground, rolling sideways away from the flying feet.

Bugsy and Gasser stood shoulder to shoulder facing the other man. 'There's nothing here for you to see, so get lost and don't come back. Just remember, you won't always be here to look after your Mum. Be a good boy and mind your own business. Now fuck off before we get warmed up and give you a real hammering.'

Faced with two crazy druggies, and reeling from the headbutt, Baz Jackson stepped backwards towards the footpath. 'You fucking nutters haven't seen the last of me. I know there's something dodgy going on in there. There better not be any more noise from here, or I'm coming back.' Baz knew that now was not the time to react, his turn would come.

Chapter 5

Heather lay on the floor of the bedroom, eyes filled with tears, as she heard Bugsy and Gasser running up the stairs again. Rachel was still lying face down on the bed where she had been pushed when Bugsy was raping her. She shook uncontrollably, quietly sobbing into the dirty bed covers.

Gasser was first through the door, and he kicked at Heather's legs. 'I told you what would happen if you made any noise. We've got that nosy neighbour banging at our door now. That was your fault, thumping the floor like that. Watty is going to go nuts when he gets back.' Bugsy reached past his mate and hauled Rachel's head off the bed by her hair. He gave her a fierce punch to the cheek, followed by one to the ribs, before throwing her face down into the covers. He started to undo his trousers again, but Gasser stopped him. 'We've had enough noise for now. Wait till Watty gets home, and we can fuck them both this time. I've always fancied his sister, but she left home before I could try it on with her.'

'Yeah.' agreed Bugsy. 'This other one needs a good wash before I'm going near her again anyway. Let's grab a beer while we're waiting for Watty.'

'Good idea. Bring me one up, I'll stay here and keep an eye on this pair. We can't leave them alone again, not until they've got the message about keeping quiet. And fetch some cardboard and some tape so I can fix the window.'

Rachel lay silently now, scared to move for fear of another beating. The caked blood on her buttocks and thighs was itchy and made her feel horrible. She ached from the punches, but more so from the rape. Her insides felt that they would never be the same again. She wanted to use the toilet, but knew that it would mean more pain, and probably more blood. The gag in her mouth prevented her from asking anyway, so she just hoped that she could hold onto things for a little while longer.

Heather was still on the floor, her shin ached where she had been kicked, and the cloth rubbing at the corners of her mouth was starting to cause sores. She couldn't speak to Rachel or even get her attention; Gasser was sitting there watching over them. All she could do was think about Darius, and the way her brother had killed her fiancé. Darius' body would still be inside his car, at the bottom of the flooded quarry. Surely his parents would know he was missing by now. His workmates would miss him, and maybe try to call his house. But nobody would be looking in the quarry for him. Her thoughts turned to their wedding plans, now all in ruins. They had found a lovely new house, on a development on the outskirts of Dunfermline, and had bought all the furniture to make it their own, giving them a comfortable first home together.

The wedding plans included both a service and the reception at a local hotel. Invitations had gone out only the week before, in perfect time for the big event on the last Saturday in August. Heather and Darius had selected their outfits in secret, Heather choosing a traditional white silk gown. Darius had originally planned to surprise Heather by wearing a full-dress kilt regalia, in Watson tartan in tribute to her family. But he had asked her how she felt about the idea before he finally decided what to do. Together, they had gone to the kilt hire shop to choose what Darius would wear, and then gone on to the florists to discuss flowers for the bridal party and buttonholes for the groom, best man, and the two ushers. Scottish heather was the obvious choice for the buttonholes, and what could be more appropriate for this wedding than lucky white heather. The florist had recommended artificial heather for the men, dressed with tartan ribbon to match the kilts, and Heather had collected them from the shop only last weekend.

Everything else was organised by Darius and Heather, with Rachel helping out as much as needed. The Drs Bakhoum had offered various suggestions, and lots of help with the wedding planning, but they understood that the two youngsters wanted to make their own plans. The doctors insisted on paying for everything, they said they could easily afford it, without making any reference at all to Heather's family situation. The cake, the favours for the tables, the wording of the service, the band for the reception, the menu, wine, and toasts were all organised. It was almost as if all they had to do now was to turn up in five weeks' time. But that was not going to happen now. She struggled to understand how she had got into this seemingly hopeless situation. And now it was all Heather could think of.

Heather Watson was an ordinary girl from Cowdenbeath, in Fife. She had struggled her way through school until the day she found out her brother was dealing drugs from his rucksack at breaks and after classes. He was three years older than her and was already on the verge of expulsion for his behaviour, although he had yet to come to the attention of the local Police. Heather's parents were no help. Both were unemployed, and spent most of their time watching daytime TV, when they were sober that is. She made her own meals, and tried hard to ignore her brother, who constantly pestered her to take drugs into the school for him. The house was dirty and untidy, unwashed dishes and overflowing ashtrays lay around until Heather could stand it no longer and she forced herself to clean up. Her brother was always bringing his friends round, to take drugs, and drink cheap wine or cider, and Heather tried to keep out of the house as much as she could. She would not be able to fight off his friends if they decided to try anything with her, and this made her feel helpless and afraid.

Heather's best friend, Rachel Taylor, was in her class for most of their subjects at High School and knew what she was going through. Gradually, Heather spent more and more time at Rachel's house, and joined in their mealtime debates. Economics, politics, local government, policing, drugs, it seemed that they covered every topic imaginable, and Heather found her interest in learning was reborn. She also enrolled in self-defence classes run by a local women's group, and watched You Tube videos almost every night to learn new moves, all designed to ensure that she would never feel vulnerable again.

But tragically, when she was at Rachel's house one night, Heather's parents lay drunk again in front of the TV in their filthy lounge. The gas fire was on as usual, but they had failed to notice that the flame was not burning with its normal colour, nor that several years of bird droppings had crusted up the flue outlet on the outside of the house. The colourless, odourless gas had been invading their home for a long time, but they had always woken up before they fully lost consciousness. But that cold winter night was to be their last, and Heather found her parent's slumped on the settee when she got home from Rachel's house. Unable to rouse them, she had called an ambulance, but sadly the carbon monoxide had taken them both.

With both parents dead, and Heather being only fifteen, the Social Work department became involved. Her brother was her only living relative, and with him now over the age of 18, he was allowed to take on the tenancy of his parents' council house. Benefits were arranged for him, and it was agreed that Heather would continue to live at home with him until she left school. She hated her brother, she hated the house, the Social Worker, her teachers, even the old lollipop man who had been guiding her safely across the road since she was a toddler on the way to primary school. She skipped school, she shunned Rachel, and avoided the house as much as possible. Her brother and his friends used it like a private smoking and drinking club, and it was always full of druggies and drunks.

But Rachel persuaded Heather to come and live with her and go back to school. But it was too late for Heather to make up for lost time in her class work, and she left school as soon as she turned sixteen, with some certificates to her name, but not enough to go on to a full-time course at college. After spending a few years working in various local shops, and with some night classes in computer studies and communications under her belt, she felt the time was right to do something better with her life.

Heather had been in her new job as a Customer Service Advisor in the Credit Card department at the Bank head office for only two weeks when one of her new colleagues mentioned the after-work classes the bank provided for staff. The facilities were state of the art, and she visited the gymnasium with her new workmate one night after work, to try out the beginners' martial arts class that was advertised. She soon found that she was well ahead of most of the others in the class, thanks to her early self-defence lessons, and her videos online, and the instructor picked her out to help with a demonstration. She was paired with a stranger, a young man with a dark complexion, and wiry black hair, who must have been six inches taller than she was. The instructor asked the stranger to rush at Heather as though he was trying to attack her with a knife. With a swift flurry of arms, and a swivel of her hips, Heather swept the stranger off his feet, and before he knew what was happening, he was flat on his back on the mat, with her knee on his throat. And that is how Heather Watson met the man who should have been her future husband, Darius Bakhoum.

Chapter 6

The Friday lunchtime traffic on the roundabout on Holyrood Place, Dunfermline was chaotic, with five exits trying to guide vehicles into or around the town centre. The roundabout sat at the main access route from the east, leading to the M90 motorway to Edinburgh or Perth and beyond. With the school holidays well under way, the historic town attracted its fair share of tourists, as well as the stay at home families trying to get through the busy junction on their way to or from the various parks.

Detective Inspector Mark McManus sat in his swivel office chair, his feet propped up on the desk, and surveyed the traffic three floors below. The jacket of his dark blue suit hung on a coat stand in the corner of his office, and his pale blue shirt fitted his muscular six foot plus frame snugly. The blue striped tie he had selected that morning hung over the jacket, having been quickly discarded when he put his feet up. His recent promotion to DI had coincided with the transfer of the Major Investigation Team from Kirkcaldy to Dunfermline, and as head of that team he had managed the move. He had selected the office previously occupied by the Chief Superintendent prior to the creation of Police Scotland. The office had lain unused for several years as the command structures in every force in the country had changed because of the mergers to create one unified Police authority. The senior officer at Dunfermline Police Station was now a Chief

Inspector, who controlled the policing of the whole of West Fife, from Cowdenbeath to Kincardine, and from the Forth Bridge to Kelty.

McManus was responsible for the investigation of crimes of murder, rape, and robbery among a few others, and currently had no pressing cases on his desk. What was on his desk aside from his size 10 feet was his personal phone, resting against a stack of papers. It was the second day of the Open Championship at Royal Portrush in Northern Ireland, and the challenging links course was proving a stern test for the world's top golfers. The coverage from Sky Sports was excellent, and the picture on his phone was perfect thanks to the station's high-speed internet links. His single earbud meant he could listen to the commentary without anyone else hearing it, but he could also hear what was going on around him.

As a keen golfer, McManus tried to play as often as he could, but he had only been in his post since April and was trying to limit the times he left work early to get in a few holes at his local club. But he could still watch the biggest event in world golf, even if it was on a small screen. His attention was abruptly diverted by a loud knock on his partly open door.

'Boss, you won't believe it! The Procurator Fiscal's only gone and dropped the charges against that fucking rapist bastard.'

DC Gill Edwards stood in the doorway, her face red as a beetroot, looking ready to charge a herd of rhinos single handed. 'I'm just back from court. The bastard pled not guilty and the PF stood up and said she was taking no further proceedings. The Sheriff dismissed the case, and our rapist just walked out. Cheeky bastard gave me the finger on the steps as well!'

'Oh shit, it wasn't the same finger....'

'I bloody hope not, dirty bastard. He can't get away with this, we had all the evidence, the victim's statement, forensics. It was all there, boss.'

Edwards was the only female member of his team, and had been the lead detective on the rape case, albeit under the supervision of DI McManus, involving a married woman who had been out for a meal with some friends. She had been attacked in the car park while walking back to her car. The rapist, Dennis Bates, had hit the woman in the face, dragged her into a dark area under a bridge and assaulted her. This had included inserting his fingers in her anus, as well as vaginal rape, and further punches to her face and body. The victim had tried to scream but her attacker had beat her again, so she had stayed quiet hoping to escape further injury. When it was over, Bates ran off, leaving the woman lying bleeding on the ground. A passer-by saw the attacker running away from the car park and went to investigate, finding the victim barely conscious. The good Samaritan called an ambulance before melting quietly into the darkness, never to be identified.

'Boss, you know me. That investigation was flawless. Because the victim was taken straight to hospital, we got all the samples we could have hoped for. She picked her attacker out of the video ID parade, and his DNA matched our samples. He's got a previous for sexual assault and lives only a few streets away from that car park.'

'Ok, Gill. I know you're angry, I hate it too when thugs like Bates get off like this. But if the PF has dropped the case, then that's the end of it. I'll give her a ring and see what happened. I'll let you know when I've got some answers.'

McManus was just as angry as Edwards had been. The Bates rape case had been a quick win for his team soon after he had taken over. It was Edward's first rape case, and he had supervised her personally. There were no flaws in the evidence. Bates should be going to prison for six to eight years at least. He picked up the desk phone and placed a call to the Procurator Fiscal's Office. Abruptly, he placed the handset back in place and stood up. The PF's office was only next door. He decided to walk over there and ask the woman herself.

McManus walked into the detective's office and beckoned to Edwards to join him outside. Together they walked along the top floor corridor to the rear stairwell where McManus stopped. 'Gill, I spoke to the PF over at her office. There's more to it than you think. The victim, as you know, lives in Stirling, where she works as a senior lecturer at the University there. It turns out she was on the point of divorcing her husband at the time of the attack, and the dinner with her friends was some kind of farewell night out. She had also been offered a more senior position at the London School of Economics, and she was going to make a clean break from her husband and her job. It seems she wants to move away, and start afresh, put all this behind her. She feels to stay around for a trial, and the publicity that would attract, would demean her and she would miss the chance of a new life on her own in London. She and the PF had a meeting yesterday, and she told the PF she would not give evidence. The case can't go ahead without the only witness, Gill. The PF had to let it go.'

'But, she had all the forensics, the identification, everything. We had him. Bates did it. He was going down for sure.'

'I know, Gill, but the witness has to give evidence, about the attack, the samples being taken, the ID parade, all of it. If she decides not to, the PF can't force her. It would only lead to him walking free if she tried to force the witness, and the defence would have a field day with that.'

'So the bastard just walks? We all know he did it, but he gets away with it, right?'

'Nothing we can do about it, Gill. He's done it once and got away with it. He'll do it again, he's that kind of person. A predator, a creepy coward, a pathetic individual, but we'll see him again soon. And we won't let him slip away the next time. Have a word with the duty sergeant, have him pass on the description so the uniforms can keep an eye out for him. Then leave him alone and move on, Gill. There's nothing more you can do about it.'

'That's easy for you to say, you've no idea what rape means to a woman. It's an awful experience. That woman will never forget what he did to her. Tom Fraser and I are going to keep an eye on him, he might just try it again now that he's got off with this one. Do you want me to call you if he does anything?' she asked.

'No, Gill. I'm off this weekend, so let DS Gibson know instead. He can arrange any follow up needed. And don't keep young Tom out too late, will you. And remember, I'm expecting you at my place tomorrow night.'

'I'll come around tomorrow, but don't think you're going to tie me face down on your kitchen table and fuck me like you did the last time. I only allow that to happen because I want it, not because you think you control me. Do you understand?' Edwards spat angrily. 'You can't just order me to appear at your house for sex on demand, even if I do enjoy it.'

'Gill, you seem to have forgotten how our last murder case in Pittenweem ended. You're here because of me, you are a Detective Constable because I made it happen, you could just as easily be in prison right now. You need to think about that a bit more before you start dictating terms.'

'And you seem to have forgotten that I know what you did in Pittenweem as well. You didn't get to be

Detective Inspector because you solved a murder, you got here because of what you did to Rutherford. I know because I helped you do it. And I know your secret as much as you know mine. So stop the bullshit about how I owe you. I think we have a mutual interest in keeping each other's secrets, so if I want to come to your house, to bend over your table, to let you fuck me, then you need to understand that it is only happening because I want it to. Is that clear, Mr fucking Detective Inspector!' and she stormed back into the station, making sure to slam the door as noisily as possible.

'Ok, I guess I'll see you about seven-thirty as usual then.' he said to the wooden door still vibrating in its frame.

Chapter 7

Adam Watson drove up to the front of the block in Cowdenbeath and stepped out of his ageing Vauxhall Astra. A lot of people he met said he should get a better car; it was not the kind of car a guy like him should be driving. But Watson was happy not drawing attention to himself by driving a flashy Mercedes or BMW like some others in his line of work. Drug dealing was about contacts, supply and demand, pricing structures, timing, and maintaining relationships. It was nothing to do with cars or jewellery or big houses, or girls or clothes or fancy watches. It was about making money and not getting caught. So far so good, he thought as he pushed open the broken gate leading to his front door.

Bugsy and Gasser jumped up nervously when Watty pushed open the front door and stepped through into the filthy lounge. He kicked one empty beer can and threw another in the direction of his two friends. 'Can't you two keep this place tidy? I've been out for a couple of hours and look at the state of this pigsty. I go out making deals so you two got shit to sell, so you can earn some cash. And what do you do while I'm out, fuck all but drink beer and laze around.'

'Sorry, Watty, but the girls gave us a bit of trouble. We had to go up there and quieten them down a bit. That neighbour came over too. You know, the army guy from next door. But we took care of him, broke his nose, sent him flying.' Gasser tried to explain before Bugsy dropped them both in the shit. 'They got their gags off and were talking, but we took care of that too, didn't we Bugsy. They won't be any more trouble, Watty.'

Watty exploded, 'What do you mean, they got their gags off. You two half-wits are supposed to be watching them. Fucking idiots!' and he ran out of the room and up the stairs.

Heather was still bound and gagged and lying on her side on the floor of the bedroom. Rachel was on the bed, also with her wrists and hands tied, a sports sock held in her mouth with a tightly tied strip of sheet. Neither looked at Watson when he came into the room.

'Bugsy, Gasser! get up here now' he shouted. 'What the fuck have you two done?'

'It was Bugsy, Watty. He fucked the dark-haired one again, and she started kicking. She broke the window. He was going to fuck your sister too, but I stopped him. That's when the army guy came shouting at the door. He must have heard the glass breaking. It was Bugsy, man. I never touched them while you were gone.'

Bugsy broke in, 'He was going to fuck them both too, but the neighbour came around. You said we could play with them till you got back, Watty. I'm sure you said it was ok.'

'Shut up, both of you, and get that mess downstairs cleaned up. We've got some business to sort out tonight, and we'll be expecting visitors. So tidy it up and get the sales gear out. Now go!'

With Bugsy and Gasser occupied downstairs, Watson turned his attention again to the two girls. 'I guess you don't feel so good now, Rachel. Bugsy likes you, Rachel, he likes you a lot. And you've seen what he does to girls he likes.' Rachel tried to squeal, but only managed a faint groan from her dried-up lips. 'And what about you, Sis. My young sister Heather. How do you like watching my friends play with Rachel here? They both want to play with you too, but I haven't let them. Not yet anyway.'

Heather just looked at her brother, eyes raging, hoping to generate heat enough to burn through him. But she knew she was helpless. No-one was coming to rescue them. No-one even knew they were here. She was starving, thirsty, in pain, and in fear for her life. Watching Bugsy rape her friend again had made her determined to punish her brother, to make him pay for killing the love of her life. He had burned Darius alive in his car, and she would make him feel the same pain. But first she had to get out of this house alive. She had to get Rachel out alive, and together they would recover their strength, and take revenge.

'Heather, wake up! I'm talking to you.' Watson shouted at her as he slapped her face. She had been caught up in her thoughts and not heard what he had said. 'I already told you what you have to do to get out of here. And what will happen if you tell anyone.' Watson looked over at Rachel, and pulled at her legs, rolling her towards him so she could see his face.

'Heather, look at Rachel here. She has been raped over and over, by each one of us. Me, Bugsy, Gasser, over and over. All that blood on her legs. Look at her eyes, how defeated she looks. She has given up all hope of getting out of here. Can you smell her. That is not just piss and shit and cum! That is fear! She is covered in it.'

Watson pulled Heather's head up from the floor to be level with the bed. 'Can you smell that? Can you smell her fear? Can you see the defeat in her eyes? She wants you to help her, Heather. Do you want to help her, Heather?'

Heather tried to nod her head, tried to speak, tried somehow to communicate her agreement. But nothing worked. Her head was held tight by the blonde hair wrapped in her brother's grasp.

'Good,' continued Watson, 'here's the deal. You both need to agree, so pay attention.' Watson laid out his plans for letting them go, as the girls began to quietly sob through their gags. 'I need to know that you won't say a word about any of this. About the quarry, or Darius going over the edge. About you two being here, or anything that happened during your visit to your brother's house. I told you before that I didn't believe you would keep silent. But here's what will happen if you don't.' Watson released Heather's hair and stood over the girls, between the two twin beds. 'Rachel has had her fun with my boys, but it doesn't look like she enjoyed it all that much. If either of you tell anyone about anything, then we will come back for Rachel again. We will find you, bring you both back here, and start all over again. We will play with Rachel, while you watch Heather. But Heather, I know they want to party with you too. Stay quiet and I'll let you both go. Tell anyone, and it will all begin again. You'll stay here till the morning, then I'll let you go. But if you try to attract attention, or try to escape, then I might just let the boys have their fun with both of you.'

Watson leaned over Rachel and said quietly 'Do you agree, Rachel. I'm going to take your gag off now, so you can discuss it with Heather.'

With her gag removed, Rachel tried to lick her parched lips to help her speak. 'Heather, do whatever he says. I just want out of here. I want to go home, to have a bath, get cleaned up. I need to rest, I'm sore all over. Help me Heather, do what he says.' Rachel began to sob quietly, her gag still undone, while Watson leaned towards Heather.

'Heather, did you hear that. Rachel has had enough. What do you say now?' and he removed her gag so she could answer.

Believing she spoke for both of them she whispered 'We promise, Adam. We won't say a word. Rachel has definitely had enough; can't you see that. Let us go now and we won't tell anyone. Promise.'

'I think it's still a bit early for me to be sure about that. I'll let you go in the morning, but not just yet. You need to believe what will happen to you if you don't stay silent. Keep quiet tonight, and you can go home tomorrow.'

Heather's face ached from where she had been punched and slapped. Her shin ached from the kick she had received. Her heart ached from her helplessness, from her failure to help her best friend, but worst of all, it ached from her surrender to the man who had killed off her hopes for a better life. She resolved to do anything now to get out of there. Sadly, her martial arts skills were no use to her here; if she tried anything they would only take it out on Rachel.

Rachel looked down at her best friend Heather, she could see she was totally defeated. 'It's ok, Heather, we'll be home tomorrow. Just do as he says. There's nothing more you can do about it.'

Chapter 8

It was after seven-thirty pm when Dr Neith Bakhoum parked her Volvo estate on the driveway of her home after a longer than usual drive home from the hospital. Her husband's old VW Passat was already there, leaking oil onto the brick paved surface, gradually expanding the stained ring of fluids underneath the car. She had lost count of the number of times she had suggested he buy a new car. What was the point of having expensive paviors if he was going to let his leaky car mess them all up? Huffing to herself, Dr Bakhoum pulled her bags from the passenger seat and set them on the ground before walking around to the tailgate. With a quick beep from her remote key fob the tailgate lifted and she looked inside. She always made a point of checking her emergency kit when she got home, just in case she got a call out from the hospital. She was part of the area emergency burns response team, and was occasionally called out from home to attend a road accident or burns incident where treatment was required at the scene. Everything in her two plastic storage boxes on the floor of the boot seemed to be in its place. Only this afternoon she had stocked up from the hospital burns unit supply room with extra surgical gauze, rolls of clingfilm, and bandages. A nurse had interrupted her as she was filling a shopping bag, reminding her to sign the requisition folder before she left. Did she or didn't she sign the folder? Dr Bakhoum couldn't remember. No matter, she thought to herself, I can do it next time, and she closed the tailgate and locked up the Volvo.

Dr Amun Bakhoum was busy in the kitchen when his wife came in the front door. 'In here,' he shouted, 'I've made a start on dinner, and there's a bottle of red open on the counter.'

'Thanks,' she responded, 'I'll be there in a minute, just get rid of these bags first.'

Once she stepped into the kitchen Neith poured wine into the empty glass set next to the bottle, then reached over to give her husband a peck on the cheek. Looking at the table, with two places set for dinner, 'Only the two of us tonight then? Have you not heard from Darius?'

'No, nothing at all. I tried calling his mobile again five minutes ago but got no answer. Maybe he's going straight to Heather's place.'

'I've been trying to call him as well. Have you tried calling Heather?'

'No, I didn't want to cause any fuss. He might have secretly taken the day off to do something he doesn't want her to know about. You know, with the wedding coming up, he might be planning some kind of surprise present for her or something.'

'But we've not heard from him since he went to work yesterday morning. There's something not right, Amun. He's usually home by seven, if he's not here by the time we've finished dinner I'm calling the Police. In fact, I'm just going to call Heather right now, see if she's seen or heard from him today.'

Amun continued with his pasta sauce while Neith went in search of her mobile phone to make the call. He wasn't worried, Darius was a sensible young man. There would be a perfectly reasonable explanation for him being out of touch for a day or so. He just hoped Darius and Heather hadn't fallen out. Amun had spent a lot of money already on the wedding preparations, and he didn't think much of it would be refunded if the wedding was cancelled. He might have been born in Egypt, but he could think like a Scotsman.

'No answer. I tried Heather, Darius, and Heather's house number, all the same. Nothing.' Neith explained when she came back into the kitchen.

'It'll be fine, come and sit down. The pasta's nearly ready, the table's set, and I've refilled your wine glass. We'll have dinner, and you can phone again after we've finished. I'm sure everything is fine. Come on, sit down and enjoy dinner.'

Chapter 9

The usual Friday afternoon briefing in the MIT incident room had passed very quickly, with nothing new to add on any of their current cases. Nothing of a major nature was outstanding, and his team were either catching up on paperwork, or were assisting the local CID in more minor crime investigations. McManus had hated how his predecessor, DI Rutherford, had handled these briefings, and he was desperate to keep them short, interesting, and very much focussed on new information. He had already told his team he expected them to be completely familiar with all aspects of their current cases, no matter how minor. He had no intention of allowing unnecessary repetition of information at every briefing, and he also encouraged his newly promoted Detective Sergeant, Ronnie Gibson, to take the lead in most parts of each briefing. He expected a second new DS to join them next week. McManus had always been aware that his MIT staff levels included two Detective Sergeants, and when he was promoted to DI, and former DS Kerr had been transferred to uniform, he had no DS at all, and had discussed staffing levels with his boss, Detective Superintendent Nicholson. Gibson had an excellent record as a DC in the team, and was an ideal candidate for promotion, which the Superintendent duly sanctioned. However, the Superintendent was aware of McManus' relative inexperience, and had decided to find a much more experienced detective to fill the remaining vacant Sergeant position. A DS from Glasgow had recently applied for a transfer from there to 'P' Division, in Fife, as his wife's mother who lived near Dunfermline was ill, and she wanted to be close by. The opportunity seemed ideal for both parties, and without consulting McManus the Superintendent had arranged for DS Liam Robertson to join the team. McManus had not been happy when Nicholson broke the news, but he quickly agreed that the experienced detective would be an asset to the Fife MIT.

With the briefing over, McManus was looking forward to wall to wall golf on his weekend off. He had entered his name for the monthly medal at his home course, and there were the final two rounds of the Open to watch as well. Pushing papers from side to side, McManus stayed at the Police Station half watching play at Royal Portrush until after seven. With his eyes sore from watching golf on the small screen of his phone, he eventually drove home to Crossford, the first village on the main road to the west of Dunfermline.

As he reached the hill to the highest point of the village, McManus had managed to banish any Police thoughts from his head with some loud music playing on his car CD player. Driving into the cul-de-sac leading to his house, he could see a woman walking a dog turning into his street from the lane that led to a wooded area further up the hill. He noticed her shapely legs first, she was wearing shorts and trainers, with a tight vest top over ample breasts, and she looked strangely out of place, but a glance at his dashboard showed the temperature outside to be still in the mid-seventies. She looked familiar, but he could not immediately place her, although he was sure she did not live in any of the houses on his street. Slowing to turn into his driveway, McManus allowed the woman to walk across the front of his Ford Kuga then drove in and parked in front of his double garage. As he stepped out of his car, McManus heard the voice calling him from the pavement, 'Excuse me. Excuse me, are you Mr McManus?'

Turning to face the woman in the shorts McManus nodded, 'Yes, that's me. Can I help you?'

'I hope so,' she began, 'I need to talk to someone about something, and a neighbour said you were a detective, and could maybe help me.'

McManus walked to the foot of his drive and stood about six feet from the woman, a bit wary of the strange dog. It seemed quiet enough, but he didn't want to take any chances. Besides, if he got any closer he might not be able to stop himself staring at the woman's chest. 'What do you need to talk about? I'm actually off duty, maybe you should go into the Police Station if you need to see someone.'

'It's about my husband. You might know about his case, he was arrested for having photographs on his computer, you know, illegal ones. Of children. He was convicted last month, and he comes back to court on Monday for sentencing. I don't know what's going to happen to him, or who to speak to about it. Can you help me?'

'It wouldn't be one of my cases, and if it was I wouldn't be able to speak to you about it. Have you spoken to your husband about it, or his solicitor maybe?'

The woman looked close to tears, and the dog was pulling at the lead sensing something was wrong. 'I'm Jane Docherty, and my husband David is in Saughton Prison, he won't allow me to visit, he won't phone me, and he's instructed his solicitor not to talk to me either. I don't know where to turn for any information. I know he's done something really bad, but I don't know any of the details. The Police took his computer away, so I can't see what he had on it, and I don't know if I really want to know any way. What am I supposed to do?'

'I understand you're in a difficult situation, but I don't know anything about a case like that. When was he arrested?'

The woman began to sob as she allowed her story to flood out with her tears. The more he heard the more McManus realised he did know quite a bit about the case. It was the one where he had overheard two men talking in the pub toilets about sharing pornographic photographs. He had followed it up by hacking into one of the men's computers to find that he was a schoolteacher, and his computer was full of graphic images of children. He had then compounded his own crimes by sending a message from the man's email account to one of his Dunfermline detective colleagues, enclosing a sample of the image files and confessing his guilt. His colleague had followed up the extraordinary email confession and arrested the teacher, seizing his computer as evidence, and charging him with numerous offences. Of course, the intervention by McManus had been wiped from the computer's history as quickly as it had taken place. His unusual technical skills were not something he wished to share, preferring to use them at his discretion to uncover evidence of crime that might not otherwise come to light.

Realising that he had been primarily responsible for her husband's discovery, McManus relented a little. 'Is your husband a teacher by any chance, who drinks in the Adamson Hotel sometimes?'

'Yes, that's him. Do you know anything about his case?'

'A little bit, but I wasn't involved in it, I'm in a completely different department. Look, we can't stand out here and discuss a current case, and I've just got off shift. Do you want to come in for a minute, I could do with a cup of coffee.'

Sitting at the kitchen table McManus handed the woman a box of tissues, she had continued to cry while he had made them both coffee and her eye make-up was smeared over her cheeks. At least she had left the dog in the garden, its extending lead tied to the gatepost outside the back door. 'From what I remember hearing from a colleague, your husband emailed the Police confessing to having illegal child pictures on his computer, and they called at your home and arrested him. A search of the computer found multiple files containing illegal images, and he was charged and went to court. You probably know all that bit already.'

'Yes, but I don't know what kind of photographs they were. Or how he got them, or what he did with them. I can't imagine that he did anything to children, he was a teacher, for goodness sake. But I don't know enough about it, or about him anymore, to decide if I want him back or not. He's been in prison for nearly two months now, he pleaded guilty when he first came to court, but they put him away, pending reports they said. What am I supposed to do?'

McManus really knew little about the case, but enough to know that it was a very serious matter. With the man being a teacher, he could expect a heavier sentence because of his position of trust, but there being no evidence of contact with any of the children made the likely sentence a bit lighter. McManus felt no guilt for having exposed the teacher's predilections and would be happy to see another paedophile go to prison. But he was seeing first-hand the effects the man's crimes were having on his wife.

'Because the case is being dealt with at the Sheriff Court in Dunfermline, and not been referred to the High Court, the usual maximum prison sentence under that court's proceedings is twelve months. With your husband having been inside for two months already, he might get released in another four months or so. But if the Fiscal charged him under what's called Solemn Proceedings, then he could be jailed for up to five years. Do you know what happened when he went to court the first time? Did he appear in the public court, or was he taken to see the Sheriff in a private room?'

'He was in a private room. I didn't even get to see him; his solicitor came out and told me that he was ashamed and didn't want to speak to me. He was taken straight to prison, and neither of them have spoken to me since.'

'In that case, it sounds very serious indeed, and you need to prepare yourself for your husband getting a lengthy jail sentence. You can be in court on Monday, the case will be held in the public court, so you'll see and hear what goes on. But you won't get any more information about the case other than brief summaries from the Fiscal and your husband's solicitor before the Sheriff passes the sentence. I'm afraid I can't help you any more than that. Your husband is entitled to keep the details from you, which is quite possibly why he pleaded guilty at that early stage, so you wouldn't find out exactly what he had done.'

'It sounds like it's really serious then. I had no idea he had these photos, or that he had any interest sexually in children. We've got two kids of our own, and there was never any sign of anything wrong when they were growing up. God, I've been so stupid, all that time he would spend upstairs on his computer, schoolwork he would say, and I believed him. What a mug! Well, depending on what's said on Monday, I might be better off without him. I know I'll never be able to trust him again, I don't know if I want him in the house again, even if he gets a short sentence.'

'Why not wait until Monday, things might not be as bad as you think. Where are your children now, do they know anything about this?'

'They're both away at university, our son is in Aberdeen and our daughter is in London. They know their father was arrested, and why, but none of us knew any more than that until now. Thanks for listening to me and explaining things a bit for me. I better get going, let you get your dinner.' With a final swipe of a tissue across her eyes the woman stood up.

'That's ok Mrs Docherty, I'm not sure I've helped your situation much, but I hope you feel better for talking about it with me. Let me know what happens on Monday.' and McManus also pushed his chair back from the table and stood up. Their fingers brushed as they both reached for the empty coffee mugs, and before either realised what was happening they were in a crushing embrace, McManus backed up against the sink unit as they fought to keep their balance. He could feel himself becoming aroused and hoped the woman would not notice. Her long legs were temporarily forgotten as her ample breasts were crushed against his chest. Tempted as he was to run his hands over her tight shorts, McManus held her round her waist as he fought to regain his composure and allowed her to continue to hug him. Gently pushing himself away from her, McManus steered her towards the kitchen door. 'Remember to let me know what happens won't you? Now that you know where I live, you can drop by when you're out with your dog.'

'Oh, that mutt? He's not mine, I borrowed him from one of your neighbours, an excuse to come round this way on the off chance I might catch you coming home. She said you usually get home about six on a

Friday. I live in the next street down, so I'll see you on Monday, let you know what happened to that bastard husband of mine.'

McManus closed the door behind her and thought back to that night in the bar when he overheard the two men discussing their pictures. At least he had helped to put one of the sad fuckers behind bars. That deserved a drink tonight, that was why he was in this job after all.

By the time Neith and Amun Bakhoum had finished their dinner it was after nine o'clock, and leaving Amun to load the dishwasher, Neith stepped out into the conservatory to make her phone calls. When Amun joined her she was sitting in her favourite chair, staring out into the garden, tears streaming down her face.

'What's the matter, my love? Have you spoken to Darius?'

'Nobody is answering, neither Darius nor Heather is picking up. Both phones just go to the answering service after a few rings. I can't get an answer at Heather's flat either. It's just not like him, or Heather for that matter, not to be in contact for so long.'

'I know, it's really starting to get a bit worrying. We've not heard from him now since Thursday morning. Did you ring the Police?'

'Fat lot of use that was.' she spat out between sobs. 'They said he's an adult. They don't consider an adult to be missing till they've been out of contact for 48 hours. I've to phone again tomorrow morning if he's not turned up.'

Chapter 10

McManus had watched the last players complete their rounds while he finished off his microwaved lasagne. Daylight in July meant the Open golfers were still playing late into the evening, hoping to qualify for the final two rounds on Saturday and Sunday. As he flicked channels on his massive wall-mounted TV, he thought about Jane Docherty, and how she had felt as he had been pressed up against his kitchen sink only a few hours ago. She was incredibly attractive, long slender legs, married, but probably soon to be separated, kids away at university, just his type really. He definitely preferred older married women, less hassle he thought to himself. It was his involvement with just such a woman recently that had nearly cost him his career, but instead he had ended up being promoted and heading up the MIT. He wondered how Georgina Rutherford was getting on. He hadn't heard from her since she separated from her husband, McManus' old boss on that last case. 'What a cock up that turned out to be.' he recalled, and he picked up his mobile from the coffee table and dialled her number.

Georgie had been cool on the phone, not returning McManus's cheery banter, choosing instead to remain aloof and distant. Gradually the conversation had grown warmer, and Georgie had explained that she was now living alone in her house in Leven, still working at the bakery, and still playing golf at Lundin Links on the weekends. Her husband, former

Detective Inspector Ian Rutherford, was living with his brother in Kirkcaldy, he had not yet found another job, and he still blamed McManus for losing his job, his wife, his home, and everything else in his life. McManus felt no remorse for any part of Rutherford's situation, he had not liked the man anyway, and it was only a matter of time before his attitude led to his downfall. It all meant that he could maybe meet Georgie a bit more often now, but he had to be careful. There was no way he wanted any long-term relationships; he was perfectly happy with his bachelor lifestyle. By the end of the call, he and Georgie had agreed to meet for dinner the following week, to catch up, but with no promises about anything beyond that.

Satisfied that his love life was looking a bit more promising than it did earlier that evening, McManus switched off the TV, loaded the dishwasher with his few dirty plates, and climbed the stairs to the top floor. He had set up one of his spare rooms as an office and computer room, with large monitors connected to a powerful computer. His red and black leather gaming chair was the most comfortable seat in his house, and he pulled it up to the edge of the workstation and opened his system. He booted up his laptop and set it to auto sync with the main computer, before opening a chatroom site and logging in. He found Gregor Aitken was online, and he sent him a quick message asking for a voice call. Gregor had been involved in his last case, the murder in Pittenweem, and had some amazing computer skills. McManus kept in touch, knowing that he was owed a favour, and would probably find Gregor useful at some point when he needed something the Police techs could not offer.

Once the voice call was live, Gregor chatted for a bit about his sister, who was on holiday in Spain with her university friend Sophia. McManus had also met the two students during that last case, and he was pleased to hear that they were both well after their experience with the two murders. But the most interesting news was about Gregor's attempts to hack into four bank accounts that McManus had identified. The accounts were located in France, and Spain, and each bank had received a cash deposit of the equivalent of 7,500 euros over the first two weeks of July. McManus knew that the accounts belonged to a serving Police officer, a senior one at that, and that the balances indicated that the deposits had been going on for several years. He also knew that the senior officer had recently been on holiday in France with his wife, close enough to the Spanish border to make easy trips to the banks concerned. Knowing that the officer was depositing chunks of cash every year was not enough to justify further action by McManus. Especially when the officer was senior to him in the chain of command. But it was enough to keep McManus interested, and he remained determined to build a corruption case eventually. But he had no evidence that he could bring to an investigation. Only suspicions and illegally obtained information. He chatted further with Gregor about monitoring the accounts before closing the call.

His next clicks of his mouse took him to a view of CCTV cameras in Dunfermline town centre. Scrolling through the various screens, he found a view of the car park in Bridge Street and searched the area for a particular car. The lighting in the area was good, and although he could not make out the licence numbers clearly, he could identify the make and model he was looking for. Reaching over to the small fridge that sat on the floor under the adjacent workstation, McManus took out a beer and settled down to watch the footage. Sure enough, his wait was rewarded as he saw a couple walking unsteadily towards the white Mercedes saloon. He recognised the car owner immediately, it was the same local solicitor he had seen before, the one who made a habit of driving home drunk on a Friday night. Clearly he had not been deterred by McManus´ last intervention. Unfortunately, he also recognised the woman with him. It was one of the paralegals from the Fiscal's office, who happened to be married to a Police Constable. PC Collins was currently working on the night shift and could not be too far away. McManus uncharacteristically hesitated, the solicitor deserved to be caught for drink driving, but the revelation of his companion's identity could cause untold damage. Not his problem, he concluded, and picked up his mobile phone as he watched the drunken couple get into the Mercedes. He had worked with the young PC before, a nice lad who had a great future in the job, and selected his number from the contact list. Dialling Collins, he simply said that he had received information that the solicitor was about to drive home while drunk, and he would be exiting from the Bridge Street car park. Every officer in Dunfermline knew that white Mercedes, and he trusted that the PC would intercept him somewhere between the car park and the solicitor's home. The rest was up to him.

McManus sipped from his beer can and watched the white car drive away. What did he care? The man was a serial drink driver, he just hadn't been caught yet. He just hoped Collins could survive the impact of what he was about to learn. McManus had talked with the young officer for hours one night, after the PC had asked why McManus had joined the Police.

He told him the story of how when McManus was just nineteen he went off to St Andrews University, and four years later he emerged with an honours degree in Economics, a plus two golf handicap, and numerous business contacts for the future. The first summer out of University, with no firm plans for a job, he interned at his father's law practice. His father was well known in Edinburgh legal circles, and he had also made millions from property deals in the capital. His father was pleased to have him in the firm, and he did everything, made tea, ran errands, delivered mail, and met many sorry people who had fallen foul of the law. That was when he learned how the law really worked, and he decided to stay on for a bit longer for no reason other than the sheer amazement he felt at the inadequacies of the Scottish criminal justice machine.

Constantly seeing guilty people escape punishment, victims failing to obtain justice, or compensation for injuries or losses, he realised there had to be a better way, and being a solicitor, or economist would not cut it. There seemed to be a massive bias in the system towards helping the criminals, the perverts, the guilty, instead of their victims. It looked like the criminals held all the power, and the system was helplessly trying to keep up. The quality of evidence being put to the courts seemed to be inadequate, the Procurator Fiscal's office only seemed to take forward cases they were certain of winning, and the sentencing policies in the courts seemed out of kilter with the crimes committed.

After a year or so he decided it wasn´t for him, he felt frustrated not being able to win against the system, against the crooks, the murderers and rapists who manipulated the courts and the justice system. His father was content to profit from the queue of criminals at his door, his reputation for winning was well known, and he regularly had good prosecution cases thrown out of court on one technicality or another. But McManus was powerless in a system where power always prevailed. What was a twenty-four-year-old economics graduate supposed to do? He had decided to dedicate his career to bringing the guilty to justice, to seize power away from the crooks and murderers, to make them pay for their crimes, and to making sure that the courts had all the evidence they needed to make it happen. He was now too well known in Edinburgh, and he needed a position where he could make changes, where he could make a difference, not just be a small fish in a big sea. He needed to find a smaller pond, so the next day he made his application to join Fife Constabulary. He was six feet four inches tall, weighed bang on fifteen stones, and had no trouble at all with the physical or the academic entry requirements.

'The bad guys have to go down, mate. That's our job. They have to go down hard, so they stay down. It takes guts, smarts, and effort to do this job, but we chose this. Let's put the bad guys down.'

Hopefully, the young PC would remember that. How he and his wife dealt with it after that was up to them. But at least the dodgy solicitor was going down this time.

Chapter 11

Neith Bakhoum and her husband held hands as they walked back to the car. 'I told you it would be a waste of time, it's been 48 hours now, and still they're not interested.'

'That's not fair, Neith,' explained Amun, 'the Sergeant took all the details, the car registration number, the contact numbers for his work, for Heather, and you gave him that photo of Darius from just last week.'

'Yes, I know. He said he would start making enquiries at once, but I don't believe he took us seriously. I know Darius is twenty-five, has his own car, good job, a new home to go to after his wedding, but it's just not like him to not call us back. We have to do something ourselves. I don't think the Police are going to be any help, they´ve obviously got better things to do on a Saturday morning.'

'Fine. Where do you suggest we start?' Amun was clearly frustrated but didn't want to upset his wife any further. They both wanted to find Darius, so he got behind the wheel and started the engine. 'Let's drive out to Heather's place, Cowdenbeath is only ten minutes away. Have you got her address?'

With the address set into the car's sat nav system they set off to find their missing son. It was still early enough that Heather or her flat mate Rachel would probably still be in bed on a Saturday morning. Full of hope, Amun drove out of the public car park of

Dunfermline Police Station and onto the busy roundabout.

The two brothers ran down the pavement with their Labrador puppy chasing after them, jumping up and snapping at their heels. They were in a hurry, they had to get home before their father woke up, or they would be in big trouble for taking the dog out on their own. Aged only seven and ten, they were full of energy in the mornings, and had tiptoed into their parents' bedroom before eight o'clock, unable to sleep any longer. Their mother had been barely awake when she sent them packing, fearful that they would waken her husband, who was sleeping off a late night at the local social club. She did not realise they had gone out, taking the pup with them, but she had fallen asleep again very quickly, and thought no more about it.

The brothers had walked up to the disused Mossbank Quarry, a place supposed to be out of bounds to them, but they liked to play there anyway. Their favourite game was to throw a piece of wood or plastic bottle into the huge flooded hole, then throw rocks at it to try to sink the imaginary battleship. They hadn't been there for a few days, but this morning a much bigger target was waiting for them. A white car was partially submerged in the murky water, with only the boot sticking up at the foot of the thirty-foot drop from the quarry edge. As ten-year-old boys do, they thought nothing of gathering up a pile of rocks, ready to launch them at the rear window of the car. No sooner had they begun dropping the rocks onto the car below, the first target being the car number plate, when they heard an angry shout from behind them. An old man, with an even older looking mongrel dog, was shouting and waving his walking stick at them. They didn't wait to hear what the old man was shouting, they hurled one last rock over the edge and ran off as fast as they could.

PC John Kerr sat in the front passenger seat of the Police patrol car, eating his warm sausage roll from Greggs. His official meal break was not till ten o'clock, and he had been hungry since he had come on duty at six. With an hour still to go before he could legitimately go back to Cowdenbeath Police Station, he had asked the young PC who was driving him today to stop at the baker's shop for a coffee and his favourite snack. Now they were parked just off the road, in the entrance to the old quarry, hidden from passing traffic by a screen of tall bushes. With the sausage roll half in his mouth, Kerr was startled by a sharp rap on his passenger side window. Coughing out a mouthful of flaky pastry crumbs, he hastily brushed his trousers and pressed the button to open the window.

'Did you see two youngsters running down here a minute ago? With a black lab puppy? They must have passed right by you.'

Kerr had no idea what the old man was talking about and said so. The old man repeated his question, looking at Kerr through the open window. 'Well, are you going to get out and do something about it?' continued the old man.

'About what, some kids running down here with a dog?'

'No, about the car in the quarry. The kids were throwing rocks at it. That's what I mean. Maybe it's been stolen or something. You should check it out.'

'Ok, give me a minute till I finish my breakfast.' But the man turned and walked away before Kerr could say any more. Kerr crumpled up the paper bag and stuffed it into his empty coffee carton. The padlock and chain that normally denied access to the track leading to the quarry was lying loose on the ground, so the young PC at the wheel drove the patrol car carefully over the rough ground. Parking as close as she dared to the quarry edge, they both got out and looked down into the flooded base of the old slate workings. The young officer had been out here a few times when they were getting to know the layout of the new patch. She was still new to the area, and frequently got lost on her way to calls. Kerr, although much more senior in service, was no use in that regard either, he had only been stationed at Cowdenbeath for a matter of weeks.

Sure enough, there was a car partly submerged in the flooded quarry. It looked like it had hit a ledge in the cliff wall which prevented it from falling all the way to the bottom. Kerr could see the registration plate, and noted the number in his pocketbook, along with the date and time. Walking around the top of the cliff edge, Kerr tried to get a better view of the car, but the water was up to the back windscreen. There was no way he could tell if there was anyone inside the car or not. Picking up his personal radio he called the station with the information about the car, hoping it might be a stolen car, and the owner would have to arrange its recovery. Then maybe he could leave and head back to the station for his official breakfast. But there was no such luck. The car was not recorded as stolen, but instead belonged to someone from Dunfermline. The controller had called the address on record, but there was no answer. Could Kerr and his colleague stand by the vehicle until the Sergeant could join him?

What for, thought Kerr. It's an abandoned vehicle. It looks like it's empty. Some neds have probably stolen it last night and dumped it here. The owner's going to be still asleep in a nice warm bed. In the meantime, I've to wait here, miss my break, and then I'll get chewed out by the Sergeant for taking the patrol car off road. Even though I wasn't driving.

While he waited, Kerr thought about the events that had brought him to this old quarry in this rundown old town. He would never forgive Mark McManus for his current predicament. The fact that it was his own drink driving conviction that had led to his demotion and transfer out of the Major Incident Team was nothing to do with how he felt. He despised McManus, he despised life as a PC, and he hated Cowdenbeath.

But that did not change the fact that a white Audi A3 lay nose down in the water below him. It just meant he would have more paperwork to do. He fucking hated McManus!

Chapter 12

Watson had been out shopping and arrived back at his house in a good mood. Not only had he managed to purchase some high-quality heroin the day before, but today he had located a supply of something a bit special. Something he could use to cut the heroin, to spice it up a bit, make it more powerful, and give a better high. It used to be called China White in the US, but his supplier told him that here in Scotland they liked to call it 'White Heather.' He was looking forward to trying it out himself, but first he had a few things to take care of.

In the upstairs bedroom, Watson had gathered his two mates, Bugsy and Gasser, to help him. The two girls were still bound and gagged, one on the single bed, the other lay on the floor. 'Girls, today is a big day for us. I'm going to take you home, but first you have to help me with something. If I take your gags off, do you promise not to scream or shout or anything?'

The reply was muffled, but both girls were frantically nodding their heads. 'That's a good start, but first here's what I need you to do. In these bags are some sets of new bedding. I want you to strip down the beds in this room, and next door, then make them up again with the new stuff. Understood?' More frantic nodding followed from the two captives. 'Then, I need you both to get cleaned up, showered, hair washed, and then dressed in the new clothes I've brought you.' Watson produced two jogging suits from another plastic shopping bag, along with two pairs of slipper socks. 'Are we all clear on what you have to do?' The girls mumbled again and nodded vigorously, seeing an end to their ordeal now within reach.

'Bugsy and Gasser, I need you to keep an eye on them while they're cleaning up. Then I want you to vacuum the carpets in both rooms, then clean the bathroom from top to bottom. There's bottles of bleach and cloths in one of these bags. We have to make sure there's no trace left of the girls in these rooms. It needs to look like they were never here.'

Reaching down, Watson untied the gag on Rachel first, then untied her hands and feet. Hauling her into a sitting position on the bed he asked her 'You know what will happen if you ever tell anyone about your visit here, don't you?'

'Yes, Watty, I know. I promise again that I will never tell anyone about this. Just let us go. Please.' pleaded Rachel.

'What about you, Heather?' he asked as he bent down to release his sister's bindings.

'We told you last night, Watty. Neither of us will tell anyone. Not a soul.' promised Heather. 'Just let us go.'

'Ok, I believe you. Get these beds changed, and then you two can get cleaned up. I'm going to drive you home myself.'

Neith Bakhoum got back into her husband's Passat, defeated and unsure of what to do next. There had been no-one in at Heather's flat, and no neighbours had been home either. They had driven around a few of the nearby streets looking for Darius' car, but there was no sign of it anywhere. They did not know if Rachel owned a car, and there was no point in driving back and forth any more. 'Come on, Neith, let's go home and get some lunch. We can wait for news from the Police there. There's nothing more we can do here.' Amun put his arm around his wife's shoulders and hugged her awkwardly in the front seat of the car.

'I suppose you're right. Maybe we can come back tomorrow?' Neith asked as her husband put the car into gear and drove off.

'We'll see what happens, shall we?'

Neither of them spotted the Vauxhall Astra turning into Rachel's street as they waited at the traffic lights a hundred yards away.

PC Kerr was still standing by at the disused quarry, he still hadn't had his break, and the Sergeant had been called away on another shout instead of coming to meet him at the quarry. Messages on his radio had told him that the owner of the part-submerged Audi could not be contacted, but that he should remain there until further information was available. What a waste of time, he thought. I could be doing something else instead of babysitting a crashed car. Anyone who might have been in there will be dead by now anyway. And the car's not going anywhere is it? He couldn't go back to the station, which is where his sandwich box was, but no-one would know if he just nipped down to Greggs for another coffee and sausage roll, would they? Especially if he went through the housing scheme, rather than round the link road. Decision made, Kerr bullied his young driver until the PC got in the car and drove him away in search of something warm and satisfying. His mind was debating whether to have another sausage roll, or go for a steak bake instead, and maybe a cup of tomato soup rather than coffee. He never saw the Passat waiting at the traffic lights, or the Astra a few streets away. Within twenty minutes he had bought and eaten his warming snack, returned to the quarry, and nobody was any the wiser.

Watson had seen the patrol car though and prayed that the two girls in the back of his Astra would keep their promise and not try to attract the Policemen's attention as they turned into Rachel's street. They kept their word, and he parked outside the flat and let them out of the car. 'Be good girls now. Tell no-one, and just remember this. I know where you live.' Watson grinned at them and drove off.

Once inside the flat, Rachel grabbed Heather by the shoulders, and they stood clinging to each other. Moving back and holding her friend at arm's length, Heather said 'Rachel, I'm really sorry. I had no idea what was happening. All I know is they pulled me out of Darius' car, set fire to it, and pushed it over the quarry edge, with him still in it. I didn't know that they had taken you to Watty's place.'

'It's ok, Heather. We're safe now. We can't tell anyone about this, you know what he'll do to me. I could never handle that again. It's not you that they're going to beat, and rape again is it? You have to promise me Heather, you must never tell anyone.'

'Rachel, it's ok. I promise. I will never tell anyone. Not unless we both agree and do it together. But I'll tell you now. He might be my big brother, but he is going to pay for what he did to you and Darius. And that is a promise I intend to keep.'

'Thanks Heather, I believe you. Now the first thing I want to do is get out of this stupid jogging suit and have a proper shower.'

The Bakhoums had arrived home and eaten a light lunch, talking about what to do next. Neith had made a call to Darius' work, but the main switchboard was connected to a message simply giving opening hours, and numbers for the various customer services centres. No-one at any of the numbers could answer her question about Darius having been at work on either Thursday or Friday. If she had thought to ask the same question about Heather, she might have learned that Heather had not turned up the day before. But that would not have helped her find her son. So Neith and Amun spent the rest of the afternoon considering various scenarios, none of which fitted with their image of their caring and thoughtful son.

It was after four o'clock when the phone rang. Amun had answered to find a constable from Cowdenbeath Police station asking about the owner of a white Audi A3 car. The car had been found partly submerged in a quarry in Cowdenbeath, and the Police were eager to speak to the registered owner, a Darius Bakhoum. Amun patiently explained the situation to the PC, and carefully noted down all the information he was given. After calling the Dunfermline station and finding out they had no knowledge of the car in the quarry, he had replayed the conversations to his wife.

'What if Darius is in the car? Do they know if anyone is in it? Are they going to pull the car out of the water?'

'I can't answer any of those, Neith. Calm down and think about this for a minute. We reported him missing to Dunfermline Police this morning. But Dunfermline doesn't know anything about the car, so we have to go to Cowdenbeath. Get a jacket, and I'll start the car. We have to see about getting that car checked and pulled out of the water. We need to know if Darius is in it or not!'

'Wait a second, phone Cowdenbeath back, see what they're going to do about the car. Then we can go.'

Amun replaced the receiver on its stand and turned to face his wife. 'They say there is no sign of any occupants inside the car, it's almost fully submerged. They can't do anything about removing the car tonight. Apparently, they need a Police dive team to secure a winch to the car, and a special crane to lift it out after that. They are making those arrangements now that they know Darius has been reported missing. They hope to start the recovery tomorrow morning. There's nothing else we can do about it just now.'

'Yes, there is. I can try calling Heather again.'

Heather diverted the call when she saw who it was ringing her mobile. She had been re-living the last two days with Rachel, both in tears, both in pyjamas, and with cups of hot chocolate. Rachel really needed to see a doctor, but she had refused to let Heather call one. Instead she had taken two hot showers since Watson had dropped them off at the flat, and Heather was still flushed from the one she had taken later once the water heated up again. She cradled the mobile against her, trying to muffle any sound it might make, afraid it would ring again at any moment. How could she possibly speak to Darius' mother? How could she tell her that her son was dead, that he had been murdered by Heather's own brother? That was a call she could not take, not until she could say the words to herself first, assuming she ever found the words to describe what her brother had done.

Chapter 13

McManus was still in bed when his phone rang at nine-thirty on Sunday morning. The caller display showed it was his boss, Detective Superintendent Nicholson, and he pushed himself upright against his pillow before answering. A quick glance to his left showed that there should be no interruptions from that direction, for the moment at least.

'Good morning, Mark. Sorry to call you on your day off, but I need you to help out with an enquiry in Cowdenbeath.'

'Oh, em, yes...... of course sir.' McManus stuttered. 'Is it a murder, then sir?'

'No, or at least not yet anyway. It's a missing person case, a man from Dunfermline, reported missing yesterday morning. His car was found in a flooded quarry in Cowdenbeath yesterday morning.'

'I see. Was there a body found in the car then sir?'

'Not yet. They are recovering the vehicle this morning, in a few minutes actually. We need someone from CID down there, but the local squad have a few DCs on holiday, so I thought you could help out. I don't think you have any pressing enquiries right now do you?'

'No sir, just a few minor cases where we're helping the local lads. What do you need from MIT, maybe a DS and one DC to start with?'

'I think that would be enough to start with, see where the recovery leads, try to find this misper, put the case to bed as soon as possible. You can allocate resources as you see fit, Mark, within reason of course'

'Of course, sir. I'll get DS Gibson and DC Edwards to make contact with Cowdenbeath as soon as I can get hold of them.'

'Thanks, Mark. You make sure to enjoy the rest of your weekend off.' and the call was ended.

McManus snuggled back under the covers and spooned against the warm back of the woman lying next to him. Reaching around her, he squeezed her breast firmly, bringing a breathy gasp from her lips, and a backward press from her hips. 'Did you hear that DC Edwards, the boss says I've to get a hold of you, he's got a job for you. But so have I, and I'm closest.'

Gill Edwards knew exactly what he meant, and wriggled round under the sheet as he wrapped his fingers in her hair, guiding her downwards.

When DC Edwards arrived at the quarry she looked quickly around at what could potentially be a crime scene. Fat chance of that she thought, it's more like a circus than a crime scene. There was no scene tape anywhere. No white suits. No barriers in sight. The DI would have a fit if this turned out to be a murder instead of a missing person or an abandoned stolen car. The access to the quarry was by a single rough track, but no-one was stationed at the entrance to restrict entry. Cars seemed to be abandoned on every available flat surface, a breakdown truck with a car trailer sat tucked behind a rocky outcrop, the driver sipping from a mug. Two police patrol cars were parked off the side of the track, in a small clearing between the overgrown rhododendron bushes that seemed to surround the site. A white truck with Police lettering was evidence of the presence of the Police Specialist Diving Unit, and a man in a wetsuit was conferring with a uniform

Sergeant at the steps leading up to the truck rear doors. The most intriguing sight was the yellow mobile crane, parked close to the edge of the quarry. Its huge tyres must have obliterated almost every other mark in the dust and gravel as it drove into position. The crane was immobile, its long arm hanging out over the edge of the quarry, a stout cable hanging from the end, and Edwards made her way towards it. As she did so, she saw that DS Ronnie Gibson was also part of the conversation with the diver, and spotting her, he waved to Edwards, beckoning her over.

'What's going on Ronnie? This place is total chaos. Do you want me to get some scene tape out and try to create some sort of access control?'

'It's a bit late for that Gill. The car was discovered yesterday morning, any number of cars and people could have been up here since. Oh, and it's good of you to join us, Gill. What kept you?'

'You know what it's like, Ronnie. Every time I was getting ready to head out, something else kept getting in the way. But I'm here now, so what gives?'

Gibson repeated the information he had received from McManus in the earlier phone call and added the update from the Dive team. 'The water is pretty murky, but they're reasonably certain there is no-one inside the car. The divers have attached a cable to it, ready for the crane to lift it out of the water. We're just waiting for the owner's parents to arrive. The owner is registered as Darius Bakhoum. 25 years of age, Dunfermline address. He's the one who was reported missing yesterday morning, not been seen since Thursday morning apparently.'

'Sounds a bit of a mystery then. So why do they need the MIT on this?' Edwards kicked at a loose rock to show her lack of enthusiasm at being called out to the middle of nowhere.

'Typical July, isn't it? Too many of the local CID boys on holiday at the same time. They all want time off in the school holidays so they can take the kids to Tenerife or somewhere.'

'Well, let's hope they pull the car out easily, we can look inside, then start trying to trace this Bakhoum lad. I was working on something for the DI before I came out here, and I know he'd like me to finish it off later if I can.'

Just then a Volkswagen saloon drove up the track, stopping beside the two parked police cars. The uniform sergeant spotted it and went to intercept the man and woman who had got out of the car. Gibson and Edwards were too far away to hear the conversation, but the man and woman got back into the car and the sergeant re-joined them. 'That's the owner's parents. He's still missing. I've asked them to stay in their car until we can lift the Audi out of the quarry and inspect it.'

'Good call Sergeant. We don't know yet what's inside the car. Pray he's not there, but the diver can't be certain it's empty. So, are we good to go?' asked Gibson, keen to get the show on the road.

The Sergeant nodded and shouted to the crane driver, who started the engine and began to slowly winch the cable upwards. The two divers, the Sergeant, the two local PCs and Gibson and Edwards all peered over the edge of the drop into the water at the base of the quarry, waiting for the car to emerge from the dark water. The rear wheels appeared quickly as the cable wound slowly around the drum of the winch. Then the rear doors showed themselves, both firmly closed, but the tinted glass kept the car's interior a secret. It seemed for a moment as if the winch failed, the cable lost tension, and the car dropped two feet back into the water. The onlookers gasped and leaned further forward, looking for any obstruction that might be causing the car to fight against the crane's powerful motors. But the winch won and the car, famed for its slogan 'Vorsprung Durch Technic', was hauled unceremoniously backwards from the water. Water poured downwards from the open front windows and the cable jerked upwards as the load lightened. Dragging it backwards over the edge of the drop, the crane finally backed away from the car, pulling it onto a flat area of loose gravel.

With the car sitting once again on all four wheels, the police officers moved in to inspect it. DS Gibson took command, and issued latex gloves to the others, instructing them to stand back for a moment. All the doors were closed, and the grey airbags hung like ghosts from the front pillars, the front windows and over the steering wheel. Gibson began by opening the driver's door and leaning in for a closer look. Muddy water still covered the floor, and odd papers, a pair of sunglasses and a single shoe lay in the muck. Without touching anything, Gibson looked around the interior, at the driver's area, at the door panels, the dashboard, and finally at the roof. It was obvious that there had been a fire in the front of the car, centred around the driver's seat. The burning was not immediately noticeable on the dark material of the car seat, but the dark stain on the white roof lining puzzled Gibson.

'It looks like there's been a fire in here, and until we know the cause, we need to tread carefully here. I'm going to call this in now as a crime scene. Gill, can you contact the Forensics Unit. Sergeant, can your lads close off the locus, put a car across the track down at the main road maybe, then put some scene tape up. We need to seal off this area till we can examine it properly. And I guess I should go and speak to the parents.'

'Mr and Mrs Bakhoum, I'm Detective Sergeant Ronnie Gibson. As you can see, we've recovered the vehicle from the water, but there's no-one in the car. There is some light damage to the car, but whether it's from the drop, or it happened previously, I can't tell yet. At the moment, we still don't know where your son is, but we will continue to treat this as a missing persons case until we find him. The registration plate is clearly identifiable, so we're certain that it's your son's car. We'll be able to check the engine and chassis numbers just to confirm, once we get all the details from the computer.'

Amun Bakhoum was not too happy and leaned forward into Gibson's face. 'All very well to lift the car from the water Detective Sergeant, but where is my son? If he is not in the car, then where is he?'

'I don't have an answer to give you just now. We need to study the car, to see what we can learn. For all we know the car could have been stolen sometime in the last three days and dumped here. Darius could be away somewhere, and completely unaware that his car is here. We don't know. You have to give us some time to figure this out.'

'Figure this out?' What is there to figure out? Our son is missing. His car turns up at the bottom of a quarry, and there is no sign of him anywhere. Is he in the water, Sergeant? Dead?'

'I'm sorry, but I don't know. But we will find out what happened here. It will just take some time. Now can you go and sit in your car for a few moments. I want to get something to show you.' Gibson gently turned Mr Bakhoum back towards his car, then walked back to his own car to retrieve some evidence bags. After taking some photographs with his cell phone, Gibson reached into the driver's foot well of the soaking wet Audi and picked up the discarded shoe. Dropping it into an evidence bag, he then went back to speak to the Bakhoums.

'Do either of you recognise this shoe?' he asked as soon as Mr Bakhoum wound down his window. Amun shook his head and passed the bag to his wife. Neith took her time, and examined the shoe more carefully, turning it over to look first at the sole, then at the inside of the heel.

'This is one of Darius' shoes. He was very particular about what he wore to work. He bought all his work shoes from the same online company. You can see their name on the insole, right at the heel there. And it's his size, a 10.' Neith turned the shoe inside the bag to let Gibson see the company name on the inside, and the size on the sole. She then clutched the evidence bag to her chest and cried out in anguish. 'Oh Darius. Wherever you are, please come home.'

Gibson could only watch through the window, helpless as Amun cradled his wife's head to his shoulder. Reaching in gently, Gibson retrieved the evidence bag from between them and walked away to begin his investigation. What kind of investigation it was to be he could not tell yet. Was it an accident, suicide, or was it a murder? He would call the DI, he could decide. Day off or not, that's what the DI was paid for after all.

Chapter 14

The insistent buzzing of his mobile phone from the other room was not loud enough to distract McManus from watching the eight sizzling rashers of Ayrshire back bacon in his frying pan. He was about to crack the two eggs that would be the finishing touch to his bacon and egg rolls. The kettle was coming to the boil for his mug of tea, and he was spreading butter thickly on both halves of his morning rolls that he had just de-frosted. With the bottle of Heinz brown sauce at the ready, his plate and mug already sitting on the tray, he was looking forward to his traditional Scottish brunch in front of the TV. The leaders in the Open Championship would be teeing off shortly, and the only item on his schedule for this Sunday afternoon was four hours of live golf. He had a small wager with the professional at his golf club, and his selection was still in contention after the third round had finished yesterday. Anything could happen over the rest of the afternoon, and he was determined to enjoy every last minute of it. He would enjoy it even more when he collected his winnings in the club shop next week.

Finally sitting in his leather recliner, McManus bit into the first of his rolls, the sticky egg yolk oozing out of the side and down his chin. As he reached for the paper napkin on the side table beside his tea, his phone buzzed again. Trying to juggle his napkin, sticky brown and yellow roll, and the tray on his knee, McManus gave up on reaching the phone, and took another huge bite of bread, butter, bacon, egg, and sauce. Chuckling to himself for a minute, he thought 'and they say this stuff's not good for you. Well, they're right, I nearly knocked over my tea.'

McManus finished the first roll, wiped his hands, took a mouthful of tea, and looked at his phone display. 'Ronnie Gibson,' he said to himself, 'Ronnie loves a bacon roll as much as the next man. He'll understand if I don't call him back right away.'

A few holes later, and with two breakfast rolls demolished and washed down with a mug of strong tea, McManus called Gibson back.

Gibson related the details of the situation at the quarry in Cowdenbeath in a concise way that left nothing out. McManus was impressed, he had selected Gibson for promotion only two months before, after having worked with him on just one case. The murders in Pittenweem and Crail, that had been his own first case in the MIT, had been solved despite all the distractions that had surrounded the investigation. Ronnie Gibson had acquitted himself well there and managed to steer clear of the scandal that enveloped the former DI Rutherford and DS Kerr. He was pleased to see Gibson was up to the job of DS in the MIT.

'Great work, Ronnie. You seem to have it all under control. But it's still officially a missing person case isn't it? Unless you find any evidence that points to anything more sinister, I want you and Gill to run with it for the rest of today. I know you said about the burnt headlining, and the shoe. But have you got anything else?'

No, Boss, we don't. The dive team is going to search the area around where the car was, but the water is too murky really. They are bringing in drag nets and a dinghy, but that will be a few hours till they get the stuff here. It's light enough until quite late, so they're prepared to work on until it gets too dark.'

'That's great, Ronnie. Keep me posted on any developments but keep it low key for just now. If any reporters show up refer them to the Press Office. Phone me if you need anything. You ok with that?'

'Sure, no problem. I've encouraged the parents to go home and stay by the phone. They're leaving now. The Forensic Unit has just pulled up, so I'm going to brief them, and I'll phone you again later, let you know what's going on.'

'Brilliant. Anything else going on that I should know about?'

'Yes, a couple of things. You'll be interested to know that PC John Kerr was one of the officers who originally called in the discovery of the car in the quarry.'

'What, that little wanker. What was he doing out there, probably sneaking a tea break or a kip no doubt? What else?'

'Well, did you hear about the young lad on nightshift in Dunfermline, couple of nights ago. He pulled over a local solicitor on suspicion of drink driving. Not only was the solicitor completely pissed, but it turns out the PC's wife was in the car with him. Seems the brief's been shagging her for months and the PC had no idea. Funnily enough, the brief was so pissed that when he got out of the car he lost his balance, stumbled, and broke his nose when he fell against the door mirror. Or so the story goes anyway. The PCs been off sick since. Seemingly the wife was pissed too, and attacked him with her handbag, broke his jaw. She had a half bottle of gin in it apparently. It was only when they all got back to the station that she realised it was her husband who had arrested the driver. The demon drink, eh?'

'I hadn't heard that one Ronnie. Hope that it works out ok for the young lad. I heard he was a good copper. But that's the job isn't it? Sometimes it all works out, other times we're just not very lucky!'

By 7 o'clock the Open had finished in a narrow victory for the home favourite, and McManus was having an attack of conscience. He could not decide if it would be a sign of lack of confidence in his team if he turned up at the crime scene or not. DS Gibson seemed to have it all in hand, but the Super might not agree. Luckily, he had been drinking tea and coffee while watching the golf unfold over an eventful afternoon on the Irish coast, and he decided to drive out to the quarry anyway. It was only to show support for his team, he told himself, and to show his commitment to the boss. After only two months in his new post he did not want the Detective Superintendent to think he was lazy. That would never do. After a quick change, McManus drove his Ford Kuga out of his two-car garage and pressed the remote to close the door behind him. He failed to notice the good-looking woman with the dog who jerked back behind a parked car on the opposite side of the street.

Chapter 15

McManus stopped his car at the entrance to the quarry and got out, approaching the PC with the clipboard standing next to the crime scene tape. 'DI McManus, MIT.' he said for the benefit of the crime scene log, watching as the PC made a note on his pad. 'Is DS Gibson still here?'

'Yes sir, over by the Dive Team vans. They've a tea urn set up there, nothing else to do till the dinghy and drag nets get here apparently, sir.'

'Thanks. What's your name Constable?'

'Morrison, sir. Anne Morrison.'

McManus could not help noticing her deep green eyes, olive toned skin and the dark hair pulled smoothly into a tight bun behind her uniform hat. The standard issue stab vest hid most everything else, but he had already noticed her long legs and slim hips clad in the black trousers of the Police Scotland uniform.

'Ok, Anne, I'll have someone bring you over a cup of tea. You've been standing here a while I imagine.'

'Thank you, sir. Only since my meal break at ten. I was meant to finish at two, but the Sergeant asked me to stay on for a couple of hours overtime. I'm hoping to be relieved soon, I'm expecting word from my Sergeant, but I haven't heard anything yet.'

'Let me check up on that and I'll let you know what's happening in a minute.' McManus said over his shoulder as he walked towards the large white van parked further up the rough track.

At first glance the area looked nothing like an active crime scene, there were no officers in white forensic suits, no detectives taking statements, and no photographer snapping away with a digital camera. Only the Police vans and cars indicated that something out of the ordinary had taken place here. It looked exactly the same on a closer inspection, so McManus climbed the steps to the rear door of the van marked Police Scotland Dive Team and went inside. The occupants were startled by the sudden appearance of the visitor, and their conversation stopped. Only Gibson reacted.

'Hi, Boss. Wasn't expecting you here, thought it was your day off?'

'It is Ronnie, but I thought I would come out and see what's doing. Nothing much by the looks of things then?'

'Eh, not really. We're still waiting for the rest of these guys' team to appear with the drag nets. Apparently, they were called out for a missing toddler at some loch up near Pitlochry, but he's turned up safe and well and they're on their way now. Should be here in the next hour I'm told. I sent Gill home, there wasn't anything else for her to do, and she had something on this evening. I told her just to go. She'll come into the office in the morning for a briefing at the usual time.'

'That's fine, Ronnie. So what else can you tell me? What's happened since we spoke at lunchtime?'

'Well, the car's been taken away to the garage at the forensic unit, the techs took tyre impressions from around the edge of the quarry, but apart from that, there's nothing else to do here. Apart from dredging the quarry of course… just in case.'

'Fair enough, Ronnie. When will we hear from forensics?'

'Not till Tuesday probably, they said. Have to let the car dry out a bit before they can examine it fully.

The parents identified the shoe I found inside the car as one belonging to their son, Darius. Apart from that, at the moment, we have nothing else to go on. Just another car sticking out of the water.'

Gibson pulled his phone from his pocket, and swiping the screen several times, he held it out for McManus to see. 'A bog-standard Audi A3, registered to our missing man. No major external damage, a few dents in the front from hitting the water, a dent in the rear bumper. The only obvious internal damage was the burning marks on the headlining. This could be anything. A stolen car dumped in the water. An accident. A suicide attempt. Murder even. But with no body...... '

'I get the picture, Ronnie. We'll have to wait to see what the dive team come up with.'

Gibson stifled a chuckle and pointed to the interior of the van. 'Cup of tea then, Boss?'

'Just a minute, there's something I need to do,' and McManus left the van to make a phone call.

The additional dive team had appeared not long after McManus had arrived and began to make preparations to search the flooded quarry. While they were getting ready McManus carried a hot cup of tea back down the track to where PC Morrison still stood at the crime scene tape.

'I spoke to your Sergeant. He wants you to stay here as long as I need you. But I think we can let you go in half an hour or so. The divers are going to use their big van to block the track, and I don't expect we'll have any more visitors tonight. Unless we find a body of course.'

'That quarry is supposed to be pretty deep. There are probably all sorts of things down there. Old washing machines, bikes, shopping trolleys, who knows. They could be there all night.' Morrison replied between sips. 'I'll be glad to get away before that happens. Besides, I've been on my feet for hours now. They're killing me.' Morrison hopped from foot to foot, trying to ease the weight on her legs. 'And I need the toilet!'

'I'm sorry I can't do anything about that, but I suppose if I turned my back for a few minutes, no-one would know. Anyway, when I come back next time you'll be free to go off duty. I can give you a lift home if you like.'

'Great, thanks. Can you hold this clipboard for me for a minute?'

The area of Dunfermline between Carnegie Drive and the small village of Townhill was populated with a variety of residential streets, full of stone built detached homes, terraced houses and traditional homes split into apartments. On her promotion and transfer to the MIT at Dunfermline DC Gill Edwards had been worried about finding a suitable place to live. Her home in Pittenweem was too far from her new job to travel back and forward every day. It had only taken a few days to find a woman PC who had recently divorced her PC husband and was now looking for a housemate to share the costs of her home. Ensuring her that it was only temporary, Gill had agreed to move in to the large two-bedroom apartment until she could find a place of her own. Edwards and her new housemate, Susan Rogers, found they had lots in common, including bizarrely a membership of Roughmeup.com. The dating website had almost cost Edwards her job but had instead led to her promotion.

That night in their upper floor conversion in a stone built detached house Edwards and Rogers were expecting a visitor. They had posted on the site that they were looking for a submissive who was willing to clean their home for them in exchange for being subjected to domination and humiliation by two strict women. They had received several responses, and after careful consideration, and several on-line exchanges, they had agreed to interview a twenty-seven-year-old plumber from Crossgates.

Edwards and Rogers had a good idea of what a stereotypical dominatrix should look like in the average male eyes, and had tried to dress accordingly. Neither wished to spend too much money on authenticity in the early stages of this new adventure, and had made do with some cheap purchases to supplement their existing wardrobes. Now dressed in various combinations of leather, latex, chains, and belts, the two expectant women sat nervously on the large settees in the softly lit lounge. When the doorbell sounded, Rogers used her phone to check the display from the security camera. A young man in overalls stood on the top step, holding a tool caddy and a small rucksack. He glanced around anxiously as he waited for the door to open, clearly unsure about the whole visit.

'Go on, quick, before he gets cold feet.' Urged Edwards.

'No. You go. It was your idea.'

'Come on, it was you too, remember. Besides, we're all dressed up and nowhere to go.'

Rogers gave in and went to the door, returning moments later, leading a nervous plumber using the front of his overalls clutched tightly in her fist. Although the fabric was bunched up badly, you could still make out the logo for Morrison Plumbing Services above the breast pocket.

Little did they know that only a few miles away, in Crossgates, the plumber's wife in full Police Scotland uniform was leading an eager DI McManus into her home. She definitely had no need to drag him by the front of *his* jacket.

Chapter 16

McManus walked slowly from the rear car park towards the first-floor back door that led to the Specialist Crime Division offices, and the separate MIT squad room, incident room and staff offices. The reorganisation of policing in Fife had been ongoing since the amalgamation of all the regional Scottish police services into one body, Police Scotland, in 2013, with Fife now being known as 'P' Division. With Fife split into 3 regions, each with its own Area Commander, the area was further divided into Wards, with an Inspector in charge of each one, supported by a varying number of Sergeants and Constables. Community teams and special units were also in place to further assist the public in preventing crime and protecting the communities. Small teams of detectives worked at each regional headquarters, following up on all kinds of crime, but the major crimes were the property of the MIT. The Major Investigation Team. But in Fife, major crime was not a daily event, and officers from the MIT would regularly assist the local detectives with any cases where they could lend support.

McManus still had responsibility for the deployment of his team, and held a briefing each morning at nine o'clock unless a major investigation was underway. Today's briefing was expected to be short; McManus was looking forward to a quiet day after last night's energetic encounter with one of Cowdenbeath's fine young officers. His back ached, among other things, and he did not walk slowly out of choice. The back door banged against the outside wall as it was roughly pulled open from the outside. Looking back along the corridor he saw the outline of DC Edwards against the light streaming through the glazed security door. As she moved towards him he noticed she was trying to hide a slight limp and appeared to be walking rather gingerly. He knew from personal experience why her gait was unusual, and he waited for her to catch up.

'Rough night last night, Gill? Is that why you went home early, to play games with some young stud?'

'I couldn't possibly comment, Boss.'

'Come on, Gill. It's me you're talking to. You know I'm only looking out for you.'

'Well, let's just say….I had the plumber in last night, and leave it at that eh. And, em, ….I noticed you're not walking so well this morning either. Been jumping fences to escape an angry husband again?

'Now Gill, careful.'

'Come on Mark. It's me you're talking to. Chasing married women is only going to get you in trouble you know. Look what happened the last time.'

McManus simply smiled knowingly. 'No comment. Now come on, we've a briefing to get to.'

Walking straight into the squad room McManus noticed the new face sitting at a desk near the window. 'DS Robertson I presume?' he said to the stranger.

'Yes sir, Liam Robertson, starting today, transferred in from Ayrshire CID at Troon.'

'Troon eh? I expect you'll play a bit of golf then?'

Yes, sir. I was a member at Lochgreen, you know, the municipal courses, all three together, next to Royal Troon.'

'I know it, Liam. Played there a few times, but not recently.'

McManus turned towards the front of the room, 'Right then, let's get started. Ronnie, lead us off, will you?'

DS Gibson stood in front of the white wallboard and listed all the cases currently under investigation, who was assigned to each one, and what stage the enquiries were at.

'There are no outstanding major cases where our squad would be lead investigators. In all of them we are supporting the local CID or providing intel to the National Crime Agency. They have an ongoing operation which overlaps into our patch. The local drugs families are under pressure from outside gangs trying to expand from down south, from Glasgow and Edinburgh, as well as from Dundee and Aberdeen. Our part is just to pass on any info we come across, no action required.'

Gibson paused for a glance at the DI, who nodded, and walked forward to the front.

'Yesterday I received a call from our boss, Detective Superintendent Nicholson, asking us to assist in a missing persons case.' He held his hand up to quell the murmurs that had broken out.

'I know, I know. It's not something we normally get involved in, and it will probably be only for a few days. But it crosses over between here and Cowdenbeath, so we're helping out, OK. Now, Ronnie has all the details. Carry on Ronnie.'

'Thanks Boss. The missing man is Darius Bakhoum, aged 25, from Dunfermline. He's the son of two local Egyptian born doctors, both of whom are quite well connected, hence the extra interest in his disappearance. Last seen at home on Thursday morning, as far as we know at the moment. His car was found on Saturday morning, part-submerged in an old flooded quarry in Cowdenbeath, empty. There were signs of a fire inside the vehicle, but it's impossible to say when that might have happened.

The vehicle was recovered yesterday, and it was taken away by the forensics bods for examination. The dive team from the Operational Support Division was on scene yesterday evening, and they will continue to dredge and search the quarry this morning.'

'Thanks Ronnie, what enquiries are needed now, and who do you need to help you?' interrupted McManus.

'Gill and I interviewed the parents yesterday, but we have still to contact his work, and his girlfriend. She seems to have been out of touch for a few days, and the parents are worried that they haven't been able to contact her.'

'Are you thinking foul play of some sort here?'

'Well, the typical scenarios are suicide, maybe a falling out with the girlfriend. Or an accident, maybe they were both in the car, talking…. or something… and the brake came off and the car rolled over the edge. Or it could have been deliberate, a murder/suicide, both of them arguing in the car, one of them wanting to leave, the other driving over the cliff. We just don't know right now.'

'So where are you taking the investigation now?'

Gibson had only known the DI for three months, but he already knew his style of leadership. He wanted Gibson to show initiative, to lead his team of detectives, and to offer courses of proposed actions rather than wait for instructions. Gibson liked his job much more than before, and believed that his career could flourish under DI McManus.

'We should interview the parents again, make enquiries at Darius' work, his girlfriend worked in the same place, then try to track the car's movements, his mobile phone's movements, and find out his movements since he was last seen until the car was found in the quarry.'

'Geez, Ronnie. Take a breath will you.' Chuckles sounded around the room and Gibson flushed slightly at McManus´ interruption. 'We need someone to go back to the quarry again this morning, the dive team are still searching you say?'

'Right, Boss, they are. I'll go to the quarry, as I was there yesterday and know the routine. I need……….'

'Ronnie, how about you liaise with the dive team and the local uniforms from Cowdenbeath. Liam, can you take DC Fraser and find out what you can from Barhoum's workplace, the bank HQ in Edinburgh where he and his girlfriend worked. Ronnie do you know her name?'

'Heather Watson, boss, aged 24, address in Cowdenbeath.'

'Thanks. Liam, you and Tom are on that. Check any CCTV in their car park as well, find out if he left at the normal time. Did they travel together? Did they…. I'm sure you know the score Liam, sorry.'

'No problem, Boss,' replied the new man, 'I'm sure DC Fraser can keep me right.'

'Good. And phone me with any info as soon as. I'm taking Gill with me, we'll interview the parents again, show them we care, then we'll follow up anything that's needed after that. All good? Right, get to it everybody, and Liam, can you see me for a few minutes before you head out.'

'Have a seat Liam.' Invited McManus as DS Robertson knocked and entered the office. 'Sorry we didn't get a chance to properly introduce ourselves before the briefing. Let me start. In private you can call me Mark, but with the troops it's Inspector, or boss, not sir please. I take it you prefer Liam to DS Robertson.'

'Indeed, my real name is William, but I've been Liam since I was at school.'

'Great. I've been the DI here at the MIT since May, when we closed out a double murder case, and the previous DI resigned after some domestic problems. I'm glad to have an experienced DS here to keep me right. Ronnie Gibson only stepped up to DS at the same time as I got promoted. We've a good team here, two clever techy types, Steven Alexander and Gerry Cairns. Bob Fowler and Brian Inglis are experienced, well organised, and intelligent with it, while Gill Edwards and Tom Fraser are both new to the team. Gill was a big help on the last case, she was stationed in Pittenweem where the first murder took place, and Tom was my DC in the CID unit here in Dunfermline, so he knows the area really well.'

'Sounds like a great team, Mark. I'm really looking forward to working here. As you know, my wife's Mum is poorly, and she needs looking after. She lives on her own, in Aberdour, and there's not much support available. That's why I applied for the transfer, we've bought a new house in Dalgety Bay, and we move in next week. We're staying at Mum's just now, till the new house is ready, but I'll tell you, it can't come quick enough.'

'I understand Liam. I've lived on my own since I left school, I couldn't imagine having to share a place, never mind with your mother-in-law. I'm happily single, and don't have any plans to change that status. Hope your new house is ready in time. In the meantime, if you want to escape for a pint one evening give me a shout. Or even nine holes at Aberdour one night after work if you like, I know the Pro there, he'll get us on no bother.'

'That sounds great, Mark. I'll let you know. But I suppose I better get to work, start off with a good impression. I'll go find Fraser and we can get away to Edinburgh.'

'Sure, just don't listen to all the stories he'll tell you. Only about half of them are true, and even he doesn't know which ones are which. Oh, and don't believe what he says about the Brazil shirt and the architect's wife!'

McManus turned away to look out the window, reflecting.

Chapter 17

'Gill, can you check the numbers for the Bakhoum doctors, find out where they are this morning. And ask the duty sergeant to check the missing person file. Did anyone search their house? I know he's 25, and won't be hiding under the bed, but it's standard procedure. I'll get the car and meet you out front.'

Edwards muttered to herself under her breath as she walked away towards the stairs to the ground floor. She just wanted a quiet morning, a comfortable seat, and a hot cup of tea to go with her paracetamol tablets. Last night had been a bit wild, and she had drunk more white wine than was good for her. McManus would no doubt be on her case for the rest of the day about her 'plumber'. He didn't look so hot himself this morning. She had been in his bed on Saturday night into Sunday morning, and then on Sunday night he was jumping someone else. She had done the same, so she considered that she had no grounds for complaining. Who would listen anyway? She checked her phone to see if there were any messages from the plumber, then sent him a short one saying she was disappointed he hadn't performed as expected and she wanted him back to do the job properly.

McManus was waiting in his car in the public parking spaces when Edwards came out the front door of the Police Station. She climbed gingerly up into the Kuga and pulled the door closed.

'I phoned the good doctors' mobiles, they're both out at the quarry right now. Watching the dive team still dredging the water. The sergeant checked the log, no search of the Bakhoum residence was done. What do you want to do now, Mark?'

'I think we need to get you a rubber ring to sit on, you look a bit tender! I saw your housemate earlier; PC Rogers isn't it? She was walking a bit funny as well. I didn't realise you two were so close already.'

'Well, you know, it gets a bit boring fucking a DI all the time. The plumber was just a bit of rough, made for a very entertaining evening. I think Susan and I are going to get on like a house on fire. Might even have to call in a firefighter one night, just in case.'

'Careful Gill. I'm still your boss remember. And I still want you round at mine every Saturday night when we're off duty. Anyway, was he really a plumber? My shower is leaking, and I need someone to come and look at it.'

Edwards pulled a business card from her purse and held it out for McManus to see.

'William Morrison, Morrison Plumbing Services, Crossgates. Well that is interesting.' was all he said as he put the car into gear and drove off.

The quarry entrance was once again strung with Police Crime Scene tape, and a red and white barrier was also blocking access to the dirt track where it met the main road. The dive team van was still parked on the level ground near the water's edge, and a second Police Scotland Operational Support van was parked nearby. A uniformed Inspector prowled the quarry edge, watching as a rubber dinghy floated on the surface, thirty feet below her. Two men in Police overalls stood on the opposite side of the quarry, pulling on ropes, while two divers bobbed around on the surface, talking to another diver in the dinghy. DS Gibson observed proceedings as closely as possible while trying hard to keep out of the way of the Inspector's pacing route. He was acutely aware that the two parents of the missing man were observing from further down the track. He had tried to keep them outside the Police tape at first but had given in to their protests. They had agreed to wait by their car which had been allowed to drive up the track to a small clearing just short of the operational area. The Inspector had not been happy at their presence, and Gibson had been forced to point out that the dive unit was here in support. Gibson had made it clear that until DI McManus arrived, he was currently the Senior Investigating Officer at the locus.

The officers with the ropes heaved away once again, and when the grappling hooks on the end were close to the foot of the cliff the two divers swam over to assist. This time the catch included a rusty bicycle frame, minus wheels, a metal bucket, and a red and white traffic cone. Between them the four men transferred the items into a rope basket suspended on the end of another pair of ropes, which were then pulled up to the surface by a winch attached to the front of the divers' van. The Inspector looked over briefly before motioning that the men should add their new haul to the growing pile of debris recovered from the quarry already that morning. Dropping the grappling hooks back into the water, the two men in overalls took a break while the divers swam the hooks to the opposite side to begin the process all over again. The divers had been working in shifts of an hour at a time due to the temperature of the water, and Gibson strolled back to the support van where the off-duty divers had a tea urn set up. The tea had barely hit the bottom of his mug when there was a loud rap on the side of the door.

'No time for tea now, Detective. Looks like your boss is here.' called the Inspector, sounding more cheerful than they had a right to be at spoiling Gibson's tea break.

As soon as McManus pulled the car up to the barrier, he knew the day was only going to get worse. The two officers manning the access road were both known to him. PC John Kerr had been a DS in the MIT when he had joined it in April, although they had known each other for years. He couldn't stand Kerr and was glad to see his career plummet after being convicted of drink driving during that last case. PC Anne Morrison was different. She was the good-looking PC he had bedded the night before, and he was definitely looking forward to seeing her again, but not so soon, and certainly not at a crime scene with Kerr.

'Look Gill,' said McManus, 'It's Juan Kerr. Doing what he was always destined to do. Minding the gate. I always said he should have been in the MOD Police. Little wanker!'

'It's not his fault he barely made the height limit, is it? I suppose the woman PC has to drive him around everywhere since he lost his licence. Can't be much fun for her either.'

Winding the front window down, McManus leaned out and asked the officers to move the barrier. Once the way was clear he edged forward and spoke to Morrison. 'Are the parents here somewhere? We need to speak to them again.'

'Yes, sir. They're parked further up the track, old Volkswagen, you can't miss them.'

'Thanks Constable. Hi there, Juan. Looks like you've put a bit of weight on since I saw you last. Who ate all the pies, eh?' McManus shouted out the window.

'Yeah, every time I…….' but McManus drove on before Kerr could finish his comeback.

McManus parked his car next to the Volkswagen and stepped out. He had not met the two doctors and walked up to the driver's door to introduce himself. Neither occupant of the car made any effort to get out, but the driver's window slowly lowered as McManus bent down to speak. After the introductions, it was clear that neither of the parents were in a mood to discuss their missing son, so McManus tried to placate them.

'I can understand that you are worried about your son, but we have stepped up our enquiries this morning in an effort to shed some light on his whereabouts. I have officers going to his work to check up on his fiancée, to check the car park cameras, and interview his closest colleagues. We are also checking traffic cameras to trace the movements of his car from the time he last left work until it was found here on Saturday. I'm sure we'll have some answers soon.'

'Well Inspector, we're certainly not getting any answers from anyone here. We've been shunted into this clearing, and nobody is telling us anything.' replied Mr Bakhoum angrily.

'I'm sorry about that, but we need to be able to work safely here, and we can't allow you to get too close. It's a health and safety requirement at all police operational locations. Give me a minute and I'll see if I can get any update for you.'

The window slid upwards without another word, and McManus motioned to Edwards to join him as he walked away towards the Police vans further up the track. 'For fuck's sake, what do they expect, it's not even my fucking case, and I'm getting lumbered with all the aggro from the parents.' said McManus.

'Steady Mark, they just want information. I'll find out who's in charge and get them to talk to the parents', offered Edwards.

Gibson had watched the exchange between the DI and the parents and was ready for the obvious first question.

'Nothing to report so far, Boss. Just an old bike, a supermarket trolley, and lots of other junk. I get the feeling the dive team are not too enthusiastic about continuing the dredging. The Inspector over there will know more. She's been here since they started at seven thirty this morning.'

'Thanks Ronnie, I'll have a word.' And McManus strode towards the uniformed figure pacing the quarry's edge.

'DI McManus, Fife MIT,' he said, hand outstretched towards the Inspector. She ignored the gesture and simply said 'Fletcher, Operational Support. What does MIT want here? Do you really think there's a body in this big puddle?'

'We don't know, it's not my case yet, but that's why you're here. To find out. Now what's the story so far. My DS said you've found nothing but a rusty bike.'

'That's about the size of it. My divers have trawled most of the quarry floor now, with nothing to show for it. Come on, let me show you how it works.' The Inspector walked away towards the two men in overalls at the far side of the quarry, with McManus following.

'These two ropes are attached to a set of four grappling hooks, which are joined together by a metal bar six feet long. Like a plough on a tractor. The divers drop the hooks at the opposite end, and they are then dragged across the bottom until these two here get them to this end, when they pull the hooks up.'

'Ok,' agreed McManus, 'so you can dredge a six-foot-wide section each pass. How much do you still have to cover?'

'We've got one more haul to do, then we'll have done the whole quarry twice. No body so far, but wait ten minutes, and we can probably all go home.'

McManus stood with his hands in his pockets as the ropes were gradually pulled through the murky water, hoping to find nothing when the hooks appeared at the surface. A dead body right now would only complicate his day, and would not be the best result for the parents waiting and watching further down the track. He turned to look at the Volkswagen and saw Edwards waving to him from the support van. She was right. It was time for a cup of tea.

With the final trawl of the quarry depths completed, the dive team convened in the van to confirm the results with their Inspector. No body had been found, and they began to pack up their gear ready to return to their base to await the next call out. McManus thanked the divers and their Inspector, made some entries in his notebook, and asked Gibson and Edwards to join him outside.

'Well, at least we can score that off the to do list. It still looks like a missing person enquiry, and maybe Liam and Tom will have some answers from their trip to the bank in Edinburgh. Ronnie, you head back to the office, chase up forensics on the car, start a log and see if we can try the cell phone tracking system for the missing man. Gill and I will speak to the parents again, and we'll meet back there later. Let's call a briefing for four o'clock at the office, everybody should have something to report back by then hopefully. I'll call the Super and get him to designate us as lead on this case. Might as well, we're doing all the fucking work on it.'

'Can we release the scene now?' asked Gibson. 'I think we've got all we can from here, and the two plods from the barrier can get back to their normal duties.'

'I suppose so, Ronnie, although it would make me happy to see Kerr manning the barrier for another few hours at least. But the young constable deserves more, so let them know they can go. Gill and I will speak to the parents again on the way out. We need to interview them again at home, maybe this afternoon, give them a chance to calm down now we know he's not in the quarry. Come on Gill, let's get this over with.'

With news of the search of the quarry being called off having been given to the parents, and a meeting arranged for that afternoon, McManus was about to get into his car when his cell phone rang. Looking at the screen he found an unknown number displayed and was tempted to reject the call. But experience had taught him that useful information could come at any time, from any source, and he asked Gill to get in the car and wait for him while he took the call.

'Detective Inspector, what a pleasure,' began the caller, 'it's been a while since we last spoke. Congratulations on your promotion, I hope you remember how you got there, and the promise you made as part of our deal.'

McManus took a moment to recognise the voice, but the words made it all too clear who was calling him. 'Of course I remember our deal. It was only a few months ago. What can I do for you Mr Adams?'

Paul Adams was a prominent businessman from Dundee, a millionaire property developer and owner of several hotels, health clubs, golf clubs and a casino. Their paths had crossed in the Pittenweem case, where McManus had also found out he was the biggest drug dealer in the North East of Scotland. Adams hid his drugs and money laundering activities under layer upon layer of legitimate, cash rich businesses.

'Why, Mark. It's purely a social call, I promised to invite you for a game of golf, remember? I know you are busy, but do you think we can fit a few holes in in the next week or so?'

'That might be difficult, I barely manage a weekend off these days.'

'Well, there's lots of daylight in the evenings just now, how about coming up to my course at Perth for nine holes after work. I've a meeting there tomorrow afternoon, do you fancy meeting about six, and we can play till it gets dark. I'll buy you dinner afterwards if you have time.'

'Ok, I'm sure I can manage that. Just golf is it, or is there something else I need to know about?'

'No Mark, it'll be just the two of us, a chance for us to get to know each other better.'

'Fine, I'll see you tomorrow then…….'

'Before you go, I have some interesting information for you. I know you are MIT right? but I have it on good authority that a Cowdenbeath dealer has been buying something dangerous. Something that could cause a lot of damage in your area. He's mixing it with the heroin he sells, telling the buyers it gives a better high, longer lasting effects, a bigger rush. But he doesn't know what he's doing.'

'Yes, but why tell me? My team doesn't do drugs investigations.'

'But Mark, surely if you can bring down a drug dealer that gives you some brownie points with the brass. And what's good for you is ultimately good for me too. Besides, I need this dealer removed, he's not good for my business. He's helping the teams from down south move into Fife. He´s hooked up with a foreigner selling drugs throughout Edinburgh. New loads of drugs are pouring in from Manchester,

Liverpool, they're all over Edinburgh already. That can only mean trouble for you in Fife.'

'Ok, I see your point. Tell me more.'

'Have you heard of the drug Fentanyl, it's been used for years to cut other drugs, but now it's become very popular, particularly mixed with heroin. You know heroin is a brown powder right, well fentanyl is white, they call it China White in most places. But here in Scotland they call it White Heather.'

'Yeah, I've heard of that, but I've never come across it here. How did you say this guy is getting it?'

'It's coming over from Edinburgh, that's all I can tell you right now. I know who the dealer is, but I can´t tell you everything right now. But this guy from Cowdenbeath has just bought a new batch of several kilos, last weekend. I also heard he had a couple of girls held at his place for a sex party over the weekend, him and two mates. I don't believe the girls were willing participants, at least that's how I heard it. Will you do something about him if I tell you his name?'

'Of course, I might have to pass it on to the drugs boys, but I'll act on it. What's the name?

'Adam Watson, he lives in Parkside Crescent. I believe he has a sister called Heather. Does that mean anything to you? Right, must go, got another call coming in. See you tomorrow night for the golf.'

'Fuck, how do you know that?' cried McManus, but the call had ended.

Chapter 18

'Right you two, come out to the car and give me a hand with this stuff.' shouted Adam Watson as he pushed open the door to his house. He knew Bugsy and Gasser were lazy shits and would not have done half the things he had asked them to do that morning before he left.

Bugsy was sprawled on the dirty settee watching TV, his bare feet giving off a sour smell that seemed to blend in with all the other odours of a drug house. The carpet was stained with god only knew what, the coffee table was covered in cigarette ash, powders of varying colours, needles, plastic bags, and empty beer cans. Watson grabbed him by the leg and hauled him off the settee and onto the floor, kicking him in the stomach as he lay on top of a carry out carton, wondering just what was happening.

'I told you this morning to get this place cleaned up. It has to be pristine, disinfected, polished, like new. No sign of drugs, girls, nothing out of place, no trace of anything illegal. I have a feeling we're about to get a visit. So get off your arse and get busy.'

'Aw c'mon, Watty, I was going to do it, but Gasser just fucked off upstairs and refused to help. Then I suppose I fell asleep.'

'Fell asleep did you. Did you fuck. You've been sampling my powder again. Well that's it, last chance, get this place cleaned up or you're out. On the street out, homeless out, out out. Get it? Good! Now get started by bringing in the carpet cleaning machine from the car.'

Watson kicked Bugsy again and stormed off up the stairs to find Gasser, repeating his message to the man he dragged off the bed in the twin room, punctuating it with boots to the ribs as Gasser lay helpless on the floor. 'I'm off out again, so you and Bugsy better have this place like new by the time I get back. You've got two hours, so get busy!'

While he had been driving round some of his better clients that morning Watson had learned something interesting. Interesting and worrying at the same time. Someone had been asking about him, about his new supply of White Heather, and about the party at the weekend, the one with the girls, and the bondage and torture. How the hell had that got round he wondered. Maybe one of the punters he had turned away at the door. Good job he had told the guys to get the place cleaned up, top to bottom. He wanted no trace of the girls anywhere in the house. He would steam clean the lounge and hall carpets as soon as Bugsy and Gasser got organised. He had already replaced all the linens in the two bedrooms, he had ripped out the bedroom carpets, and new ones were being fitted that afternoon. All the old stuff was already under hours of new rubbish at the council recycling depot, all mixed in with everyone else's DNA and bodily fluids. If the Police got wind of what he had done at the weekend, with Heather and Rachel, then good luck to them proving anything if they came to search his place. Another few hours and the whole place should look as clean as gold pants, as the Andrex advert claimed. Meanwhile, he would drive round to Rachel's flat to remind her and Heather to keep their mouths shut.

McManus and Edwards were also on their way to the same place. A phone call from DS Robertson told them that Heather Watson had not turned up for work that morning, and armed with her address, they had agreed to check out her home on the way back to Dunfermline.

'6 Muir Place, that's it here,' said McManus drawing up to the kerb. The property was typical of an old Scottish mining town, in a street of two-storey stone-built blocks with eight flats in each. The four ground floor flats had doors on the front, with a small walled garden to each, while the upper flats were reached via an alley up either side of the building leading to two external staircases at the rear. Each staircase rose up to a concrete landing, open to the elements, with iron handrails, and two doors. Also perched on the landing were two small brick sheds, one on each side, which would have originally been the outside toilets for the upper flats. The toilets for the lower flats were tucked away under the staircase. McManus had visited many similar homes while a Constable in Dunfermline, and always thanked his lucky stars that he been born in Edinburgh, as the son of a wealthy solicitor.

As they walked up the alley to the rear of the block, they could see that the rear garden was well tended, someone obviously took a bit of pride in their surroundings, despite the grim grey stone block that cast a long shadow over the back gardens. A painted white arrow on the wall pointed upwards; Number 6 was an upper flat in the middle of the row, and McManus and Edwards climbed the steps to stand together on the top landing. The door was painted dark blue, and the number 6 hung down from a single screw, making it look like a drunken scrum half in a Scotland shirt. Anyone in a Scotland shirt had every reason to be drunk after that last visit to Twickenham, thought McManus, recalling watching the second half while jumping up and down on his couch, beer spilling everywhere.

The sudden sound of Edwards banging on the door brought McManus out of his reverie, and he waited impatiently for the door to open. Edwards banged again, and this time the door to number 8 opened slowly and an old man peered out, his eyes blinking in the sudden light.

'They're no' in.' was all he said, and he began to close the door again.

'Wait a minute, we're Police.' Edwards held up her ID wallet. 'Does Heather Watson live here? We need to speak to her.'

'I don't know a Heather whatever, there's two lassies live in there, Rachel something, I can't remember her last name, and her pal lives there too. I just like to keep myself to myself, you know what it's like these days. I don't want any bother.' the old man replied.

'When did you last see either of the two women? They're not in trouble, we just need to speak to them.' added McManus. 'Do either of them own a car? Do you know where they work?'

'Look, I told you I don't know anything. I need to go.'

'Wait a minute, can you think of....'

'I told you I need to go...., ' and he closed the door.

'Well that was a lot of good.' said Edwards as they walked back down the stairs. She stopped at the foot and looked up at the rear window, a kitchen she assumed. There appeared to be a shadow behind the net curtain but she couldn't be sure, and she stood still, watching for a twitch of the lace film that would betray the occupant. The only thing that moved was the venetian blind at the window next door, the old man was watching them leave.

'We'll come back later, Gill. Make a note of the numbers of the cars parked out front, maybe we'll get one registered to Rachel somebody.'

With the numbers noted, McManus and Edwards drove off, intending to be back at Dunfermline for the planned briefing at four. Edwards put her notebook away in her bag for now; if she had done the checks on the vehicles parked on the street at the time she would have identified the Vauxhall Astra registered to Adam Watson, Heather's brother. Watson was at that very moment holding a knife to the throat of an old man in the flat at number 8.

Chapter19

All of the team had made it back to the office in time for the afternoon briefing and McManus started off first. 'Ok, the missing person, Darius Bakhoum. The search of the quarry is finished, with no body recovered. The car pulled from the water yesterday is to be examined by forensics tomorrow once it has dried out a bit more, but so far, other than the burning to the roof lining of the car, there is no sign of foul play. For the moment this is still a missing person case unless anyone has any evidence to the contrary. I would really like to do all we can in the next few days and then pass it back to the locals. What else did anyone find out today?'

DS Robertson stood up from his seat at a desk at the front of the squad room. 'DC Fraser and I went to the Bank HQ this morning and asked around. Neither Darius nor his girlfriend Heather Watson have been at work since Thursday. Neither has answered any calls to their phones from work since then either. None of their work colleagues have heard from them or seen them, nor did they know of any plans for a trip or a holiday over the weekend. It seems that both of them are missing. Whether they are together or not is anyone's guess. Fraser, you're up.'

'Right Sarge, as you know we checked the CCTV footage from the bank offices. Also the coded access staff entry system. Each employee has an ID pass which records their access and exit at the main staff doors, of which there are several. It looks like they left together at five twenty-five pm on Thursday. Their ID cards were swiped consecutively at entrance B, which leads directly to the staff car park. Neither of them has entered the building since. At least not with their own ID cards anyway. CCTV from Thursday afternoon shows them leaving that door together.'

'Can you tell if they both left in the same car?' interrupted McManus.

'Yes, Boss, I was getting to that. The car park access is not secured by their ID cards, but the CCTV shows them both getting into Darius' white Audi about that time. The car drove out of the car park without incident. Stevie did some extra checks for us, didn't you Stevie?' and Fraser turned towards DC Alexander.

'I looked at the footage from the road bridge cameras and found the car crossing the bridge northbound at five fifty-five pm, a reasonable time since leaving the bank car park. That doesn't give them any time to stop off anywhere along the way. I then followed the car up the M90 as far as the cameras allow, at the Halbeath junction, where presumably they turned off for Cowdenbeath at six twenty. The car was spotted again on a Number Plate Recognition camera in the town at about nine fifteen pm. I can't tell where it went between those times, Boss.'

'Great work, Stevie,' added McManus. 'What about tracing their cell phones?'

DC Cairns got to his feet with a sheaf of papers in his hand. 'That was me, Boss. I traced both numbers this afternoon, no movements since Thursday night, but they follow the same route as the car took. Both phones are clearly together all evening, at various locations in Cowdenbeath. It looks like they might have stopped for about two hours at Heather's home address. A call to a Chinese takeaway is recorded on Darius' phone at just after seven pm. Then no activity until both phones go dead around ten. It looks like they might have been together in the car near the quarry, Darius' phone went off first, then fifteen minutes later Heather's also went off. Interesting thing is that his phone is still off, but Heather's came back on late on Saturday afternoon.

'Thanks Gerry. Any calls on Thursday that are out of the ordinary, unknown numbers, flagged numbers, anything like that?'

'Nothing, Boss, sorry. Heather hasn't made any calls since her phone came back on either.' confirmed Cairns.

'That´s a bit odd. Anyone else have anything?' queried McManus. 'Anyone checked their bank activity?'

When no-one answered McManus began to pace across the room, deep in thought. 'If they were together all night on Thursday, their phones went off the grid about the same time, and they've not been seen since, what does that mean? Are they both missing? Are they together somewhere and just not told anyone? Are they both together at the bottom of that quarry? Come on, anyone any ideas?

Edwards answered for them all. 'We need to speak to the flatmate, Rachel. She must know something. The parents clearly don't know everything about their son and his fiancée, maybe Rachel can shed some light on where they are.'

'Ok, Gill, we'll just have to go back there later. The rest of you keep on with what you are doing, and we'll meet up again in the morning. I need to speak to the Super.'

The briefing moved on to the more routine matters under investigation and McManus zoned out as he thought about what to say to his boss, and how he could dump this case in someone else's in tray. After all, he thought, MIT stood for Major Investigation Team, not Missing Idiot Trackers.

'This is surely a job for the Cowdenbeath uniforms sir. There's no evidence of a crime, no body, a crashed car in a quarry and nothing else. The guy and his girlfriend are off on a jolly somewhere, or they've got cold feet about their wedding and run off together. They're bound to turn up in a day or two.'

'Well, Mark, when they turn up, then you can pass off the case. But until then I want your full efforts employed in finding this missing young man. His mum has been calling all over the place. She goes to some book group with the Chief Super's wife and he wants to be kept in the loop about our enquiries.' explained Detective Superintendent Nicholson. 'So no, you can't pass the case off anywhere. But minimum expenditure of resources on our budget, it's not even a high risk misper, so keep time and costs to a minimum. But I still want you to get to the bottom of it, even if you have to jump in that quarry yourself.'

'Ok, sir, I get the picture. I've not met the Chief Super's wife, but it sounds like she's someone worth keeping on the right side of. I'll do all I can to find the guy, and keep you updated as we go.' conceded McManus.

'As you should, Mark. Remember, you've only just made the step up, you're quite young to be in charge of an MIT, and if you want to go further……. Once you make it to senior rank, progress is all about contacts, details, communication, procedure, and keeping your bosses happy. Their wives included in this case. Keep me posted, Mark.' And with that Nicholson ended the call.

McManus looked at the phone handset in bemusement. Had his boss just said he had to keep the Chief's wife happy? He had never met her, sure, but he had seen her picture. During the last murder case he had seen her picture on a website, *Spa-Girl* she called herself. He was fairly sure she did not spend all her time reading books.

Returning to the squad room he called to Edwards, 'Gill, you and me, back to Cowdenbeath to see Rachel again. The Super wants all out action but with no budget costs on this one. But let's get a coffee and some grub first, meet me in the canteen in ten and we can talk about how we deal with her. Assuming she's in this time of course.'

Turning to Alexander, McManus asked 'Stevie, can you take that list of car numbers Gill has and do a check on them. Also find out if Heather Watson owns a car. And Rachel Taylor as well while you're about it. I'll need that in half an hour, ok?'

Turning towards the door, McManus said to DS Robertson, 'Liam, sorry we've not had much time today to get acquainted, maybe we can get together for a coffee tomorrow sometime. Gill, canteen in ten minutes please.' And he walked out leaving Robertson to contemplate his first day in the new job.

Chapter 20

'This is a weird one, Gill, isn't it? What do you think?' McManus asked as he parked once again outside Rachel Taylor's flat.

'Don't know what to think yet. The Bakhoum lad is reported missing, last seen leaving work on Thursday night with his fiancée, yet she appears to be missing as well. And both their phones have been switched off since Thursday night, and they were clearly together. Or at least their phones were in the same place. Then we have Heather´s coming back to life on Saturday.' Edwards thought for a minute. 'According to his parents, the fiancée, Heather, lives with her pal Rachel. Hopefully, she'll be home this time and we can ask her.'

'Looks like we might be in luck. That's the car we think Rachel uses. It's registered to a local car dealership where Rachel is a receptionist. Maybe she gets to take cars home at night. Come on, let's find out.' With that McManus got out of the car and strode towards the narrow alley leading to the rear stairs, Edwards running to keep up.

'Usual signals, Gill. I'll lead, and if I want you to take over, I'll ask you a question, ok. Until then, you observe, body language, eye motion, all that stuff they taught you on that course, and we can compare notes afterwards.'

A few hard knocks on the door of number 6 brought a dishevelled looking young woman to the door. 'Rachel Taylor? I'm DI McManus. We're looking for Heather Watson, her fiancé Darius Bakhoum has been reported missing and we need to speak to her. May we come in?'

The woman stepped back into the narrow hallway allowing the two detectives to enter. 'I'm Rachel, Heather's in the kitchen, go through and I'll tell her you're here.'

McManus and Edwards almost filled the small sitting room as they stood waiting for the two women to join them. 'Did you see her face?' whispered Edwards. 'That looked like a broken nose to me, and two lovely shiners to match.'

A different woman came into the room, hesitating at the doorway, looking back over her shoulder towards the hallway. 'I'm Heather, what's this all about?'

McManus did the introductions again and asked if they could sit. A three-seater sofa was pushed against a wall, facing a large flat screen TV on a wall mount opposite. A table and two chairs stood underneath the window overlooking the street, and the only other furniture in the cramped room was a wooden bookcase and a coffee table which had a pizza box and two Fanta cans on it. Heather reached down and lifted the debris from the takeaway dinner and handed it to Rachel as she came through the door. Otherwise, the room was clear of any clutter, the coffee table had some magazines on the shelf underneath, and a bowl of fruit took centre stage on the small dining table. The two detectives took the chairs at the table by the window as Heather sat in the corner of the sofa farthest away from them.

McManus looked around the room, eyed the bookcase, it held a whole variety of titles, but one caught his eye. He had the same book at home, part of his crime fiction collection from an American author. Nothing unusual in that he thought, and turned back to look at Heather, then at the door, before finally settling his gaze on Heather again. 'Is Rachel going to join us, I think it would be helpful if she did. I understand you live here together, and you're due to get married in a few weeks.'

Heather looked nervously towards the door, waiting for Rachel to re-appear from the kitchen. 'Yes, Rachel's parents were very kind to me when I was younger. They took me in after my own parents died, and then when Rachel and I got jobs, we decided to share a flat to save money. So what's all this about. I heard you say something about Darius being reported missing?'

McManus paused as Rachel came back in and sat on the sofa beside Heather. 'Yes, Mr and Mrs Bakhoum reported Darius missing on Saturday. They were worried as he hadn't come home from work on Thursday night. He hasn't been in touch with them since he left for work on Thursday morning. They're very worried.' McManus paused again to watch Heather's reaction, but Rachel had leaned forward blocking his view. McManus once again was treated to the awful sight of Rachel's broken nose and two black eyes.

'Heather, when did you last see or hear from Darius?'

Staring straight at McManus, Heather coolly replied, 'He drove me home from work on Thursday, he finished work a little earlier than usual so he could drive me home.'

'And what time would that have been? Talk me through your journey home and what happened that night.' asked McManus.

Heather began nervously, 'We left work as usual and Darius drove me back here, we were going to get a Chinese carry out for dinner. We wanted to eat it before Rachel came home from work, she works late on a Thursday because the car showroom is open late.'

'So what time did you get here that night?' asked McManus, glancing at Edwards across the table.

'Must have been about seven maybe, we called the Chinese take away as soon as we got in. It arrived quite quickly, probably about a quarter past. We ate that and watched TV for a bit, Emmerdale first, then EastEnders, I think. But we knew Rachel would be home about nine, and we had a lot to talk about, wedding plans, you know, that sort of thing.' Heather finished her explanation and looked at Rachel before studying her hands clasped tightly in her lap. 'When Rachel got home, she heated up some of the takeaway we had kept back for her, and we talked about the wedding. Darius left to go home about ten and Rachel and I just sat up and chatted.'

'That was good of them Rachel, keeping you some dinner back. What did you have?' McManus asked.

'My favourite, crispy chilli beef. It's what they always get me on a Thursday night, isn't it Heather?' replied Rachel rather quickly.

From his position at the dining table McManus could see into the cramped kitchen. A white carrier bag sat on the sink drainer, and the shape of the contents were remarkably like two take away cartons stacked on top of each other. 'That's one of my favourites too, I'm always starving if I get home late from work. What shop do you use?'

Heather reached for her handbag, then stopped quickly, sitting back again against the sofa cushions. 'The Golden Duck on Junction Street. I thought I had their number in my phone, but I remembered Darius phoned in the order last time.'

'If Darius left at ten o'clock to go home, when did you see him next?' McManus leaned forward knowing the answer was important.

'I didn't see him again. I only knew he was missing when you turned up tonight. What's happened to him, surely you know what's happened.' cried Heather and she buried her face in her hands and began to sob. Rachel put an arm round her and hugged her tight.

'What about the next day at work, you must have seen him at some point. Did you try to call him? On Friday?' continued McManus. 'Come on Heather, you have to know something, he's been missing for four days now.'

'I don't know what happened to him. I lost my phone and spent all weekend looking for it. I don't know if he called me or not.'

'You could have borrowed Rachel's phone, surely. Darius' parents have been trying to ring you all weekend. You too, Rachel. Did you two have a fight, Heather? Is that what happened? Has Darius just gone off somewhere because you called off the wedding?' McManus could sense that something was not quite right here, it was very strange that a young couple would not be on the phone all day to each other in the weeks leading up to their wedding. He could see Heather looking up into Rachel's eyes, as if seeking approval or permission for something. Rachel looked back at McManus, her black eyes and swollen nose suddenly seeming more important now than ever.

'What's going on you two? There's obviously been a fight somewhere. Darius is missing and it's our job to find him. You need to tell me what's been going on.' McManus got to his feet and walked over to stand above the two young women on the sofa. Turning away, he stepped into the kitchen and opened the white carrier bag, pulling out two aluminium cartons, white lids still firmly in place. With a flick of his thumbs he prised open the first lid. The smell from the carton was instantly recognisable. Walking back into the sitting room with the carton, McManus bent down to show it to the two women. 'I guess the crispy chilli beef wasn't so good this time.

Gill, can you take Rachel into the other room, I need to speak to Heather alone.'

Fifteen minutes later McManus and Edwards huddled in the narrow hallway after interviewing the two women separately. McManus began, taking occasional glances at his notebook. 'It seems Rachel had messaged Heather that there was a party at Heather's brother's house, Rachel went straight there after work. She phoned later and asked Heather to meet her there once Darius had gone home. They had ordered the takeaway by then, that's Rachel's meal still in the kitchen. Heather went to the party sometime after ten. That's when it all seems to have got out of hand. Heather's brother is Adam Watson, or Watty, a well-known local drug dealer. Heather says they were experimenting with some new drug Watty has gotten hold of, that and the drinking, and they can't remember very much about anything until they woke up on Sunday morning. Seems they had been taking drugs all day Friday and Saturday. At some point there was a fight, some guys tried to gate-crash, and Rachel got in the way. Neither of them was able to get up at all yesterday, they were sick and hung over, and only felt back to normal this afternoon. Watty drove them home late on Saturday afternoon. Heather is pretty shaken up about the whole thing, embarrassed obviously to be telling us this at all, and still says she did not know about Darius being missing.'

Edwards took the pause as her cue to begin, 'Rachel says the same thing. She didn't come back here after work on Thursday but went straight to the party. She hasn't seen Darius at all since the weekend before. She's a bit confused about the whole weekend, and obviously her face is a bit sore as well. She has no idea who did it to her, and just wants to forget about the whole thing. They have both missed two days at work, and are really worried about that, as well as Darius being missing of course.'

'You know what Gill. I don't believe them. I think they are both lying and we should take them both back to the office; let them stew for a while. We can see if their stories are the same in a few hours. I think Darius is missing because of something that happened here on Thursday night. Or at that party. And Heather and Rachel know a whole load more than they're telling us.'

'You might be right, Mark, I don't entirely believe the story either. But this is a missing persons case, we've no suspicious circumstances, and no grounds to detain them for questioning, or statements, or anything. And besides, you told me the Super wants you to be low key on this, limited resources and all that.'

'I can just feel it, Gill. There's something odd here, they're lying about something, not just getting shitfaced at a party and missing work. Funny thing about the cell phone traces on Darius and Heather we got earlier. It put their phones together until about ten that night. That ties in with their story. But what about Rachel's phone. We need to track that as well, the same time period, see where she was over the weekend. Come on, I want to try something.'

'Wait. You didn't tell them about finding the car, or the search for Darius at the quarry'

'Very observant of you, Gill. We'll make a Detective of you yet. I don't intend to tell them just yet, keep it quiet for the moment when you speak to them again, ok?'

McManus pulled out his phone and searched his folders as he walked back into the sitting room. Heather and Rachel had again taken seats on the sofa and huddled together, heads together, muttering to each other. 'DC Edwards is going to speak to you again for a minute, I have to go out to the car for something, but I'll be back in a bit.' McManus pressed a button on his phone and looked around the room as a ring tone sang out from a handbag at the side of the sofa. 'Good. I see you found your phone Heather.'

McManus had spent five minutes on the phone to DC Alexander asking for a cell phone tracking history on Rachel Taylor's phone since Thursday night. Alexander promised to have it in the morning, which McManus accepted as good enough for now. After a further five minutes rummaging about in a briefcase in his car boot, he finally found what he was looking for. Mobile phone in hand he pressed a series of buttons, spoke a few words, looked at his phone screen, pressed more buttons then put his phone back in his pocket and closed the boot. He didn't bother to knock when he got back to the door of the flat and found Edwards still at the dining table questioning the two women.

'If you know anything about Darius' disappearance you have to tell us. His parents are worried sick. He could be injured, ill, anything could have happened to him,' Edwards was saying as McManus walked back into the room.

'We've told you all we know. I haven't seen him since he left here on Thursday night. I just hope he's ok. I know it was stupid to go to that party, to try those new drugs. It wasn't Watty's fault,' cried Heather.

McManus picked up on this immediately, 'What wasn't Watty's fault? What do you mean Heather?'

'The drugs of course. It was our choice to take them, he had nothing to do with it.'

'So your brother was supplying drugs at the party, is that what you're saying Heather?' continued McManus.

'No, it wasn't like that. I don't want to get my brother in trouble. We took drugs, that's all I can say. It was our own fault we got in over our heads.'

'I see, so if we go round there, to Watty's house, we search it, from top to bottom, we will find the drugs? Is that what you're saying?'

'No, Yes, oh…. I don't know…….. I don't want to talk about my brother. I just want to forget that weekend, don't we Rachel.' Heather buried her head in Rachel's shoulder and began to cry again.

McManus used the distraction to reach beneath the dining table to place a tiny sticky pad onto the underside of the table. Edwards looked at him sideways and whispered, 'What the fuck…?' but McManus simply stood up, looked at the huddle on the sofa and stated 'That's all for now, but we might need to speak to you again. Oh, and Rachel, I really think you should get that nose seen to.'

Chapter 21

As soon as they were outside the door and walking down the stairs Edwards turned to McManus, 'What the fuck, Mark. They were doing drugs at a party in a known drug dealer's house. They must know something about Darius, what happened to him. We can't just walk away from this right now.'

'Gill, it's a missing person enquiry, it's not our department. We've just been asked to help out the locals, and to keep our budget on this to a minimum. Did you learn anything remotely useful in there?'

'No, but…..'

'Well just bear with me for a bit, Gill. I think we're about to find out what really happened between Heather and Darius on Thursday night.'

Edwards couldn't help herself, 'But how. You just walked away at the good bit.'

'It's fairly clear they're hiding something, they're lying about the times, the phones, the take away even, but I don't think they were about to tell us what that is.'

'Aren't you supposed to say something like 'We'll be in touch'?' she persisted.

'They only say that on TV, Gill, now come on.' McManus walked away down the steps and back to his car without another glance at Edwards, who was scowling furiously at his back.

Once inside the car McManus waited while the Bluetooth system connected his phone to the car speakers. Pressing an app on his phone screen brought some strange screeching sounds for a moment before voices became clear. It was Heather and Rachel talking inside the flat.

'What have you done, Mark? You can't just plant a bug in someone's house, you need a warrant.'

'I know that Gill, I also know that whatever we hear can't be used as evidence in court, if we ever get that far. But it can help us in our enquiry, it can help us get to the truth about Darius' disappearance. Now just shut up and listen, and put that notebook away, I want no record of this conversation.'

Edwards dropped her notebook back into her bag, let the bag slide to the floor and sat back in her seat. Looking out of her window she could see the light on in the flat they had just left. 'I take it they have no idea we're listening?'

The conversation coming over the car speakers was incredible, punctuated with sobs, curses, and long moments of silence. It was Rachel who had started off the most revealing part of the discussion between the two girls. 'Well, that's just fucking brilliant, isn't it Heather? Watty tells us not to talk to the Police, and what is the first thing that happens as soon as we get home, the Police are on our doorstep.'

'It's not our fault, Rachel, they're looking for Darius. It makes sense that they would come to speak to me, Watty will understand that.'

'Your brother is a fucking drugged up maniac. He will never believe this. He'll think we went to the Police, not the other way around. What are we going to do?'

'Rachel, come on, it'll be fine. He doesn't need to know. How will he ever find out if we don't tell him. It's not as if he's parked outside watching us, is he?'

Edwards sunk down into her seat as she saw the curtains in the flat being pulled aside, Rachel's face coming into view as she looked down onto the street. Rachel looked up and down the street before withdrawing her head from the window and allowing the curtains to fall back into place. Her gaze had passed over the Ford Kuga parked opposite the flat, not noticing Edwards or McManus in the front seats.

The conversation inside the flat resumed, the car speakers once more coming to life with female voices. 'He'll find out, Heather. He knows almost everyone in Cowdenbeath, including that nosy old bastard next door. It won't be long before he finds out the Police have been here.'

'But they were detectives, Rachel. Not in a Police car, was there a Police car outside when you looked just now? Right then, we're safe.'

'Safe,' shrieked Rachel. 'Did you say safe? We're never going to be safe again. As long as we're alive, he knows we can grass him up, put him in prison. For life, Heather. For murder.'

McManus shot upright in his seat, clearly shocked at what he had heard. But before he could comment to Edwards the voices continued.

'What else can we do Rachel. If we go to the Police you know what he said he would do.'

'Oh, I remember all right. I was there when his mates raped me, punched me, kicked me, spat on me. I will never forget that weekend at your brother's house, never. My arse is still sore, I never want to feel that again. It was horrible. And they just laughed when I cried and begged them to stop. The two of them just fucked me harder and harder. I hate to think what it was they used on me when they were tired out. I never saw it, but I felt it right up inside me. Fucking bastards. They don't deserve to live, none of them, including your fucking brother. He just stood and watched, laughing.' Rachel's sobs could be clearly heard as she shouted at Heather. 'It was alright for you. They didn't touch *you* . You were only tied up, I was tied up and fucked like a dog, for the whole weekend. Just to deliver a message. To you, my best mate. *Don't tell the Police!*'

'Right, right, come on Rachel, we won't go to the Police. I'm sorry this happened to you. There was nothing I could do about it. Like you said I was tied up too, in a different room most of the time. I could hear you moaning and crying but I couldn't get free to help you. I'm sorry Rachel. Really sorry. My brother's a real bastard, but what can we do?'

'Let me think for a minute. Oh yes, we could grass him up then leave the country. Start a new life somewhere else. Oh, that's right, we've no money, no new identities, no jobs to go to. Fucked up, that's what we would be if we tried that.'

'What about if the Police could get us protection, you know, like a witness protection thing like they do on TV? We could start a new life somewhere else.'

'But when Watty gets out? He'll come after us. He has mates all over the place, he could send someone to look for us, hunt us down. Then it's more rape, more beatings and all that shit, all over again. No, Heather, I'm not going down that road. It's not your arse that's at stake here. They didn't fuck you, did they?'

Edwards looked at the car dash in shock, her eyes riveted to the speaker outlets. McManus turned his head to her and said 'Not one word to anyone about any of this, am I clear? Not a word. We need to think about how we deal with this. How the hell did these two girls get mixed up in all this, and how the fuck are we going to help them?'

The speakers were quiet for a few seconds. 'I know what he said. If we tell the Police then they come after you again, do all those things to you again. I promised you Rachel, I will never go to the Police. We'll just have to keep quiet. My brother's mates raped you, beat you and hurt you badly. My own brother set fire to my fiancé in his car, pushed him over the cliff, murdered him, and there's fuck all either of us can do about it. Does that about sum it up?'

'Pretty much apart from one bit.'

'What bit?'

'The bit about what we can do about it. I think we should kill the fuckers.'

'What? Are you mad, Rachel? We'd never be able to do that. I couldn't do that.'

'Yes, I am mad. In fact I'm fucking furious right now. Those fuckers are not going to get away with what they did to me. We are not going to the Police; we're going to do the exact opposite. We'll take care of this ourselves. You and me are going to kill all three of them.'

Edwards had her hand on the door handle before McManus could restrain her. The door opened slightly before he could reach over and pull it shut.

'What, Mark. We need to get up there, they witnessed a murder. They were victims of abuse over the whole weekend. We need to speak to them again, they're key witnesses.'

'Gill, we have to think about this for a minute. Listening to this conversation was illegal. But at least now we know what happened to Darius. And who did it.'

'That's all very well, we know what happened, but what can we do about it? Mark, come on, we need to do something.'

'Let's leave it overnight, if we went back in there right now then they would know that somehow we've been listening to them. That would be career over, for both of us. Tomorrow, we go back with the same questions as tonight. If we get the same answers then we take them in for interview at the office. We can take it from there.'

'But we've still not found Darius. We know he went into the quarry inside his car, but the divers didn't find a body. So where is he? And what can we do about the brother and his mates raping Rachel. Any evidence we might have found must surely be gone by now.'

'True, but that depends on what we find out when we interview the girls again tomorrow. We have to base our actions on information legally obtained, not some illegally recorded conversation.'

'But what about the threats to kill the brother and his mates. You heard them, they're 'going to kill the fuckers', they said.'

'To be fair, that doesn't sound like a bad idea. Let's hope they don't act on that tonight!' and McManus started the car and drove off.

It was not late when McManus drove up his street towards home. He had dropped Edwards off at her flat before driving through the narrow streets north of the Police Station towards the Glen Bridge. He didn't stop to glance down through the stone balustrades guarding pedestrians from the long drop down to the car park. He missed the drunk solicitor staggering down the steps from Bruce Street on the opposite side of the car park. He also missed the figure in black pulling the solicitor to the ground and kicking lumps out of him. As he was missing all of that, he was sure he recognised the figure in black as the young PC he had called on Friday night about the drunk driver.

There was still a bit of daylight as McManus parked his Kuga in the driveway, the street lights had not switched on yet, but there was enough light to see a woman approaching his car from the street. She was not dressed in running gear this time.

Instead she wore a tight vest top over a long flowing skirt with a split running almost to the top of her thigh.

'Hello again, Mrs Docherty, you seem to have lost your dog.' he said as he smiled at her.

'Touché, Inspector, guilty as charged. My husband was back in court for sentencing today, remember I told you about the case on Friday night.'

'That's right, I remember. How did it go today?'

'He was sentenced to four years in prison. The judge was pretty fierce in his remarks about him. Child pornography not to be tolerated, a teacher in a position of trust and so on. I really think I'm well rid of him. I just want to get on with my life. I've still to tell the kids what happened. I'm not looking forward to that.'

'Your kids as you call them, they're at university, aren't they? At least they're away from the local gossip that's bound to be doing the rounds after a case like that.'

'Yes, I suppose that's a blessing at least.' She moved towards McManus, stopping short with one hand on her hip which was thrust forward, pushing her bare thigh through the split in her skirt. 'I was thinking it was very kind of you to listen to me last time I stopped by. I wanted to thank you, and to let you know I appreciated the information you gave me.'

McManus looked at her thigh, then at her vest top showing a generous cleavage, and said 'It's been a long day, Mrs Docherty. I'd love to chat longer, but I've got fish and chips going cold in the front seat here, and I've not eaten all day.'

'Sorry to hold you back from your dinner. I know how easily hot things go cold outside, even in July.' She smiled and pulled her skirt a little, allowing the split to ride higher on her leg, a flash of white underwear just visible.

'You're right, where are my manners. Why don't you come inside and I'll just pop my fish supper in the oven?'

Chapter 22

McManus felt like a half-shut knife as he trudged through his morning routine, dragging his way around the bathroom, the bedroom and finally making it to the kitchen where he sagged into a chair while the kettle boiled. What the fuck am I doing, he thought, rubbing his aching back with one hand while scratching his balls with the other. With mug of coffee in hand, he stood at the kitchen window looking at the reflection of his bloodshot eyes. 'I need more sleep,' he heard his brain say. 'Yes, but three different women in three nights,' he heard his cock say. He knew which one he should be listening to, but it was easy for him to stray. His liking for older women was going to get him in trouble, again. He had narrowly escaped a major problem during that last murder case in Pittenweem. Christ, he had been lucky that time, and look how that had turned out. A promotion, salary increase, and he didn't even have to move office! Still, maybe he should try to behave for a bit. But that young woman PC from the other day, well she was something a bit special. Younger than he was normally attracted to, but married, so that bit was ok. Plus, her husband seemed to be into some kinky stuff, playing away while his wife was keeping the public safe from harm. And then there was Jane Docherty from last night. That had been a real surprise, she was very athletic and adventurous in bed, and McManus had struggled to keep up with her, in spite of their age difference. Now, with her husband going to prison for a few years, her kids away at University, she was going to be lonely. And she only lived around the corner.

McManus shook himself out of his daydream and finished his coffee, dumping the mug in the sink before picking his car keys off the hook by the door. Moments later he was driving away when he suddenly braked to a halt, before slamming the gear stick into reverse. 'What's the matter with me.' he muttered. 'I'm losing it here.' He had completely forgotten the most important part of his whole day. He was playing golf that evening with Paul Adams, and he hurriedly opened the garage to get his golf clubs.

The MIT morning briefing started a few minutes later than planned, McManus had insisted on getting another cup of coffee and a bacon roll from the cafeteria before he could begin. McManus waved everyone to silence with his greasy roll, and gestured at DS Gibson to begin. Gibson was always in the office early, and McManus felt sure he would be totally up to speed on the Darius Bakhoum case.

'Initial reports from forensics on the Audi recovered from the quarry are a bit limited so far. Examination by the techies showed the keys were in the ignition, the engine was switched off, the gearbox was in neutral, but the handbrake was off. That is a bit strange, but no explanation from forensics about that.'

'So why would the car be parked at the edge of the quarry, but the handbrake off.' asked DC Edwards from the back. 'Does that not seem a bit dangerous to anyone?'

McManus could think of a number of reasons why a couple in a car would have let the handbrake off. It could be decidedly uncomfortable if it got in the wrong place at the wrong time. But he kept quiet and waited for the rest to figure it out.

'Ok, park that for a minute,' Gibson continued, a few groans sounding out at his attempts at humour. 'The underside of the car showed scraping on the sills and floor pan, from the front wheels all the way back to the rear wheels. The exhaust system also showed damage consistent with the car sliding over the quarry edge. The inside, in the area of the driver's seat, showed burning to the seat, the headliner, the door panel, and the carpets. The airbags were deployed in all front passenger and driver locations. There was no sign of scorching or burning of the airbags. It's likely that any fire in the car was extinguished when the car hit the water at the bottom of the quarry.'

'Thanks Ronnie,' interrupted McManus, 'but can we have short words this morning, remember DS Robertson is from Ayrshire.'

Robertson raised a cheery hand as the rest of the team laughed at the new guy. 'Thanks, boss, but I got most of it, apart from extinguished. Does he mean the fire went oot when the car hit the watter?'

DS Gibson smiled at the translation and continued. 'Sounds about right. Apart from that, no further info yet, but fingerprinting and DNA sampling could only get going once the car had been de-humidified, that's 'dried oot' for you Liam.'

McManus was quietly pleased by the way his team was bonding, humour went a long way in getting people to work together, and his new DS seemed to be fitting right in. He was feeling more like a DI now that he had finished his coffee and roll and decided to move the briefing along. 'Thanks Ronnie, now what else do we have?' What about any credit or debit card activity on the missing man's accounts? What about the phone records I asked for from the girlfriend, Rachel?'

DC Alexander looked up from his laptop on a side desk. 'That was me, boss. There's been no bank activity on Darius' accounts since last Wednesday, the day before he went missing. Nothing either on his girlfriend. Rachel's phone is shown at her work on Thursday, until that evening, when it moves to a location somewhere in the housing estate near the quarry. The same location where Heather's phone last pinged before it went dead for the weekend. Rachel's phone was also dead for the same period, possibly they were together at the party at Watson's house like they said. We can't pinpoint the exact place, too many different buildings working off the same cell towers.'

'Thanks, Steven, good work. Can you tell where the two girl's phones are right now?'

Alexander pressed a few keys on his laptop and looked up at McManus. 'System shows both phones at the same location, somewhere in the area of Rachel's address. Can't pinpoint the exact....'

'Yeah, yeah, I get it, too many buildings working off the same cell towers.' McManus waved a hand at the ceiling, 'seems like Big Brother can't watch all of us eh. If only everyone had a GPS chip in their necks, like a cat or a dog. It would make our job a hell of lot easier.'

Turning to the white board behind him, McManus began to assign tasks. 'Gill, you come with me again, we need to go back and re-interview Rachel and Heather. The Super wants a tight budget on this case, it's still technically a missing person case, and we're only supposed to be helping out the locals. Liam, can you write up a statement on your enquiries yesterday at the bank, then see if you can contact the parents again. Find out if they can think of anything else that might help. Ronnie, can you keep in touch with Dundee for any forensics updates, phone me if you get anything. The rest of you back to whatever you were on before.'

Murmurs rose from the team as they went about their tasks, and McManus beckoned Edwards to follow him into his office. 'Gill, you know why I can't say anything about this to the rest of the team. But those two girls are withholding information, information about some serious stuff. A murder. Multiple rapes, imprisonment, assaults, who knows what else happened at that house over the weekend. We need to get them to make statements, to tell us on the record. So far all we have is a transmission from an illegal bug. Which I have to get back sometime as well, and soon. Before they find it under that table.'

'So, what can we do. Beat them up again?'

'Of course not. But we have to get them to trust us, show them we can protect them from Watty and his mates. Maybe get the drug squad to turn Watty's place over, keep him occupied. Surely they'll find something that would keep him locked up for a while.'

'They haven't managed to pin anything on him so far. Everyone knows he's a dealer. But no-one comes forward with any evidence, and the drug squad won't do anything without a guaranteed case. You know how they are about their success rates. It's all politics with them. They might have fancy cars, leather jackets and designer stubble, but you won't catch them actually working. They won't do a search unless they know they're going to find something substantial. I don't think we can count on them to help us. You would have to take that up with the Super.'

'You're such a cynic, Gill. You're beginning to sound like me. But how do we get Watty and co banged up for this. The only way is to get the girls on board. So go and find out where they are right now. Be sneaky, we don't want them to know we're coming for them. We'll bring them back here, to Dunfermline. Then hopefully Watty won't know we're talking to them again.'

Watty was upstairs inspecting the bedrooms which Bugsy and Gasser had finished cleaning up, again. Their first attempt had fallen short of his expectations, and Watty had read them the riot act. Now the two rooms looked pristine. The walls had a new coat of paint, the new carpets were laid, the windows had been cleaned, the broken glass replaced and the beds had new linens and pillows. The old stuff had been taken away and burned according to Bugsy. Gasser had been busy cleaning the bathroom with several bottles of bleach and a pair of Marigolds. The cupboard at the top of the stairs no longer held any drug supplies, scales, or plastic bags. Watty was satisfied that at least the upstairs would pass muster if the drug squad stopped by unannounced. And, more to the point, no trace of the girls remained.

Downstairs had been subjected to similar treatment over the last two days since the two girls had been returned home. The carpet and sofas had been steam cleaned using the hired carpet cleaner, after Watty had removed all his drug stocks and taken it to his storage unit. The only stuff left was low enough in quantity as to be argued that it was for personal use only. He had a stash of powder and syringes hidden under a drain cover in the back garden, and most of his cash was all in a money belt around his waist. He kept more in the garden shed, well hidden in a bag of grass seed beneath some old paint cans. 'Come along anytime,' he thought. 'You'll get nothing on me here.'

As Watty relaxed into his reclining sofa section his phone rang. Fishing it out of his back pocket he looked at the screen in surprise. Number withheld. Answering it anyway, he suddenly shot upright when he recognised the voice on the other end of the call. His face paled as he listened, trying several times to interrupt. To protest his innocence. To explain. Fearfully he nodded in invisible agreement with the caller. Making promises. Giving assurances. Selling his life to a man he had only met once. He waited a lifetime after the other man had finished speaking and ended the call before he could breathe again.

'Bugsy, Gasser, get the fuck down here. Right now! Do you hear me? Right fucking now!

Gasser was first to come hurtling down the stairs and into the living room, with Bugsy close behind. 'What's up? What is it, Watty? We thought this place was all cleaned up. You said it was all ok.'

'Shut up, just shut up, both of you. We've got a problem. A big fucking problem. A fucking life or death kind of problem. That was the supplier on the phone. The head man in Edinburgh. Not the guy I usually deal with, this was the boss man this time. He said I hadn't paid him for the last load of stuff we got. Last week. Remember I went out to get stocked up? Well. Seems like the guy I deal with didn't pay over the cash to the boss man. He's done a runner with a lot of the cash. The boss man says we still owe him.'

'That can't be right. If your middle man stole from the boss man, that can't be your fault Watty.' suggested Bugsy.

'That's what anyone would think, isn't it? But he says I owe him. I got the stuff; he didn't get my money. He wants ten grand the day after tomorrow, and another ten in advance before he gives us any more stuff. That's what the big fucking problem is. We don't have the ten grand unless you two get out and get selling. But we'll have to cut it down even more, so we can get the extra ten grand for the next lot. Now do you see what the problem is. We need twenty grand in the next few days just to stay in business.' They didn´t need to know about his seed money. What they didn't know they couldn't tell.

'How the fuck are we supposed to get twenty grand in two days?' Gasser farted loudly and turned away as the other two swatted at the air. 'Sorry, you know I can't help it when I get nervous. You're lucky it's just a fart. Twenty fucking grand. No way can we do that.'

'Well, we just have to fucking do it. There's no other fucking way. The man said he'll cut off my bollocks and choke me with them if I don't get him the money. He said it'll be slow, and painful. Very painful. And I'm not ready for that just yet. So here's what we'll do.' Watty reached down the front of his trousers, just for reassurance. His face was still white, and cold sweat trickled down from his forehead onto his nose. Comforted slightly by the warm feeling in his fingers, he withdrew his hand and slapped at his mates. 'You two. Get all the stuff out of the drain. I'll shoot over to the storage unit and bring back all the gear we have left. For the rest of today you two will be making up packages, I'll be on the phone getting in some orders. Then tomorrow, it's sell, sell, sell. Right? My fucking bollocks are at stake here. You got that! And if you can't do that, then your balls are coming off first.'

Chapter 23

The MIT had their own suite of offices on the top floor of the three storey Dunfermline Police Station, but all the interview rooms were on the ground floor, close to the prisoner reception area. This area was reached from the lower level rear courtyard, which allowed cars and vans to drive right up to the back door. McManus and Edwards had escorted Heather Watson and Rachel Taylor from their Cowdenbeath flat after finding them both there instead of at work. After getting the two women into separate interview rooms, Edwards had gone to get them checked in with the custody Sergeant while McManus parked his car in the upper-level staff car park.

Meeting again in the reception area McManus and Edwards discussed their interview approach. They huddled together to avoid eavesdroppers and whispered. 'We know what happened that night at the quarry, but we have to get them to tell us. We can't let anyone know we bugged their flat.'

'Too fucking right, Mark. My job's on the line here, again, might I add. And yours. Pittenweem was a fuck up, that last case, but we've got past that now. Let's not go there again, please.'

'Why? What's wrong with Pittenweem?' chuckled McManus, nudging her in the ribs.

'You know exactly what I mean. This is serious. We've got to get one of them to crack. We can't go after Watty and the other two without a statement putting them in the frame for Darius' murder. It was only Heather that was at the quarry, so she has to tell us. One way or another. Or we might as well pass the whole thing back to uniform, and Darius can just stay missing!'

'Ok, ok, I get the picture. Let's start with Rachel. She's the one who was raped and beaten. Surely she's the most likely to turn them in. You lead, I'll observe to start with, usual kick under the table if I want you to shut up? Right, let's get it done.' McManus went in search of the Sergeant with the keys while Edwards waited outside Interview Room 2.

Edwards began by assuring Rachel that she was only there to help with their enquiries into the disappearance of Darius Bakhoum. They wanted to check her movements on Thursday night, the night Darius had last been seen.

'Look, I told you already. I was at a party at Heather's brother's house. I got a phone call while I was at work telling me it was on that night. I went home and got changed first, then went straight there.'

Edwards looked up from her notebook. 'Well, that's the thing Rachel. When we spoke to you last night you said you went straight to the party from work. Which is it? Home first, or straight to the party?'

McManus gave the slightest nod in Edwards direction, encouraging her to pursue this first lie. Edwards persisted. 'How did you get to the party, Rachel?'

'Ok, I forgot, Watty came and picked me up in his car. I phoned him to let him know when I was ready to leave work and he met me there.'

'He met you at work?'

'Yes.'

'What time was that?'

'It must have been about nine. I always work a bit later on a Thursday night to get ready for the salesman having their big sales push at the weekend. Anyway, the showroom's open till eight most nights. What's the big deal here? I told you I didn't see Darius that night.'

'Like I said earlier, we want to find out what happened to Darius, Rachel. But you've told us three different stories about Thursday night. Which one should we believe?'

McManus interrupted, 'Why don't we go and ask Heather about Thursday night. Maybe we'll get a different story from her. Come on Gill. Let's leave Rachel to think about things for a bit.'

Heather stuck to her original story when Edwards questioned her in Interview Room 1. McManus sat back and observed as she lied her way through the story. He knew she was lying, Edwards knew she was lying, and Heather knew she was lying. But none of the detectives had any way of proving it.

'So, Heather, what you're saying is that you last saw Darius when he left your flat about ten o'clock on Thursday night? Is that right?'

Heather simply nodded, face down, looking at the tabletop. McManus slammed his hand down on the table, causing Heather to jolt upright, panic evident on her face.

'We don't believe you, Heather. I think the last time you saw Darius was when he was trapped in his burning car. Being pushed over the edge of the quarry. Screaming. Dropping to his death. Pushed there by your brother. Murdered by your brother!'

Heather screamed and jumped from her seat. 'No. No it wasn't like that. Watty would never hurt him. We were going to be married. We had bought a house together. I don't know what happened to him. I don't know where he is. Maybe he's hurt somewhere, you need to find him!'

'That's not going to work. We know what happened, Heather. Rachel has been very brave, but we've figured it out now. Tell us the truth. What happened at the quarry on Thursday night?'

'I don't know what you mean. I've told you all I know. Darius left the flat about ten o'clock. All I know about the quarry is what you told me. About finding his car there. I was at Watty's, at the party. I haven't seen him since Thursday night.' Heather slouched forward over the table and began to cry, head buried on her folded arms. 'Leave me alone,' she shouted, the words muffled through her tears.

Outside the room McManus and Edwards regrouped. Undeterred, they considered their next move. 'We could always try the old trick, tell Rachel that Heather has come clean. That we know the real story now. What do you think?'

Edwards wasn't convinced. 'Rachel was repeatedly raped over the whole weekend and Heather is lying to stop that happening to her again. She won't tell the truth till she knows her friend is safe, that it'll never happen again. We can't promise that, can we? No, not without putting Watty away for this.'

'That's the problem. We know what happened, but we can't do anything about it. Fucking bastard is going to get away with murder! I hate the prick, and I've never even met him! Fuck! We have to do something, Gill.' McManus kicked the wall in frustration, adding another black scuff to the fading plasterwork.

'Come on Mark. One last go at Rachel. Like you said. Let's just bluff her, see what happens.'

Thirty minutes later, the two detectives sat in the cafeteria, coffees steaming away in front of them. Neither of the two women had changed their story in spite of more questioning. In the end, McManus had consulted with the custody Sergeant. Detained in connection with the suspicious disappearance of Darius Bakhoum, and conspiracy to pervert the course of justice. They relied on the law that a suspect can be held forcibly in a police station for a maximum of 12 hours to allow him or her to be questioned about their suspected involvement in a crime. That was the best they could come up with while they continued enquiries. That was the official line at least.

'Nothing else we could have done, Mark. Not without putting us in a shitload of bother. Maybe forensics will come up with something.'

'Yeah, right, Gill. Fucking forensics. The car was in the water for nearly three days. They'd need to be really clever to find something linking Watty to that car after this amount of time. I fucking hate it when this happens. We know what happened. Who did it. The murder. The rapes. And there's fuck all we can do about it. Bastard will just keep on selling drugs like it's a normal day. Meanwhile the Bakhoums don't get any answers about their son. We look stupid, can't even find a missing person in a flooded quarry. Where else could he be for fuck's sake?' Come on, finish your coffee and we'll go visit Watty before he gets wind that we've got his sister locked up.'

McManus and Edwards stood on the doorstep with ID badges held up as the man opened the door. 'DI McManus and DC Edwards, we want to speak to Adam Watson. Is he here?'

'Nah, he isn't here mate. Come back later.' The man began to close the door as McManus pushed it open again.

'I just need a word. Who are you then?' McManus was fairly sure that the man at the door with the protruding eyeballs was Bugsy, one of Watson's drug runners. McManus continued to lean on the door, preventing it from closing. "Look, we just need a quick word. Is he here?"

"I already said, he's not here. Now piss off. If you want to come back later I'll tell him you called, Detective Inspector. And bring a warrant if you want to go any further than this door.'

The two detectives were walking down the path back to their car when a man from the house next door waved to them from his window. Curious, the pair went in the next gate and waited till the door opened and the man beckoned them inside.

'Are you with the Police? Is it about all that ruckus at the weekend? What a bloody rammy that was.'

'Can you slow down a bit, please. What ruckus?' McManus stepped into the small hallway beyond the front door, Edwards close on his heels.

'It started on Thursday night, after ten it was. That guy next door, you know, the drug dealer you lot never seem to do anything about. Well, he came back here about half past ten, him and his two mates, and they had a girl with them. She was in a right state, kicking and shouting she was, they pulled her into the house and slammed the door.'

'And you're sure this was Thursday night, Mr.....'

'Jackson, Captain Barry Jackson, Paratroop Regiment, retired. I'm here visiting my mum for a bit, I live in Colchester, but I'm between jobs just now, so I visit when I can.'

McManus stepped back as the burly ex-serviceman leaned over him to push the door closed, his muscles stretching the sleeves of his thin t-shirt. Jackson rubbed his nose, drawing attention to the bruising around his eyes.

'I went round there to complain about the noise, one of them lads got lucky with a head butt, but I'll be ready for them the next time I see them.'

'Looks nasty, tell us what happened, Mr Jackson.'

By the time Jackson had finished his story of the Thursday night, McManus and Edwards were convinced that the all weekend party Rachel and Heather had told them about was in fact only five people. Jackson had watched Watson's house all weekend and had seen no one enter or leave the house until the Saturday morning. All of which was contrary to the story given by the two girls currently detained at Dunfermline Police Station. McManus was also fairly certain that Jackson had a score to settle with Watty and his two mates Bugsy and Gasser. He was quite happy to let that develop without any intervention from the Police. Besides, it was Cowdenbeath Police's patch, nothing to do with him.

Heather and Rachel had been released from detention and driven home by McManus and Edwards. The twenty-minute drive had been completed in silence, much to McManus' consternation. He had hoped the women's relief at their freedom would encourage at least some conversation, but despite Edwards' initial efforts to chat with the girls they had remained silent for the whole journey. The two detectives now sat in their car around the corner from the women's flat, listening to the sounds coming through the car speaker from the listening device still hidden under the dining table.

'It's ok, Rachel. I will never let them do that to you again. I promise I will never tell the Police anything. We've been friends for what seems like forever, but now we need to stick together more than ever before, it's our secret. A dirty little secret to be sure, but we can't tell anyone. Ever.'

'I know Heather, but what about Darius' parents. They'll want to know what happened to him. You need to call them. They'll be suspicious if you don't.'

'Right, and tell them what? That my brother burned their son alive. That they set fire to him in his car then pushed it over the quarry edge. The police dredged the quarry, they didn't find him. They will never find him. I'm never going to be married, never live in our new house, never have his children.' Heather burst into tears and ran sobbing to her bedroom, throwing herself on the bed.

Rachel followed her and lay beside her friend, an arm around her shoulders, trying to bring her some comfort. Heather looked up at Rachel, but her eyes were drawn to the garment bag on a hook on the back of the door. 'And I'm never going to get to wear that dress. Remember how we spent weeks looking for just the right dress, you came with me every weekend for months until we found the perfect one. Oh God, all the wedding arrangements. What am I going to do about all of that?'

'It's ok, Heather, we'll work it out.' Rachel rubbed her friend's neck, don't worry about that just now. We need to speak to Darius' parents. They'll know what to do.'

Heather leapt from the bed, shouting, 'Really? Will they really know what to do?' She pulled the garment bag off the hook and threw it to the floor. She pulled open her wardrobe door, 'And what about these?' she shouted, pulling a pair of white high heeled sandals from inside. She grabbed open a drawer in her dresser and threw it on the bed. 'And will they know what to do about these?' she screamed as she pointed to the brand-new white lingerie spilling from the designer labelled shopping bag. 'Or these, or maybe I should just keep it all for the next time? If I ever meet another man like Darius, he can wear this in his buttonhole.'

She tipped a small box onto the bed, and the contents spread out over the duvet cover. Five buttonhole corsages made from white heather and purple thistles lay in disarray, and she plucked one from the heap. 'The woman in the shop recommended the artificial ones, more chance that they will keep their colour and shape all day she said. 'Good idea', I said, and here they are. 'Lucky white heather' the woman said. Especially when I told her my name was Heather. Not very lucky now, are they?' Heather collapsed to the floor in floods of tears, clutching at the folds of her wedding dress which had slipped from the garment bag.

'Heather……Heather, help me.' Please!' Cried Rachel. The blood was spreading from her thighs and bottom, soaking into the pale blue duvet cover, turning it a bright purple shade. Her face had lost all colour and her lips were turning blue. She fell sideways to the floor as Heather just began to turn around, confused by her friend's words.

'Oh shit. Rachel, where did all that blood come from. Ok, stupid question. But we need an ambulance.'

'No, no we can't. We can't tell anyone, I can't go to the hospital, Watty will find out and come back for us. Just help me to the bathroom. Please.'

Heather got her hands under Rachel's arms and helped her off the floor, half dragging her to the bathroom. Bloody drips on the carpet followed their progress as Heather struggled to help Rachel into the shower cubicle. With the shower turned on full, together they managed to undress Rachel completely, and Heather supported her friend as the water cascaded over them both. This was the first time Heather had seen the full extent of the bruising to Rachel's body. She gasped in fear as the blood and water mingled before swirling down the drain. 'I promise you Rachel, I will never tell another living soul about this. But, I will also promise you this. Those bastards cannot be allowed to live after what they did to you.'

Edwards brought her fist to her mouth as she listened to the scene unfolding in the flat. 'Mark, we have to do something. They need help, we can't just sit here and listen. She might be seriously injured.'

'What, and tell the boss that we just happened to be outside, listening to an illegal bug planted in their flat. I don't think so, Gill. They won't talk to us and we have nothing to go on here. No evidence. No statements. No hospital or doctor reports. No forensic examinations. Nothing!'

'But she could bleed out, maybe even die. We have to help her.' She turned in her seat and reached for the door handle.

'Sorry Gill, but I like my job. I thought you did too.' And before Edwards could jump from the car McManus had engaged gear and was driving off.

Their next stop was back at Watson's house, where this time the car registered to Adam Watson was parked outside. 'We're in luck, Gill. Looks like he's in this time, come on, let's see if he'll let us in.'

Watson opened the door in response to the knock, and the detectives stood there once again, ID badges held up. 'Detectives, welcome back. Sorry if my friend was a bit rude earlier, he was just following instructions. It's not his house after all, is it? Can't just be letting strange policemen in at any old time of the day, can we? What can I do for you?'

'We just want to ask a few questions about a party you had here at the weekend. May we come in?'

Once inside McManus was amazed at how orderly everything appeared. And the smell of fresh paint. And newly shampooed carpets. And not a syringe, balance scale or plastic baggy in sight. 'Nice place you've got here Mr Watson. Bet it wasn't as tidy at the weekend. Tell us about the party.'

'Yeah, had a few mates round, my sister and her pal were here too. It all got a bit messed up, drinks spilled, someone was sick in the back bedroom, you know how it is. It ran on a bit longer than we expected. Was just supposed to be Thursday night over into Friday, but some people didn't leave till Saturday. I suppose we were a bit noisy, did the neighbour complain?'

'Yes, we spoke to him earlier, seems there was a bit of a fracas. He's got two black eyes and a bloody nose. He said there seemed to be a lot of screaming coming from the bedrooms upstairs. Mind if we take a look?'

'Sure thing. That must have been the games on the PlayStation. It was a bit loud sometimes, but we turned it down after he complained. We spent a bit of time tidying up after though, so there isn't much to see. This way.' Watson led McManus towards the stairs and they went up. McManus was confused. This was supposed to be the house of a drug dealer, yet there was no evidence anywhere of anything other than a normal house. It was so tidy they must have spent hours working on it. The carpet in both bedrooms was clearly new, the bedding was also new, tightly stretched over the beds, and the paint on the walls also looked fresh.

'I see you've had a bit of a makeover since the party.'

'Yeah, well, it was a bit of a mess and well overdue for a freshen up. Seemed like a good time to do it. The two lads, Bugsy and Gasser, really mucked in. Couldn't have done it without their help.'

'Where are they now, the two helpful lads. I think it was Bugsy we met earlier?'

That was him, hard to miss him really. Them eyes give me the creeps, even now. I've known him since school, but he still gives me the heeby jeebies when he looks right at you.'

'And where are they?'

'Gone to buy supplies, we ran out of everything this weekend, fridge is empty, cupboard is bare Inspector. I'm sure you know how it is. However, gave us a nice chance to do a spring clean, even though it was a bit late in the year. Pity Heather moved out, she would like it here now, all clean and tidy.'

McManus had one last look around the upper floor, noting the strong bleach smell in the bathroom, before heading downstairs again. He was flummoxed. This was supposed to be the stronghold of one of the area's foremost drug dealers. It looked more like the house of someone from a TV reality property programme.

'Come on DC Edwards, there's nothing more for us here. Let's go and get something to eat, it's been a busy morning.'

Chapter 24

A short stop at a supermarket petrol station got his tank filled, and sandwiches for lunch for Edwards and himself. They ate in the car on the way back to Dunfermline and as they bounced over the potholes McManus could hear his golf clubs rattling in his golf bag in the boot. He was already thinking ahead, mentally checking off what he needed for later; clubs, shoes and a change of clothes for his game with Paul Adams that evening. He hadn't got over his disappointing morning, but it was looking brighter for later. That optimism wasn't to last long.

The first thing he saw when he entered his office was the balding crown of Detective Superintendent Nicholson, his head bent low over his tablet computer. 'Sir! I wasn't expecting you today. I just had to pick up a sandwich for my lunch. I would have been happy to share but I finished it in the car on the way back from Cowdenbeath. Can I get you something from the canteen, Sir.'
'No thanks, Mark. I've just come from lunch with the Procurator Fiscal. We were looking at rape and murder stats for our little piece of Police Scotland. Thought I'd drop in, see how your missing person case was going.'
'Well, I think it's more than just a misper case. I think there's been a murder, Sir. Tag on a suspected rape and kidnapping, and I think that covers the basics of it.'

'Explain, Mark. This should have been over by now, I told you to keep the budget tight, and wrap it up in a couple of days.'

'You did, sir. But… It's difficult to explain, sir. You see, the man's car was found in the quarry in Cowdenbeath, as you already know. But forensics found evidence that it had been on fire and found traces of accelerant inside. And the misper's shoe. With no sign of a body when the Support Unit dredged the quarry bottom. At the very least it's suspicious.'

'So what enquiries have you made? Is he the suicidal type?'

'No sir, he was due to be married in a few weeks, new house was nearly ready. It looked like he was getting his life in order, his parents are sure he was very happy about the future. So we checked out his work, and spoke to his fiancée, he hasn't been seen since Thursday night.'

'But that hardly makes it a murder. It might appear suspicious, but we don't have a budget in MIT for that. Pass it back to the locals, it's a Cowdenbeath uniform case. Let them have it.'

'But Sir. I believe that the man's fiancée was held prisoner over the whole weekend, kept against her will, by her brother. And that the same brother and his two friends killed the misper, setting fire to his car before pushing it into the flooded quarry. They also imprisoned the fiancée's friend in his house in Cowdenbeath and repeatedly raped and beat her over the same weekend.'

'You *believe* the man was murdered, his fiancée's friend raped and beaten, and both were held captive *for a whole weekend.*' Nicholson sounded incredulous.*'* I hope you have some solid evidence of all of this.'

'Technically, not really. Just what the man next door heard. But I think that's what happened.'

McManus could feel his face turning red with the frustration he felt at not being able to explain fully. He turned to face the window while he drew a deep breath. 'The neighbour we spoke to this morning said he heard some strange goings on at the brother's house over the weekend, women's screams, thumps on the wall, but no-one left or entered the house from Thursday night late until sometime on Saturday. The brother is a well-known drug dealer, Adam Watson. Neither of the two women, the fiancée or her pal, was willing to tell us anything. But I think they both know what happened to Darius Bakhoum on Thursday night. That at least one of them was there when he was murdered, and Watson has some hold over one or both of them to prevent them telling us. The house is absolutely spotless, fresh paint, bleach smell everywhere, new carpets, new bedding. Something must have happened there for them to do a clean-up like that.'

'Well, that's a hell of a theory, Mark. But what evidence do you have that we can take to the PF. You say forensics have nothing, there is no body, no witnesses, so what do you have?'

'But Sir. Darius Bakhoum has been murdered. I'm sure of it. He's in that quarry somewhere. We just haven't found him yet.'

'That's all very well, Mark, but we have budgets to consider. Until we find a body there is no murder. When the two women agree to talk, *then* you can investigate the kidnap and rape you *believe* happened. But in the meantime, Mark, this is only your third month in charge of the MIT here. Don't screw it up.'

'But Sir....' The Super simply held up his hand to quell McManus' protest.

'The Chief and I supported you to get this promotion. Even though DI Rutherford screwed up and you closed that last case. Every other MIT in the force, except us here in Fife, has a DCI in charge. You have a good record so far in your career, I think you can go far. But….. you're in a management role now. You have to lead. You have to manage and control people and resources. We have no money for continuing a speculative enquiry that you can simply sign off as an untraced misper. Hand it back to Cowdenbeath, Mark. It's that simple.' McManus was about to fight back but bit his tongue instead as the Super picked up his briefcase and tablet and walked out. What the fuck did he know about the case? McManus knew he was right, and he would prove his boss wrong. He might just have to do it on his own time though, the Superintendent would never know.

McManus thumped his fist into the padded back rest of his swivel chair, rocking it back into the wall, then kicked the wastepaper bin into the corner of the room, spewing the contents over the floor. The bin was still vibrating when McManus' cell phone also started to hum and spin on the polished desk surface. It was Paul Adams, texting to change the time for their golf round that evening, could McManus make it for five o'clock, get a full round in before dark. McManus was distracted by the phone buzzing and looked down at it, feeling suddenly drained. He wanted to stay angry, to vent his feelings about the way the Superintendent had brushed his concerns aside. He wanted to kick the bin all the way to Cowdenbeath and back again. But he knew that would do no good. He was management now, he had to lead. The Super was right, if McManus was to progress his career, he had to consider budgets, statistics, results, manpower resources, and not take on unsolvable cases that could be passed onto some other team. His team stats were important, he had to control his resources, meet his budgets, lead his team on winnable cases, not lost causes. He sat down in his chair and pulled himself closer to the desk, taking out a large notepad from a drawer. He thought carefully for a few moments then began to make notes on the pad. What did he know, what did he not know, what evidence did he have, what was fact and what was conjecture? Who were the witnesses, and what had they said, or not said? It took him nearly an hour to write down all his thoughts into separate pages for each heading and read it all again carefully. Viewing it like that, completely and dispassionately, he reached a conclusion. It wasn't his case. He would hand it over to uniform as an ongoing missing person enquiry. Strictly speaking, although Bakhoum lived in Dunfermline, he was last seen by his fiancée in Cowdenbeath when he dropped her off at her flat on Thursday night after work. It was their case, and he picked up his phone to call the Duty Sergeant at Cowdenbeath.

Exactly at three o'clock McManus walked into his squad room and stood at the front, looking at the whiteboard with all the details of the Bakhoum enquiry. He picked up the black marker and drew on the board for a few seconds before standing back to admire his handiwork. A picture of a golf hole, complete with flagstick, was prominent in the bottom corner, and a golf ball was drawn bouncing towards the hole before falling in.

'Listen up, everyone. The Super has decided that this missing person enquiry should be handed over to Cowdenbeath uniforms, and I've spoken to them already to tell them we are sending over all our notes. So, finish up whatever you are working on for this case, get Lynn to package it together and give me a hard copy. I need to take it to the Duty Sergeant at Cowdenbeath. I think there might be a few loose ends to tidy up first, so listen up.'

He could see some of the team getting notepads out ready, others listened closely.

'Confirm the location of Bakhoum's passport. Check any bank transactions since Thursday. Try again to locate his cellphone signal, or at least re-check the last known movements. Get written statements prepared from the Dive Team, his parents, his workplace, anyone else you've spoken to. Gill, can you do the statements from the fiancée and her friend? Right, any questions?... Good, can you get that done by this time tomorrow. Liam, Gill, can I see you in my office for a minute please?'

Once the office door was closed behind them, McManus, DS Robertson and DC Edwards stood around the desk. 'Look, I know you've done a lot of work on this enquiry, and that we have our suspicions about the actual events that took place on Thursday night, but the boss has spoken. It's no longer our case, it's a missing persons case, and it's getting passed over to uniform. Quite frankly, I can't see us getting any further with it anyway, not without the cooperation of the fiancée, and she's sticking to her story about the party.'

'But Mark, we know there's something not right here. You know what we heard from those two girls…'

He interrupted quickly, 'Gill, that's pure speculation. We have no evidence to justify us spending any more time on this. I know you're disappointed, but that's the way it is.'

'But…..'

'Liam, can you excuse us a minute, clearly Gill wants to get something off her chest.'

McManus waited until he and Edwards were alone. 'Gill, what we heard is not admissible as evidence, technically we obtained it illegally, so forget that you ever heard anything. I know what happened, but we can't prove anything. The Super wants the case shut down, so just write up your statements and let it go.'

'But that's another potential rape case just getting dropped. That's four rapists allowed to walk away in the space of two weeks. That's not right, Mark. Those bastards deserve to rot in jail.'

'Fair point, Gill. But remember, we only gather evidence, admissible evidence, to help put the guys away. The rest of the job is up to the PF to decide what cases are winnable. She brings the evidence to the court to get a conviction, not us. Once we pass a report to the PF it's out of our hands. And we don´t have enough to even send a report. Now go do your job, finish the paperwork, and move on.'

'It's not that easy, Mark. You know it's not. You know my story from the last case, I don't think I can ever move on. '

'Ok, Gill. I'll speak to the PF tomorrow, see if she thinks it's worth us pursuing Watson and his two mates, but don't hold your breath. And another thing, when you've done with the statements just go home. This case is over, and I've got to get going. Close the door on your way out!'

Chapter 25

McManus and Paul Adams walked down the 17th fairway of the picturesque Moorhall Golf Club. The views of the rolling Perthshire hills were spectacular as the sun still shone down in the late evening. Adams had owned the golf course and hotel resort for many years, it was one of his legitimate businesses that actually made a profit for him. Having come to Scotland from Poland in his late teens, Adams had begun work as a carpenter and builder, but soon progressed into property renovation and development. A lucky break brought him the seed capital he needed to expand, and now his property business, PA Properties, was worth tens of millions of pounds. His illegal businesses produced more than that every year, from prostitution, people smuggling, drug dealing, and security work. McManus was clever enough to know what he could and could not prove, and satisfied himself that he stayed on the right side of the fine line in his dealings with Adams.

McManus had met Adams during his last murder enquiry in the spring, when Adams had helped McManus to arrest and convict the murderer. The two men had reached an understanding during that case, and McManus believed that Adams could be useful to him in the future as he built his career. As long as Adams did not bring his drug business into McManus' jurisdiction, then McManus would not try to investigate Adam's businesses outside Fife. Adams though still remained a useful contact to have, and McManus was happy to tread that line for as long as he received information from Adams. The tip about Watson and his supply of White Heather was a good example. Adams had also told McManus another interesting bit of information as they were golfing that evening.

'The drug trade in Fife is run between two old families, The Stewarts control West Fife, from Cowdenbeath, through Dunfermline and out through Newmills and Valleyfield as far as Kincardine,' explained Adams. The Stewarts have been around the Dunfermline criminal scene for generations now, the father runs the show, but he has two young sons eager to step up and take over. A lot of their stuff is supplied from the big Edinburgh firm, but the Russians are trying to break into the market in Scotland from their bases in Manchester, Liverpool, and Newcastle. There's a battle going on for control in both Edinburgh and Glasgow, but the locals seem to be holding their own so far. As you know, I have the market north of the Tay, and I can't see that changing.'

'I know the Walker family runs the trade in Kirkcaldy, but we've never been able to make a serious dent in their operation. A few convictions among some of the soldiers, but we can never get evidence to stick against the family. They control the rest of Fife, up to your boundary, as I'm sure you know, Paul. We thought it was the Walkers bringing in shipments into Pittenweem in my last case, until we figured it all out, with a bit of help from you, of course.'

They continued to play down the 17th, both getting pars, before walking over the road to the par 3 final hole. Adams' phone rang as they were getting ready to tee off, and McManus delayed his shot while Adams finished his conversation. He hated mobile phones on the golf course, but Adams owned the course, so what could he say.

'Sorry Mark, business calls. I was hoping we could have dinner in the hotel when we finished our round, but I'm afraid I have to go as soon as we finish the 18th.'

'Can't be helped, Paul. But you're still one down, so you need this hole for a half.' McManus swung smoothly and watched smugly as his tee shot avoided the bunker and ran across the green towards the hole. Adams made his club selection and stepped forward onto the tee, making a hurried practice swing. Teeing his ball up, he swung his club, making perfect contact with the ball, and followed the trajectory of the ball as it arced onto the green, coming to rest two feet from the flag. As they walked towards the final green they were both confident of making their birdie putts.

'Sorry I can't stay for dinner tonight, Mark, but if you get down in two from there I'll buy you dinner at my casino tomorrow night if you can make it.'

'But what if I sink the putt for a birdie, Paul? It looks pretty straight from here, I think I've a good chance of holing that.'

'Sink that and I'll get you dinner tomorrow night, and free access to the hotel spa tonight, with a new pair of swimming shorts thrown in!'

'Right, you're on.' McManus laughed as he lined up his match winning putt. It had been ages since he had enjoyed a sauna and a swim, it was just the thing to help him relax after the round. With a firm stroke McManus sent his ball rolling towards the hole, using the contours of the green to help it turn as it died into the front of the cup.

'Great putt, Mark. Looks like you'll be living the high life on my tab for the next two nights.'

'Thanks, I'm looking forward to it. Just don't tell my boss will you.' McManus walked over to Adams' ball, picked it up and threw it to him. 'I'll give you that one, nothing like halving the last in birdies.' The two men shook hands and headed for the side of the green to collect their clubs, before walking towards the clubhouse and the locker rooms.

McManus had read a golf magazine while he sat alone at his table, eating a substantial helping of steak pie and chips from the golfers' menu in the clubhouse bar. His bottle of Hee Haw was empty in front of him and he was contemplating another before crossing the car park to the hotel, and the promise of free entry to the spa. His watch showed it was already nearly nine o'clock so he dismissed the idea of another alcohol-free beer, replaced the magazine in the rack, and said goodnight to the barman. He was still in his golf shirt and trousers, his golf shoes and clubs were safely stowed in the boot of his Kuga, and he made his way up the steps to the front door of the hotel. Following the signs for the Health Club, he approached the spa reception and explained who he was, that Mr Adams had made some arrangements for him that evening. The young woman on reception was incredibly attractive, dressed in a polo shirt and sports shorts bearing the logo of the hotel. However, McManus was unimpressed by her long blonde hair and tanned legs. She was far too young for his liking, although he gave her his best smile while she got him a key card for access to the facilities. Armed with a brand-new pair of shorts from the health club shop McManus swiped the card on the changing room door and went through.

Chapter 26

The facilities were quiet on this mid-week evening, and McManus had the swimming pool to himself as he put in some lengths. He felt his muscles had tightened considerably in that short period of exercise and looking toned and fit he showered before entering the sauna cabin. He was surprised at the size of the sauna, it looked like the tiered benches could easily seat a dozen people, but there was only one other occupant. A woman sat wrapped in a towel on the middle tier of three benches along the longer wall of the sauna. She looked familiar, possibly in her mid-forties, with long dark hair pulled into a loose ponytail. In spite of the towel covering most of her body, McManus could see that she was curvy in all the right places, with slim legs and hints of muscle showing on her arms. His eyes were drawn almost immediately to a tattoo on her ankle, a tattoo he thought he recognised. The last time he had seen that cartoon image of a girl in a bikini under a shower was during his last case. It was from a picture on the internet, on a sex dating site that had been central to his investigations, and he felt sure he was looking at a woman whose picture he had seen before. He said nothing but sat down on the top tier of the benches, at the end farthest away from the woman, trying not to stare at the tattoo.

The woman glanced his way sleepily and smiled. He smiled back but was unsure of whether he wanted to start a conversation. After all, the woman was the wife of his Chief Superintendent, the most senior officer in his division, in the whole of Fife. If he was right.

'Do I know you?' the woman asked. 'You look familiar.'

'I don't think we've met before, I'm Mark, I've been playing golf with the owner, and he said I could use the facilities. He had to leave early on business.'

'Oh, so you know Paul. My husband and I are friendly with him too. He's so nice, isn't he?'

'I don't really know him very well, but I think I might know who you are.' McManus was reluctant to say more, she had just played the husband card, and he valued his career. He knew exactly who her husband was now, and he already had his suspicions about their relationship with Adams. He had suspected for some time now that Chief Superintendent Keith Hodges was taking bribes from Adams in return for information about Police investigations.

'Are you Mrs Hodges? Mrs Hodges as in the wife of Chief Superintendent Hodges?'

'Why yes I am. How do you know that?'

'I'm Mark McManus, Detective Inspector Mark McManus. I met your husband when he promoted me recently, after DI Rutherford retired.'

'I remember your name, Inspector, my husband told me all about you. He also told me about DI Rutherford, why he had to retire, how he had such a beautiful young wife, who was divorcing him. Did you know him, Inspector?'

'I did, Mrs Hodges, I worked with him on the last case before he retired. I got his job.'

'I believe you got more than just his job, Inspector. How is Mrs Rutherford, Georgina is her name I think isn't it? It seems your reputation precedes you.' The woman looked directly at McManus. 'Do you mind if I call you Mark?'

'Not at all. Do you mind if I called you *Spa-Girl*?'

The woman continued to look directly at McManus, showing no recognition of the name he had just uttered. 'Why would you want to call me that?'

McManus looked her over without trying to hide his interest. 'I recognise your tattoo, Betty Boop in the shower, isn't it? The last time I saw that tattoo on such a shapely leg was in a profile picture on a website. A website called *Roughmeup.com.* The profile name was *Spa-Girl*. She described herself as 'A bored housewife from Glenrothes looking for some fun.' Sound familiar? It was all part of our investigation into the murders of two fishermen from Pittenweem in April. Apparently this housewife from Glenrothes was so bored that she met up with one of our murder victims for rough outdoor sex, nothing to do with the murder as it turned out, but interesting though, don't you think? That seems to me like the kind of thing a woman would want to keep secret from her husband. Especially when the man you met for sex was such a fat slob, not quite up to your usual standards I'm sure.'

'You think you know all about me, Mark, don't you? You honestly think that was me on that website? Do you really think I have sex with strangers, rough sex, just with anyone?'

'We both know the answers to those questions, Mrs Hodges. Why pretend otherwise? I can keep a secret; I don't ever meet your husband in my day to day work. Besides, here we are, two bored people in a sauna, just the two of us, miles from home, late at night, nothing between us but a towel and a pair of shorts. And I do like your tattoo!'

McManus slid along the wooden bench towards her, before dropping down a level to sit at her feet. He reached out and gently began to stroke her ankle, caressing her around the tattoo with one hand, while the other worked on her calf.

Without warning the woman drew back her hand and slapped McManus hard across the face, while at the same time kicking out at him, catching him in the chest. 'You obviously know nothing about me. Gentle caresses do nothing for me. Like my profile says, 'I Like it rough!'

McManus looked up at her from the low bench, rubbing his cheek. He stood quickly, surprising her, and grabbed her towel, pushing her forward, face down onto the top bench. Pulling at the bottom hem of the towel he found to his surprise that she was naked underneath, and wasting no more time he dealt her two hard spanks to her bare cheeks. 'Looks like we have a match then, *Spa-Girl*. But we can't play here, anyone could walk in.'

She struggled against his hand, turning her head enough to see the bulge in his swim shorts. 'I don't really care. Are you going to use that, or is it just for display?'

'Sorry, but we're both guests of the owner, it wouldn't be quite the done thing to get caught screwing in the sauna. If you want it rough, then meet me in the car park once you're dressed. My car is the dark grey Kuga in the clubhouse car park, at the far end, under the biggest tree. Don't take too long, or I might have to come looking for you.' He gave her bare arse one more hard slap before adjusting his shorts and walking out of the sauna.

An hour later McManus drove south again on the M90 motorway his mind full of images of *Spa-Girl*. She had arrived at his car not long after him, and a quick look round showed they could not have picked a better spot. His car was the only one left in the golf car park, and the overhead lights did not penetrate the darkness in the corner where he was parked.

There was an empty slot between the Kuga and the high hedge that bordered that part of the pitch-black golf course, and he had pulled her into the space and pushed her against the back door. She struggled against his grip as he unfastened his trousers, but she relaxed as he gripped her by the hair, turned her, and forced her down onto his cock. She took him in willingly although he hung onto her long hair now released from its ponytail. He remembered how she bit him lightly, and how he reacted by slapping her hard, pulling her up and round, pushing her face against the car door.

'Rough, I like it rough.' she breathed out. 'Come on, fuck me hard, Mark. Fuck me.'

And so he had pulled open the back door of his car, pushed her face down on the back seat, her legs still standing outside, and dragged her skirt up over her waist. He had fucked her there, face down, then again with her on her back, before finishing off with her bent over the floor of the open boot. He had rolled off her, exhausted, he had played 18 holes already that evening, and those extra exertions in the car park had been the icing on the cake. He hadn't reached the end though, as she rolled back over towards him and took him in her mouth one last time.

A loud buzzing sound brought him back to reality as his car drifted across a lane and the warning tone forced *Spa-Girl* from his mind in time to correct his steering direction. He safely reached his exit and was about to turn right for home when he had a fleeting thought. Turning in the opposite direction, he drove towards Cowdenbeath, where five miles later he turned into Adam Watson's street and parked fifty yards from his house.

McManus sat in his car and watched as two men left Watson's house, turning down the footpath towards him. Rolling his window down, he called to the men. 'Is that the house where I can score?'

The men eyed him cautiously but saw no obvious signs for concern. 'Aye, that's the White Heather Club'

'The White Heather Club?'

You'll no see Andy Stewart, but if it's White Heather you're after, then you're in the right place, mate.' and they laughed and walked on.

McManus sat in his car for another thirty minutes, and two other men separately arrived at the house, leaving again soon after. It was clear that Watson was dealing from his home, but it was nothing to do with him. The drug team would know about it, and he didn't want to piss on their lamppost. He was tired, and needed to sleep, but when he drove away from Watson's house he found himself driving deeper into Cowdenbeath, not escaping back to the main road. He pulled out his phone as he neared the flat where Heather Watson and Rachel Taylor lived, and pressed the listening bug app. It was still working.

'Rachel, come on, come to bed. It's late and I've got work in the morning.'

'I'll be there in a minute, the bleeding has stopped but it's really sore every time I go to the toilet. I can't stop thinking about what they did to me. Is it going to be like this every time I sit on the toilet? Will I have to remember every time one of them stuck his cock in me?'

'Of course not, Rachel. Everything will be fine. You'll get better, it just takes time. Maybe we should take you to the doctor?'

'No way. We can't. I'm feeling better now anyway. They'll ask too many questions; we have to keep this secret. Watty will find out, and he'll do it again. I couldn't stand that, Heather. Your brother is a bastard who should hang for what he did to me.'

'I know he is, but we can't do anything about it unless we tell the cops. Maybe Darius is still alive, maybe he escaped from the car and is hiding somewhere. If he came back, then he could tell the cops what happened, we wouldn't have to.'

'Even you can't believe that, you saw him being burned alive in that car. You were there when they pushed him over the cliff into the quarry. He's not coming back, Heather.'

'I know you're right. I just have to accept it all, it's going to take some time, we were so happy together. And my own brother, how could he do that to me? To you? You're all I've got now, Rachel. I need you Rachel, please help me, come to bed. I need you now, more than ever'

'I'll be there in a minute, we need to figure out how to pay back the bastards that did this to us. We can't let them get away with this.'

Chapter 27

McManus wore cream chinos and a blue jacket as he left for work on Wednesday morning, electing to take his Mazda MX6 out for the day. He had opened the garage deep in thought, edged past the Kuga and squeezed his tall frame into the bucket seat of the red sports car. Easing it carefully out onto the driveway, he left the engine running while he got out and went to the front to open the bonnet. Quickly checking the oil and water levels, he was satisfied that the car was running as perfectly as ever, and looked forward to his drive up to Dundee that night. He stepped back into the hallway of the house, picked up the suit carrier containing his best navy suit, a clean blue shirt, and a maroon tie. He wanted to look smart for his dinner with Paul Adams at his casino, and he could shower and change at the office after work.

The throaty sound of the 2.5 litre V6 engine put a broad smile on his face as he negotiated the morning traffic through Dunfermline, finally pulling into the staff car park at the Police Station just before eight am. He sat listening to the idling engine as he gathered his thoughts for the briefing he was about to lead, the briefing that would officially close this current case. The one he was convinced was a murder, but there was no way he could prove his suspicions without putting his career in danger. If last night was anything to go by, he thought, I might just have found someone to help me progress my career.

No harm in being on good terms with the Chief's wife, and it would even be fun to meet her from time to time. She was just his type, older, wiser, more experienced, and above all, married. He had found that most of the married women he had slept with had no intentions of leaving their husbands, they just wanted some fun and adventure, with no strings attached. Just the way he liked it.

Standing at the front of the squad room, McManus looked out at his team. 'Today we are closing up our investigation into the disappearance of Darius Bakhoum. The Detective Superintendent has instructed me to hand it back to Cowdenbeath for them to continue enquiries. We are a Major Investigation Team, and we have done our bit to help out while we have nothing major going on, so the Super has decided that we should pass it on. Now what do we have before we pass it over.'

'Right Boss, I'll start shall I?' began DS Robertson, getting to his feet. 'There has been no sign of the missing man since he was last seen after work on Thursday night. He dropped his fiancée off at her flat, and she hasn't seen him since. His phone has been off since that night also. His car was found in a flooded quarry in Cowdenbeath, the car was hauled out, no occupants. The quarry was dredged by the Dive Unit, no body found. No witnesses traced so far either, other than the two young boys who reported the car on Saturday morning. Forensics report that the vehicle interior showed signs of a fire in the driver's area, on the headlining, carpets, door panels, but no human tissue was found in the car. There was also evidence of an accelerant present, confirmed as lighter fuel, no specific brand identified.'

'Statements have been prepared from Bakhoum's work colleagues, his manager, and his parents, and they are all in the evidence pack ready to hand over.

Essentially, he has just fallen off the face of the earth. No phone calls since Thursday evening, no bank transactions, no credit card activity, his passport is still in his room at home. His wallet is missing, containing his driving licence, credit cards, presumably with him when he disappeared. There's nothing much else to add, really. Anyone else got anything?' Robertson was obviously finished his report and sat back in his seat.

DC Edwards jumped to her feet before anyone else could answer. 'I think it's all a bit suspicious, this is a young man with everything to look forward to. He had a good job at the bank HQ, he was about to marry his fiancée in a few weeks, they had bought a house together, it was nearly finished and ready to move into. His parents are well off, both respected doctors, he was never in trouble, either at work, or with the Police. It just doesn't feel right, Boss. I think we need to dig a bit deeper. We know his fiancée and her best pal went to a party at her brother's house on Thursday night. That's the night Bakhoum disappeared. Maybe he went to the party, either with the two girls, or maybe later. Maybe there was a fight and he got hurt, or worse. We know the friend has a black eye, from a gate-crasher she said, but it's definitely worth checking up on.'

McManus interrupted her flow sharply, 'Gill, we've checked up on that angle. You know we interviewed the two girls, and the brother. They all have the same story, Bakhoum dropped Heather off at her flat, and that's the last anyone ever saw of him. We have no probable cause to search the house, besides when I went there it was spotless, fresh decoration, new carpets, nothing out of place. Nothing suspicious. It's a dead end, Gill. We've been ordered to pass it over, so get all the remaining paperwork in order, and put it on my desk. I want to take the whole file to

Cowdenbeath personally after work this afternoon. So get back to it everyone. Thank you.'

McManus could smell Edward's perfume behind him as he entered his office after finishing the briefing. 'What is it now Gill? We've been over this. We can't do anything else. We have to forget what we heard on that listening bug; we can't act on any of it.'

'But you heard them, you know what they said. Watson murdered Bakhoum, he did it, and now you are going to let him get away with it. And there's every chance now that the two of them will try to take some kind of revenge against Watson and his two pals. We can't sit back and wait for there to be more murders.'

'You better watch your tongue, Detective Constable. Can you not just give it a fucking rest? I'm not sitting back waiting. I'm doing what the available evidence dictates, and I suggest you sort out your paperwork accordingly and get it on my desk. I've told you already, our job is not just about getting to the truth, it's about what can we prove in court. We can't put the bad guys away without evidence, Gill. You know that from your last rape case, we've already discussed this.'

'Well, if you're not going to do anything about these two rapists and a murderer, I might just have to do something on my own. Fuck you very much for your help, Detective Inspector.' Edwards kicked out at the visitor chair, sending it bouncing into the desk, before she left the room and slammed the door.

Adam Watson and his mates, Bugsy and Gasser, were playing video games and drinking beer when a loud knock sounded on the front door. Gasser farted loudly and Bugsy knocked a beer can over in his hurry to escape the fumes. 'What the fuck, Gasser, now look what you've made me do.' Bugsy reached for the can to try to salvage the remnants of beer trapped in the bottom.

'You know that happens when I get nervous, and I hate loud noises, you know that. I'll get you another one from the fridge, just calm down.' Gasser was heading in the direction of the kitchen when the loud knocks came again.

'Forget the beer, get the door, Gasser!' shouted Watson without looking up from his game.

Moments later Gasser appeared back at the door to the lounge, a stranger standing behind him. The man was as tall and as broad as the doorway, and stood motionless, his hands clasped in front of him. 'Who's Watson?'

The three mates looked at each other quizzically. They had no idea who this was or what he could want in their house. He said nothing else and stepped into the lounge, reached up to the television set and tore it from its wall mounting. Lifting the set above his head, the man threw it into the corner of the room, smashing the screen and sending shards of glass in all directions. 'I said, who's Watson?'

Watson stood up from the settee, not wanting to give the stranger any further height advantage. 'Me, who are you and what do you want?'

'Just a message from my boss. If you agree to take a supply on a monthly basis, then that means he will supply you with product every month. You will pay for said product every month. That's the message. Bring your cash tonight, and you'll be supplied with your product for this month.'

'But….. I don't want any more stuff, the cops were round here yesterday, nosing about. I can't take any more just now, it's too dangerous. Anyway, I've still got half of last month's left.'

'That's not my problem, Mr Watson. You made a deal to take a monthly supply. My boss will give you a monthly supply, every month. You will pay for your monthly supply, every month. It's simple. It's like a book club, you keep paying, we keep supplying. If you don't want the product, tough, you still keep paying until we say you can stop. Now, so far you owe my boss ten grand. He asked me to collect that from you today.'

'But I don't have ten grand. The boss said I had two weeks to pay, it's not time yet. I'm working on it.'

My boss said I have to come back with either the money or you. One way or another you have to pay. Today. Or there could be a very nasty accident. Too bad, looks like you have a nice place here. Just needs a giant TV screen on that wall there to finish it off.'

Bugsy and Gasser shrank back away from the big man, leaving Watson to work it out on his own. This was way above their pay grade.

'Look, I can get some money now, maybe three grand, I can give you that right now. I can get more this afternoon and bring it over to Edinburgh for you. Come on, man, give me a break will you? It's the best I can do today.'

'Ok, give me the three grand. I'll take it back, tell the boss you'll bring the rest tonight. But remember this. If you don't have the rest when you come tonight, there might be another accident here, and it won't just be a TV.'

Once the man had left with the cash that Watson had retrieved from his money belt the three pals sat down again in the lounge. Watson was still shaking, Gasser had farted several times, and the rancid smell still hung in the air. Bugsy's eyes were sticking out further than usual, making him look like a giant frog.

'What are you going to do Watty?' asked Bugsy, still trying to press his eyeballs back with the heel of his hand. 'Have we even got another seven grand?'

'No, we don't, but I'll have to go over there tonight and explain. Try to buy us some more time to pay. This thing with the sand dancer and the cops and the two girls has really screwed up our sales. You two need to get packaging more stuff, do it tonight while I'm out. We can start a sales drive tomorrow and over the weekend. Surely we can pull together seven grand before Monday. I can promise them the money on Monday. But you two have to do your bit, ok?'

'Yeah, sure Watty. But can you not just call the boss? Do you really have to go over there? It might be dangerous.'

'Of course it's dangerous you morons. Everything about dealing drugs is dangerous for fucks sake. But it's not your neck on the line is it?'

'But the man said there could be an accident if you didn't pay. You won't be here, you'll be in Edinburgh. What if he comes back and we have an accident?'

'You'll be fine. Just work on making up packets, just you two. Nobody else needs to know about our cashflow shortage. If anyone comes to the door, sell them some stuff, but don't let them in, ok? Anyway, you'll need something to keep you occupied till we can get a new TV.'

Chapter 28

Dressed in his fresh navy-blue suit and maroon tie, McManus felt like a million dollars as he walked into the grand front entrance of the Kingsway Casino. He had been reluctant to park his car in the big car park at the rear of the casino, but Adams had told him to drive up to the front door and one of the valet parking attendants would take his car round to the secure VIP parking garage. His Mazda was his pride and joy, he had spent too many hours to count restoring it since he bought it from his savings while he was still at University. It still served him well, with a boot big enough for his golf clubs and trolley, and a suitcase. It was full of memories as well, and he hoped a forensic team would never get near it. God only knew whose DNA they might find in there.

He had been to several of the casinos in Edinburgh but had never visited this one in Dundee. It was well located on the outskirts of the city, close to the main city bypass road that gave it the name Kingsway, and easy to get to, by car anyway. This establishment clearly did not expect any walk-in guests. Formerly an elegant mansion owned by one of the city's jute barons, the casino was now housed in a fully renovated and extended building that could have easily been mistaken for a luxury hotel. Set inside several acres of walled gardens, the long tarmac driveway curved through mature trees before finally spilling visitors out on a massive gravel turning area. The front of the casino was subtly lit with muted floodlights housed among the trees, and there was no gaudy sign advertising its identity. The only clue to its purpose was in a brass sign fixed to the gatepost at the entrance from the main road. That and the Kingsway Casino branding on the front of the valets' jackets.

McManus watched apprehensively as the valet got into his car, slammed the door, and took off with screaming revs and a spray of gravel. Clutching his parking ticket, he walked up the magnificent stone steps towards the hostess waiting for him at the entrance. She was tall and graceful, dressed in a beautiful purple evening dress, and he stopped in front of her.

'I'm here to meet Mr Adams for dinner. My name is ………'

'I know who you are Mr McManus, we've been expecting you. Welcome to the Kingsway.' The hostess turned and gestured to another woman standing inside the main door, again, she was tall and also wore a purple evening dress. 'Rebecca will show you to the restaurant, I'll let Mr Adams know you are here, he'll be waiting for you at your table.'

McManus followed the purple gown through the entrance hall, past a sweeping double staircase, and through into a large open gaming room where it looked like hundreds of people were gathered round dozens of tables. He could see all the usual games, roulette, blackjack, baccarat, poker, and dice, and the croupiers were all busy in their smart white shirts with purple waistcoats. Rebecca led him to a reception desk, next to the cashier's station. 'We just have to complete a few formalities for our guests. Mr Adams has signed for you as a temporary member for the evening, but we still need you to provide some proof of identity. It's all a formality I assure you. Even we have to comply with the Data Protection Regulations you know.'

McManus reached into his inside pocket and pulled out his Police Scotland ID card, pushing it over the desk to the waiting receptionist. 'That'll do nicely, sir" and she pushed it back after noting the details.

The hostess led him back through the gaming room into the entrance hall, pointing out the cloakrooms on the way, before turning up the grand staircase. On reaching the next level she turned right and continued down an open corridor with a waist high balustrade on the left. McManus paused for a moment when he realised where he was. He could see down into the gaming room, with a clear view of almost every part of the room, and was immediately impressed by the design of the upper floor. The hostess had stopped to wait for him, standing patiently at a set of double glass doors, and when he caught up she turned and pulled open a door, motioning for him to enter ahead of her. A man in a purple dinner jacket with matching bow tie stepped forward to greet him, 'This way, Mr McManus. Mr Adams is already seated.' The purple dress turned and left as McManus gazed in amazement at the private dining room, with only one table, and only one diner.

Adams stood to greet his guest, and they shook hands warmly. Once seated Adams explained that he had made a special menu choice for his guest this evening, it was to be a roast loin of venison, something that he only served occasionally for special guests. The starter would be Cullen Skink, with a selection of Scottish cheeses to finish, and the wine would be selected by his sommelier to accompany each course. McManus was impressed, partly by the menu, but also by the confidence of his host in making all the decisions without consulting his guest. He was not unhappy with the choices and settled into his seat. Declining the offer of wine, McManus ordered sparkling water, citing his need to drive home without interference from the traffic division. He knew from his last case just what a disaster it could be for a serving officer to be stopped for drink driving.

The conversation flowed as if the two had been friends for years, they had much in common it appeared. A love of fast cars, golf, holidays in the sun, and of course, women. But the talk eventually turned to business, the drug business, and McManus and Adams reaffirmed their agreement reached a few short months before. Adams would not conduct any illegal business in Fife, and McManus would not pursue investigations into Adams' illegal businesses outside Fife. Adams would continue to help McManus with information that might help him with investigations in Fife, not just relating to drugs, but anything of interest that he came across. McManus knew his recent promotion to DI was partly a result of collaboration with Adams, he knew he was treading an exceptionally fine line in even meeting Adams, but he also knew that information from Adams could be especially useful in the future. Particularly in the private investigation he was mounting into the corruption of Chief Superintendent Hodges. He decided not to mention Hodges to Adams until he had more information about their relationship. He was going to play that one close to his chest.

Dinner was over and the table was being cleared when the purple jacket brought a phone over to the table, handing it to Adams with a muttered apology. Adams listened for a moment before beckoning the man back to the table. 'I'm sorry, but I have to deal with something downstairs. Please take some time to experience the tables, drinks in the gaming room are on the house, and I have something here to help you enjoy the rest of your evening.' Adams rose from the table, hand outstretched for a shake with McManus, and continued in one swift movement towards the doors. McManus looked down at the small disc Adams had pressed into his hand. It was black and white around the outer edge with a bright red central disc, the Kingsway logo embossed on one side

'I don't think so, Paul,' he said softly, as he laid the casino chip on the table, the £500 sign face up, before following Adams out the double doors.

Outside on the balcony overlooking the gaming room, McManus felt like he had been transported back to his childhood in Edinburgh. The primary school he had attended was laid out in a similar design to the casino, with classrooms around the perimeter of the ground floor, with an open, central communal space. The first floor followed the same pattern, but the upper classrooms were accessed from a balcony, with a balustrade separating the passageway from the long drop down to the ground floor hall. Looking down from the casino balcony he felt he could hear the squeals of children playing indoors during break time on a wet day, or the rattle of cutlery when the hall had been set out for school dinners. Dragging himself back to the present, he looked down on the gaming tables, watching young women dressed in purple gowns hurrying back and forth to the tables with trays of complimentary drinks for the members. He watched the hostess he had met earlier, Rebecca, serving drinks at a roulette table where there seemed to be much more excitement than at any other table. Looking closer, he could see a tall blonde woman leaning over the shoulder of a man sitting in one of the chairs reserved for players. She whispered in his ear as he stretched out to place chips on the numbered table, seemingly in some random pattern that McManus could not make out. As he sat back, the man accidentally brushed his jacket against the stack of chips in front of him, scattering them over the table.

The croupier patiently waited while the man and the blonde gathered the spilt chips together again, before spinning the wheel and sending the silver ball flying around the rotating track. Less than a minute later the wheel came to a halt amidst a mix of groans and cheers, the croupier placed his marker on a number and began to scoop chips towards him with his hands, leaving those chips around the winning number. Paying out winning bets, the croupier pushed stacks of chips in the direction of the different winning players, but none arrived in front of the man with the blonde companion. Another loser apparently. The blonde leaned over the man's shoulder again, her hand brushing against his back, consoling him, as she pressed her ample breasts against his cheek. As the man turned his head to speak back to her McManus instantly recognised him. It was none other than Chief Inspector Keith Hodges.

McManus was not surprised, he had long suspected that Hodges would have been a regular visitor to Adams' casino. It would have been an ideal place to meet, for information and money to change hands, and for hospitality to be extended. McManus now further suspected just what kind of hospitality Hodges was receiving, was the tall blonde woman part of the deal? And if Hodges was here, was he here alone, or was his wife somewhere nearby while he played the tables? Looking around the room below, McManus saw no one else he recognised and continued to watch Hodges at the roulette table. He seemed relaxed, and appeared to be known to the croupier and the pit boss standing nearby. He placed seemingly large bets on each spin of the wheel, winning occasionally, and his pile of chips seemed to remain at a constant level. McManus moved around the balcony to get a closer look from directly above Hodges' table, and he could see at least one black, white, and red chip amongst the stack in front of him.

With no idea how much any of the other coloured chips were worth, McManus assumed there to be anywhere between £500 and £1000 worth of chips on the table in front of Hodges. Not bad going for a night at the casino, depending on how much you started with obviously. Hodges took a large gulp from the drink at his hand, slipped his free hand below the level of the table and ran it up the thigh of his blonde companion. She responded by leaning over again, her cleavage almost rubbing his nose, as she also reached her left hand down into his crotch while rubbing his shoulder with her right. The art of distraction, thought McManus, nothing like it when you are planning a little deception. You are definitely worth watching Chief Superintendent.

A tap on his shoulder interrupted McManus' wandering thoughts and he turned hurriedly to find a woman standing behind him. 'We meet again, Detective Inspector, and so soon.'

'What a pleasant surprise Mrs Hodges, I didn't know you were a member here.'

'Well, you know how it is, Mr Adams is very generous, and he invited us to join here ages ago. My husband likes to come here, but I usually let him come on his own. Gambling is not my forte, I prefer something a bit more natural, maybe even more energetic you might say. I think I'm much more of an outdoor kind of girl, you know what I mean?'

''I do know what you mean, we had a perfect example of your preferred pursuits only last night. I had hoped we might meet again, but I didn't expect it to happen so soon, as you said. I've just been watching your husband, enjoying himself at the roulette table, he seems to be doing quite well. Must be some luck rubbing off on him from his companion, the one in the green dress.' McManus pointed down to the table below, and Mrs Hodges turned to look down.

'Oh her, she's one of Paul's girls, she gets paid to encourage the punters, play up to them, get them to spend more than they can afford. Keith usually ends up fucking her in one of the back rooms once he's lost all his chips.'

'Does that not bother you, him playing around like that?'

'Not really. He does what he does, I do what I do. I like it rough and hard; he wants love and attention. That's not really my thing, so I get my kicks as *Spa-Girl*, literally sometimes, he gets free hookers from Paul. Everybody wins. Thing is, he thinks I don't know. One night I'm going to surprise him, walk in on them while they're at it, give him the fright of his life. Can't have a Chief Superintendent fucking prostitutes now, can we? That would never do.'

'Just like we can't have a Detective Inspector fucking the Chief's wife?'

'Oh, come on now, I never said that. Did you not have fun last night? We could do it again right now, the private dining rooms up here all have locks on the doors, and they're all empty. The staff have finished up here, they're all in the downstairs restaurant with the all-night customers. Come on, I'll show you.' She grabbed his hand and pulled him to the end of the balcony, down a short flight of stairs to a small landing, where she turned along a short corridor leading to a single closed door.

'Come on, in here, there's no one about.' She pushed through the door, dragging McManus along, and locked it behind them. It was a small dining room, with one table that could seat four or six people at most, the table was covered with a cloth and nothing more, no cutlery or glasses spoiled the smooth white surface. A side cabinet stood against a wall, a sofa and two chairs formed a casual seating area and a set of dark curtains were drawn over the only window in the room. 'Perfect,' she said as she turned and forced her body against McManus in a hot embrace, one hand reaching for the front of his trousers. McManus knew when he was on to a good thing and pushed back against her, lifting her dress to find a hot, wet spot waiting to greet his surprised fingers as he probed roughly at the top of her thighs.

She laughed out loud at his expression, 'I saw you on the balcony, watching, it gave me time to nip into the powder room to get out of my knickers. Here's a present for you from *Spa-Girl*,' and she pushed a tiny piece of lace into his jacket pocket.

McManus gazed at his reflection in the mirror in the gent's toilet on the upper floor, his freshly washed face and newly re-knotted tie hiding the inner glow he felt having just fucked the boss' wife again, two nights in a row. 'Christ,' he thought to himself, 'I need to watch out for that one, she's wild.' The scratch marks on his back still stung from her long nails, and he was sure her cheeks would still be rosy red from the spanking he had given her. He began to count silently on his fingers, 'Saturday night was Edwards, Sunday night was WPC Morrison , Monday night, that was Jane Docherty, and now we've had *Spa-Girl* on both Tuesday and Wednesday night. I'm getting too old for this, either that or my dick's going to fall off.' He checked his wallet to find that he had used his last condom. 'Fuck me, trying to remember this week is like a game of Cluedo, Mrs Hodges in the dining room with the last Durex.' He chuckled to himself as he left the toilet and wandered along the balcony to see how the Chief was doing at the roulette table.

Hodges was still in the same seat at the same table, the same blonde woman draped over his shoulder. But the pile of chips had almost disappeared. McManus watched as Hodges spread the remnants of his stack across the numbers, before the wheel spun once again. The silver ball rolled round and round, bouncing noisily as the wheel slowed to a stop, the ball finally coming to rest in a numbered slot. 'Black thirteen,' the croupier announced and cleared the table with a flourish, leaving only the winning chips behind. Hodges accepted the stack of chips pushed towards him with a hand held up, 'Cash me in, please, I'm done for tonight.'

The chips were counted and exchanged for chips of the correct cash values, but McManus could not see the values of the chips now laid out in front of Hodges. Except for the black, white, and red one he knew to be worth £500. It mattered little anyway, Hodges slid one of the new chips back to the croupier, slipped the £500 chip into his jacket pocket, and stood from the table. As the blonde in the green dress took his arm, McManus almost missed the subtle transfer of the chips from Hodges hand into the little green purse the hooker carried on her arm. The two continued together to the cashier counter where Hodges took the cash chip from his pocket and handed it over. He spoke a few words to the hooker, who turned and left him, heading towards the back of the gaming room, while he waited for the cashier.

McManus could not clearly see what was happening at the counter, it was on the opposite side of the room to where he stood on the balcony. Taking out his phone, he turned on the video camera, pressed the record button and used his fingers to zoom in on the counter below, allowing him to see the single chip resting on the flat surface. Slowly panning the camera, he could see the cashier's hands counting out bundles of notes, the notes were twenties, in bundles of a thousand each. Ten stacks meant she was about to hand over £10,000 in exchange for a single £500 chip, and the stacks all fitted neatly into a small leather pouch which she pushed across the counter to Hodges. 'So that's how they do it,' he said to himself, 'five hundred turns into ten grand, just like that. Fuck, how often does he visit the casino?'

Wild thoughts were flashing through his mind as McManus drove home from the Casino. In no time he found himself speeding down the motorway towards his exit. Should he turn right for home, or left for Cowdenbeath, as he had done the night before to listen in to the bug still hidden in Heather Watson's flat. McManus knew he had to tread very carefully here, he needed more information, and he thought he knew just how to get it. He had no time to spare eavesdropping on Heather and her friend.

If he had turned left, and parked outside the flat in Muir Place, he would have heard the two women discussing their plans for that night, to wait until the early hours before driving over to the estate where Heather's brother lived. To park the car several streets away and walk through the dark back gardens to the rear of the house, where they would find a way in and exact retribution on Watty and his two pals. The men who had brutally raped and beaten Rachel, the men who had killed Heather's fiancée, the men who would never let the two women lead a normal life ever again. But McManus did not hear any of this, nor did he see the two women, dressed in black running gear and caps, leave their flat and drive away in Rachel's car. Instead his thoughts were full of the corruption of the Chief Superintendent, the man who was stashing away thousands of pounds of dirty money he was receiving from a major criminal. McManus was aware that he was socialising with the same criminal, but he believed that it would have a good outcome, that he would gather information that would help him solve crimes and convict criminals, not fill his own pockets.

McManus was torn between following procedure or exposing Hodges his way, he wasn't always in favour of doing the right thing, but he knew what needed to be done. He needed to call Gregor Aitken, get him to run more checks on Hodges' bank accounts. The problem was, the payments were probably all in cash, just like this one. But where could Hodges park the cash in such a way that he could use it legitimately? He already knew about the foreign holidays, and the banks in France and Spain, but Hodges lifestyle was nothing out of the ordinary, no flashing cash on fancy cars or clothes, and the hookers looked like they were on the house. His suspicions about the Chief appeared to be correct, but how could he prove it, and more importantly, who could he take the proof to? Or was he getting in over his head?

Chapter 29

The morning was passing quietly, McManus was working on his office laptop, compiling the monthly budget and overtime reports for his MIT. His case report summaries were all done already, the missing person case file had been handed over to Cowdenbeath yesterday afternoon on his way to Dundee, and he was on track to have all his paperwork ready to go to his boss by the Friday midday deadline. Superintendent Nicholson wanted him to form good habits when it came to the new skills needed to lead the MIT, budgets, case reports, manpower allocation and resource management. McManus just wanted to catch and convict criminals, in his case, rapists, armed robbers and murderers, but there just weren't many crimes of that nature in Fife. He had worked on one murder since April and it was the end of July already, with nothing major being investigated by his Major Investigation Team. His team had helped out on some enquiries that the local CID team had going, but there was nothing there that had needed his close attention. The lads on the team had it all under control.

He thought about paying a visit to the Procurator Fiscal's office, he would think of some pretence or other to speak to Michelle McAllister, the woman in charge of prosecutions at Dunfermline Sheriff Court. He had met her several times during his service, mainly to discuss pending cases, or to provide additional information when cases had come to trial.

She was married to a Queen's Counsel, and lived in Edinburgh, making the daily commute to Dunfermline by train, as far as he could remember. Her husband as a QC mainly appeared at the High Court in Edinburgh, or the Court of Session across the road from there on Edinburgh's Royal Mile, so there was little likelihood of bumping into him anywhere near Dunfermline. She was just his type, married, older than him, exceptionally good looking, and he had sensed some sort of mischievous sexual connection when they had met only the week before.

Tidying up his final reports, McManus closed down his laptop, picked up his jacket and phone and walked out towards the rear exit leading into the Police car park, and the private gate that would give him access to the court car park. Once inside the court building he headed up the stairs to the PF's office where he asked for Mrs McAllister, only to be told she was in court. A quick glance at his watch showed him it was late, court would probably be breaking for lunch soon, and he considered waiting around to see if she appeared. His rumbling stomach helped him decide against waiting, but he walked back downstairs to the Sheriff Court and quietly pushed open the door. Michelle McAllister was standing at the prosecution table at the front of the court, her back to the doors, addressing the Sheriff. It looked like she was giving details of an indictment, and kept glancing to the short, stocky man stood in the dock behind her, as she told the Sheriff of the nature of the charges. McManus took an empty space on the back bench of the public gallery and watched as she went about her business before the court. He soon realised from the content of the proceedings that the PF might not be finished for a while. From where he sat he could only see the back of her head, her shoulder length auburn hair falling onto the top of the flowing black gown that was her in court uniform. His stomach gave out a particularly loud rumble, causing the teenager sitting in the row in front to turn and laugh at the noise. 'Maybe another day,' thought McManus as he stood and left the courtroom, marching off towards the Kingsgate Shopping Centre and a Greggs pie or two for lunch.

The only way to eat a hot pie from Greggs was straight out of the bag, and McManus was an expert at eating on the go. His mouth was full of a bite of his second pie as he gazed at a shop window, ever wondrous at the amazing array of things you could buy in Poundland. He was about to walk on when his phone rang, making him fumble his pie from one hand to the other as he reached inside his jacket before the ringing stopped. ¨Fuck' he muttered as he dropped both his pie and his phone, maybe just as well or he might have tried to answer the pie and eat the phone. Scrambling on the tiled floor he recovered the phone and brought it to his ear as he tried to salvage the half pie that had miraculously managed to stay inside the paper bag. Too late, the ringing had stopped, but just as he was about to bite again into the greasy pastry he thought better of it and looked at the caller display. 'DC Edwards.' The phone rang again moments later and this time he mumbled out an answer, 'What! I'm trying to eat my lunch, I'll be back in the office in five minutes, can't it wait till then.'

'I suppose so. It's only two dead bodies in Cowdenbeath. I'm pretty sure they'll still be dead when you get back here. See you in five, Boss'

¨Very fucking funny, Gill, very funny indeed.' but she had already hung up.

As soon as he walked back into the squad room McManus could feel the excitement in the air, as if the whole team sensed that this could be just what they needed. Two dead bodies found in unnatural circumstances. Death was what an MIT lived for, what they hoped for, as long as they were not personally involved of course. McManus had found it strange at first, when he first became a Constable, how his colleagues actually wished for something to happen, something bad, something major, gruesome even, to give them a purpose and an active investigation. As he progressed to Detective Constable, then DS, he had not lost the enthusiasm for the big case, the questions, the answers, and the solving of the crime. Eventually every Police officer gets bored with the routine, the mundane, the petty offences, the dog fouling reports from squabbling neighbours, the road traffic collisions that take up hours of time, reams of paper, with very few of them resulting in meaningful prosecutions. Which is why most officers of rank at least up to Inspector went on shift hoping for something exciting to happen, something to get their teeth into, something on which they could use their skills. Maybe the team could smell the aroma of a major investigation coming off the two dead bodies five miles away in Cowdenbeath.

McManus pulled his car to a halt outside the house in Parkside Crescent, he had recognised the address as soon as Edwards had told him back at the office. DS Gibson and DC Fraser had already left for the scene before McManus had returned, so he had driven out with Edwards and Fowler, leaving the others behind to nurse their disappointment. The scene looked to be under good control, a uniformed officer was stationed at the gate leading to the garden of the house, and another stood at the open front door, holding a clipboard. Some interested bystanders stood on the other side of the street, whispering to each other, and pointing at the house opposite, while McManus recognised the figure of

Barry Jackson standing at the window of the house next door.

'You two stay put just now, I'll see what the story is. No sense in everyone traipsing about all at once, is there?' Stepping out onto the pavement, McManus showed his ID to PC Kerr as he headed towards the open door. 'Hi there, Juan. I see they've got you minding the gate again. Pleased to see you've found something you're good at.'

He heard a muttered response, but ignored it, being sure it was far from complimentary, and approached WPC Morrison with her clipboard. 'You still teamed up with that wanker? Want me to have a word with your gaffer, get you someone decent to drive about with?'

'That's all right, Sir, thanks. But I've got him under control, why do you think he's at the gate and I've got the clipboard? He's being nice to me because he thinks my man is going to refurbish his bathroom, having a plumber for a husband can come in handy sometimes, you know.'

'I certainly remember how handy it was when your man had to go out on an emergency call last Sunday night. Maybe we can do it again sometime?'

'Maybe, we'll see. I'm putting your time of arrival down as fourteen twenty-five. The ME is already inside, and Sergeant Baillie is the senior officer in charge at the moment. See you later, Sir.'

McManus stepped across the threshold into the hallway of the terraced house, following the stepping plates until he reached the door to the living room, where a bulky uniform blocked his path. Sergeant Liz Baillie stood over six feet tall, and was well built, to the extent that McManus could not see into the room beyond her. He had met her before during his time as a DC and DS at Dunfermline, when enquiries would often cross over into Cowdenbeath territory. 'Good afternoon, Liz, what have you got for me then?'

She turned sharply, startled by the voice behind her, but smiled broadly when she saw the newcomer. McManus tried to peer over her shoulder, he could hear music playing softly accompanied by strange grunting sounds, but she moved to block his view again. 'Nothing for you to see here, Detective Inspector. The ME says it's probably an accidental overdose, two known druggies, in the house of a known dealer. What more can I say? We're waiting for him to finish up, then the forensics boys can have a look just to be sure, but it'll probably be an occurrence report, a sudden death, report to the PF, job done! I'll get Kerr to do the report, keep him out of mischief for a few hours. That guy is a pain in my arse. Why couldn't you keep him in MIT?'

'Nothing to do with me, Liz. He was over the limit, belting up the M90 in the rain and Traffic pulled him over. He wasn't much of a DS anyway, had a chip on his shoulder the size of Gibraltar, what is it they call it, Napoleon Complex or something? Just keep an eye on him, make sure his bad habits don't rub off on that young Morrison you've got at the door. So where were we? Who discovered the bodies?'

Baillie scowled at him, still standing tall in the doorway. 'Two young girls came to the house this morning, probably to buy drugs. They claim they were here last night till gone midnight but left some keys or something. That's why they came back this morning, about elevenish. They called emergency services; they can give you the exact time of the call if you need it. We're holding them at the station in the meantime, till we can check out their story. But I told you, it's an accidental overdose. The ME will be out in a minute, he'll tell you that himself if you hang around.'

'This address was a place of interest in our investigation into a missing man, just last week. Remember the car found in the quarry? Well, the fiancée of the misper, and her pal, claim that they were at a party here for the whole weekend. It's her brother's house, Adam Watson, AKA Watty, he lived here with his two druggie pals, Bugsy something and a bloke called Gasser. We think they may have had something to do with the missing guy.'

'That I do remember. Kerr and Morrison spent the whole of Sunday out at that quarry, left me shorthanded for the entire day. And I had to grant them overtime by the time you let them go.'

'It wasn't my fault, Liz, my Super forced the case on my team. We're still not sure what happened to the missing guy, but the Super told me to shut it down. In fact, we declared it a missing person case and I took all the paperwork into your office only yesterday. But then we've got this today. Are you going to let me have a look or what?'

She turned in the doorway to let him pass through and took a deep breath as she did so. The uniform shirt she wore was stretched to bursting over her breasts as McManus squeezed past, trying hard not to make contact, but it was inevitable that he brushed his chest against hers on the way. 'Just make sure you don't touch anything, Inspector,' she winked as she nipped his bum, a big grin on her face.

The curtains over the front window were drawn closed, but the ceiling light was on casting a dull glow over the room. The ME was recording notes on a small digital recorder as he stood looking at the two bodies splayed on the couch. Each corpse was reclining against a corner of the deeply padded couch, as though sleeping with their eyes open. But McManus could tell they were not asleep, their mouths were wide open as though screaming, the fronts of their trousers were also open, and the smell of urine and faeces was overpowering. A hypodermic needle was sticking out of the left arm of both corpses, the plunger fully depressed in each case. The coffee table in front of the couch was littered with small plastic bags containing a pale, dirty looking powder. A small set of scales, loose powder on a metal tray, and a box filled with empty plastic bags also lay there in full view. Some used needles lay among the debris, and yet more needles sat in their paper packaging in another open box. The music from the 24-hour porn channel on the open laptop continued to play as a sordid backdrop to the gruesome scene, and a smashed widescreen TV set lay on its back in the corner.

The ME stopped recording and turned to McManus, a puzzled look on his face. 'Didn't expect to see you here Inspector. It's looking like an accidental overdose, nothing else suspicious so far, you can clearly see the needles still in their arms, and all the stuff on the table makes it pretty clear what happened.'

'So no chance of someone else administering the injections? No obvious injuries, no signs of a struggle? You're sure, Doc?'

'One can never be absolutely certain until the corpses are on the table, but first impressions are exactly as I said. Your forensics guys can test the syringes for fingerprints obviously, but failing that, there's nothing else to say. Can you tell the Sergeant that she can arrange for the forensics team to come in now? When they are finished I can get the corpses transported back to my mortuary for a full post-mortem examination, you can expect the results tomorrow if you want copied in.'

'If you could please. This could be part of an ongoing investigation, there might be more to this than meets the eye, so keep me in the loop if you would.' McManus looked back over at Sgt Baillie, still blocking the doorway with her hands on her hips. 'Ok if I have a quick look round, I know my way, I was here only a few days ago.'

McManus wasted no time in exploring every other room in the house, finding it just as tidy and fresh as he had seen on his last visit. Nothing looked out of place, nothing appeared suspicious, it was just a normal house. Unusually clean and tidy for a house occupied by three men in their twenties, but that was not illegal. Just unusual, and in itself suspicious, and it niggled at McManus. Something was not quite right about this case, the missing man, his fiancée, her friend, the two dead men, and the brother, who was nowhere to be seen. A shout from outside disturbed his thoughts and McManus turned to look out of the bedroom window. PC Kerr was still at the front gate and was restraining a man from entering the garden. The man was shouting again, waving his arms about trying to evade Kerr and force his way towards the front door, where PC Morrison had dropped her clipboard and moved up the path to assist Kerr. It was Adam Watson, the householder, and McManus watched on as the two officers wrestled him to the ground and subdued him. McManus ran down the stairs, past the unflappable Sgt Baillie and out into the front garden. Baillie followed him, and promptly sat on Watson as he lay on the ground flapping about like a stranded trout. "Now what Inspector?'

McManus motioned to Edwards and Fowler who were approaching the gate having seen the commotion from the car. 'Get him into our car, we need to speak to him.' indicating Watson who was slowly being crushed by the black Baillie bulk. Kerr had already handcuffed Watson which made it easier to lift him up and escort him to the kerb outside the gate, where McManus held the Kuga's back door open ready to receive their guest. McManus looked at Baillie, nodded at Watson, and said 'Ok if we take him back to your place till he calms down?'

'Sure, let me ring the office, tell them you're coming, get the interview room ready for you,' and she picked up her radio to make the call.

'Gill, Ronnie, take this idiot to Cowdenbeath office, he's not under arrest, but detained in connection with the deaths of ….. Liz, what's their names again, those two inside, Bugsy and Gasser what?'

'I don't know, they've always just been Bugsy and Gasser. I'll find out and let you know.'

'Right Gill, on you go, the two of you. I need to speak to the neighbour here, but I'll catch up with you at the office. Find out where he's been in the last few days, where the drugs are from, and speak to the two girls who called it in. Oh, and by the way, you better let him know his pals are dead as well.'

The ME came to the door and beckoned to Baillie, 'You can let the forensics boys in now please Sergeant, I've done all I can for my bit.' He marched up the path, kit bag in hand, stepped out of his white paper suit and drove off in his car. McManus watched him leave, saw the forensics white suits walk in the opposite direction and enter the house as PC Morrison made the notations on her clipboard. Kerr meanwhile was back at his post at the gate, breathing heavily while he leaned on the fence. McManus brushed past him, giving him a pat on the stomach on the way, 'Too many pies, Juan. I told you about that on Sunday.'

Barry Jackson opened the door before McManus reached it, he had seen the detective approaching as he watched from the front window of his house next door to the commotion. Inviting him in, Jackson closed the door behind McManus and motioned him towards the living room. Jackson's mother sat in a chair next to the small table underneath the front window and McManus chose a seat on the settee opposite. 'I got the impression you wanted to talk to me Mr Jackson, you've obviously been watching all the goings on next door.'

'I have, and so has mother here. What exactly has happened next door. I saw the man Watson being dragged away, what has he done now?'

'I'm not so sure that he has done anything yet. All I can say is that his two pals who live there have been found dead this morning. So what's the story then?'

Jackson launched into it breathlessly. 'I told you the last time I saw you that there was something going on in that house over the weekend. Well, last night there was another party going on. Watson had left in his car about eight o'clock or so, and soon after these two young girls turned up. Couldn't have been more than eighteen at most, then the music started, but that didn't last too long. I could hear the TV playing but it was too low to hear what was on.'

'Who do you think was in the house apart from the two girls?'

'Only the two pals as far as I know. There had been nobody else go in or leave all day, so it could only have been them, those two oddballs that Watson has as lodgers.'

'Right, so tell me anything else that you saw or heard between the girls arriving last night and the Police arriving this morning.'

Mrs Jackson interrupted from her window seat, 'It was me saw them leaving, them two sluts, staggering all over the road they were, hardly any clothes on either, skirts up to their backsides, giggling and holding onto each other. Blind drunk, the both of them.'

'What time was this?'

'Must have been after midnight, I don't sleep very well, you know, and they slammed the door as they were leaving. I had dozed off here, right in this very chair, the TV was still on. It was that shopping channel on ITV, and that doesn't start till half past twelve.'

That's good, Mrs Jackson. What else did you see?'

'Nothing, nothing at all. Not till this morning when them two girls came back again, they were dressed a bit different this time, but it was definitely the same two. Must have been about eleven or so. My Barry was here, he'll remember the time, I said to him that the girls were back.'

McManus looked towards Jackson who nodded in confirmation, tying in with the time he had been told by Sgt Baillie. 'That's when the girls came running back out of the house, screaming their heads off. One of them made a phone call in the front garden while the other one was throwing up out on the pavement. The next thing, one of your cars arrives, a man and a woman officer it was, those two that are still there. The man went into the house while the woman officer stayed outside with the girls. He came out pretty quickly, got the two girls into the Police car, and the next thing there's three more cars on the street and blue tape going up everywhere. The car with the girls in was driven away by another officer, and that's it until a doctor arrived, then you turned up.'

'That's great Mr Jackson, thanks Mrs Jackson. Are you quite sure no one else has gone into that house after the girls left last night?'

'As certain as I can be. They woke me up when they left and I couldn't get back to sleep, I just sat here in my chair. I might have dozed off, but their gate makes a hell of a squeak when it opens. They need to get that fixed.'

McManus suppressed a chuckle as he stood up to leave, 'You've been extremely helpful, I might have to send an officer back to see you, just to note down your statements, but it won't take long. You might also find that things next door might be a bit quieter from now on, let me know if you get any more trouble.'

McManus didn't really mean it, but they felt that help was available if they needed anything. It wouldn't be him though. That was a uniform job, like taking statements, holding the clipboard, and minding the gate. No, thank God, all that was behind him.

Chapter 30

The Cowdenbeath Police Station was quiet in the middle of the afternoon, shift change had come and gone, and only the civilian and Police office staff were left in the building. The Duty Sergeant, Liz Baillie, was still in charge at the scene of the suspicious deaths, and Edwards and Fowler were sitting in the canteen drinking coffee when McManus walked in. 'Well, this is cosy. I thought I asked you to interview Watson and the two girls.' His face was flushed and his voice harsher than normal.

'Sorry Boss, but after the girls told us their story we thought it best to wait till you got here to interview Watson.' Fowler looked sheepish, caught coffee handed so to speak. Edwards tried to placate McManus, 'We think you'll like what the girls had to say, Boss. Should be able to put Watty away for a long stretch at last.'

'Ok, go on then, what's so good about what the girls had to say? I'm all ears.'

'The girls confirmed that they had gone to Watson's house the night before to buy drugs. They knew the house was a place to buy heroin, and fentanyl, White Heather as they called it. Apparently, they can mix it together to give a longer and better high. They got there some time after eight last night, but Watty wasn't there, just the other two, Bugsy and Gasser. The guys persuaded the girls to stay, to try a free sample and to watch some videos. The guys were watching a porn channel, the girls got high and they started fooling around. But they said the guys were getting a bit too heavy for them, wouldn't stop pestering them to play games like they were watching on the laptop, so they left about midnight and walked home. They stay on the same estate as Watty's house.'

'Ok, that ties in with what the neighbour said, the times they arrived, the times they left, and that Watson was not at home. So what else?'

'Well the girls can confirm that they went there to buy drugs, that they knew Watson was going to sell them drugs there, and that there were baggies, scales and raw powder on full show in the house while they were there. We took the baggies they bought into evidence as well. So we can get Watson on possession with intent to supply, it was his house, he's the official council tenant. That's good isn't it? Boss?'

'Yeah, but Watson wasn't in the house at the time the girls were there, he's not been in the house since last night at eight o'clock, which is before the girls arrived. He could claim that the two pals were the dealers, using his house without his knowledge. I know, tenuous at best, but there's some wriggle room there. What about when the girls came back in the morning?'

Fowler spoke up this time, trying to deflect the heat from Edwards. 'The girls thought that one of them had left their keys at Watson's house when they were there last night, so they both went back this morning. The door was unlocked when they got there, the two guys had been pretty wasted when the girls left, so the girls had left the front door unlocked. Probably thinking they could go back and steal some stuff later, but they didn't go back till about eleven this morning. That's when they found the two guys unconscious on the couch. The porn channel was still playing, and they reckoned the guys had been playing with themselves, their flies were undone, but then they saw the needles sticking out of their arms. The girls ran out of the house, and one called us while the other puked up in the street. Our response unit was Kerr and Morrison, and they have confirmed all of that when we spoke to them by radio.'

'And do you believe their story?'

Fowler and Edwards nodded their agreement, so McManus instructed them to release the two girls while he got himself a cup of coffee.

Like every Police interview room he had ever seen on TV or read about in detective novels, Interview Room 1 at Cowdenbeath Police Station had plain walls coated with light green emulsion paint, a single table, four hard chairs and a recording device fastened to the wall. There was a small window high in the wall opposite the door, but they still needed the ceiling light on as McManus and Edwards sat facing Adam Watson. He had shown no emotion when he was told of the death of his two friends, and adopted a cocky and superior manner when the detectives had begun to question him. He clearly believed he had nothing to fear.

'I was nowhere near my house last night, I left about eight, and didn't get home again till you saw me arriving this afternoon. What happened to Bugsy and Gasser was nothing to do with me. Stupid pricks should've known better than to take their own stuff. I know nothing about any drugs you might have found in that house. Yes, it's my house, but they were just lodgers. They were running a drug business out of my house, obviously while I was away, so that I was never aware of their activities. If I had known about it then I would have stopped them.'

McManus decided it was time to use the information he had received during his dinner with Paul Adams. 'Look Watson, we know you were in trouble, your supplier in Edinburgh was leaning on you. You had missed a payment, you had to pay him by the end of the week or you were in big trouble. We know you went to Edinburgh last night for a meeting with your supplier. We know who he is, we know all about your drug deals, we know Bugsy and Gasser worked for you, we know you sold drugs out of the house, we know you're mixing up heroin and white heather. Now tell us how you think Bugsy and Gasser died. Did your Edinburgh dealer send someone over to give you a message, even while you were meeting with him to sort out a payment plan.'

'No, it was nothing like that. They must have accidentally shot up too much stuff. I told you, I don't know anything about drugs. I didn't even know they were taking the stuff.'

'Well if all that's true, maybe we should just let you go. See if you end up dead tomorrow morning. Your Edinburgh man will be happy to see you again tonight, I'm sure. Maybe he's waiting outside for you right now?'

'No, you can't do that! What if you're right, maybe there is someone out to get me. I don't know why, but you might be right. I don't know what's going on here. I don't deal drugs, it was those other two. They're the ones who were dealing, not me!'

'Nice try, mate. That´s what we call the Billy Connolly defence, 'a big boy done it and ran away!' You're seriously trying to blame two dead guys who can't answer back. Well, we'll wait until we get forensics results from the search of your house. I'm sure we'll find your prints on some of the stuff, on the baggies, the scales, the new plastic bags, the holdall under the table with the powder in. In fact I'm going to suspend this interview so I can go check with the forensics guys, they must be finished at your house by now. Your prints are in the system from that previous possession charge you have, so we won't be long.' With that McManus paused the interview and left the stuffy room, but as soon as McManus switched his phone ringer back on it began to belt out the ring tone, displaying the name of the caller he dreaded most.

'Good afternoon, Sir.' he said with a sinking feeling in his stomach as soon as he accepted the call.

'There's fuck all good about it, Inspector. I've just had a call from Inspector Philp. You know Inspector Philp, don't you? The Inspector in charge of the station where you are standing right now. Where you are currently interfering in one of his team's investigations. Without his permission. Or mine, come to think about it. What the fuck are you playing at!'

'Well, Sir, it's that missing person case you asked me to help out on last weekend.'

'I distinctly remember telling you to hand it over to uniform, I specifically told you that only the day before yesterday. Why are you still fucking about in Cowdenbeath?'

McManus was taken aback by the anger in the Superintendent's voice, his face went white and he sagged back against the corridor wall. Edwards was watching, her mouth hanging open, clearly able to hear both ends of the conversation, unsure of whether to stand still or make a run for it. McManus made it clear what she should do. Covering the phone he turned to Edwards and mouthed 'Fuck off!' at her and waved his arm in the direction of the exit. Edwards got the message and promptly turned and hustled down the corridor before she got caught in the crossfire.

'Two dead bodies have been discovered in a house here, the house of the brother of the missing man's fiancée. We think the householder had something to do with the man's disappearance. So two DB's turning up in the same house seemed suspicious. When we got the call from the Duty Sergeant here, about the address being linked to the misper enquiry, well I came out here for a look.'

'You came out for a look? Is that your best excuse after I told you to drop the enquiry? Inspector Philp says the ME thinks it's an accidental overdose. Lots of drugs lying about, needles still in the arms, a known drug dealer's house, need me to go on, Inspector?'

'Er, no sir, I know how it looks. On the face of it....'

'On the face of it? For fuck's sake man, the expert says it's accidental. Two less druggies to worry about is what I see. Now get your arse back to Dunfermline and leave Cowdenbeath to tidy up their own mess.'

'But Sir, I'm in the middle of interviewing the householder, a known drug dealer, and I think he's scared of someone bigger. He's fucked up on a drug deal this week, and I think his bigger dealer may have taken some sort of retribution. I think we might be looking at a double murder here, Sir.' McManus was shaking now, partly in shock at being bawled out, again, by his boss, but mainly because he felt he was onto something with the two bodies and Watty in the interview room. He tried again to get his argument over to the Super.

'I think the dealer may be able to tell us more, Sir. We've only had him in here for an hour so far. Forensics have just finished up at the house, and the PM isn't being held until tomorrow. Let me interview this guy again, at least until we get the science back. I've just got a feeling here, Sir. There's definitely something off about the whole scene, their connection to the misper, to his fiancée, the house was spotless apart from that one room with the bodies. It's all a bit suspicious to my mind, Sir.'

'I already told you to close down your investigation into the missing person and hand it over. I've now told you to leave this new business alone. We don't have the budget for wild goose chases, just because you have a feeling Inspector, that's no justification for you being where you're not supposed to be.'

'But Sir, it was a reasonable call, the same address involved in the misper case, the house where the fiancée and her pal spent the weekend, the same night the guy's car went over the cliff. I'm sure something went on in that house that connects to the missing person. Then two potential witnesses turn up dead a few days after. It doesn't smell right, Sir. Let me have a crack at this guy we've brought in, I'm sure there's more to it than an accidental overdose.'

'For fuck's sake, Inspector, you are not listening to me.' There was a pause on the line, no sound, but McManus could hear his boss breathing. 'Ok, Mark' said the Superintendent, softening his tone a little. 'Given that you are there now, I'll give you two more hours on this. But if you are not back in Dunfermline when I call you again in two hours, then you might need to look out your uniform again. I took a risk promoting you, and here you are three months later, unable to follow simple instructions. Two hours Inspector. Two hours to decide your future, Detective Inspector in charge of MIT or uniform Sergeant in charge of fuck all. Your choice; speak to you in two hours. Hopefully, you'll have made your mind up by then.'

Going in search of Edwards, McManus prowled the halls of the station, finding Sgt Baillie back in her office. 'Did you grass me up to Philp. I've just had my Super screaming in my ear for being at the scene; nothing to do with me he says. Not my case he says. But it connects to that misper case I passed over to you. How did Philp find out I was there?'

'Nothing to do with me, Mark. He saw us come back once we'd closed up the house, the forensics guys were all finished and away, and he asked to see the visit log from the scene. He's shit hot on compliance, so Morrison took it into his office, making sure all the times in and out were noted correctly, all the names spelt properly, ranks and so on. That's when he saw your name. Wasn't me. Just one of those things. Are you in bother about it then?'

'Just a bit, but he calmed down eventually and said I could follow up my interview with Watson. I've got a couple of hours to come up with something or I've to back off. So I better get to it. Any idea where DC Edwards and DC Fowler went?'

'Probably in the canteen. I saw Fowler making eyes at Morrison earlier, and she just went on her break. He's likely in there chatting her up. Edwards was with him.'

'Thanks Liz, I'll go chase them up. I'll pop my head in to say cheerio when we're done. It might be an idea to call the Drug Squad, let them know Watson's in here. I'm sure they'd be interested, especially with all that stuff you recovered from the house.'

Once again McManus and Edwards sat opposite Watson in the interview room and resumed the questioning. 'Your dealer threatened you about the missed payment, is that what happened to Bugsy and Gasser?'

Watson was unmoved and hung one arm over the back of his chair. 'No idea what you're talking about. I told you, I don't deal drugs.'

'So what was all that stuff in your house then? '

'I told you that as well. It must have been the other two, dealing behind my back. I know nothing about it. If they took some of their own stuff, then that's their problem, isn't it?'

The interview continued on with Watson giving nothing away and the detectives' frustrations growing by the minute. McManus knew he was running out of time in spite of the absence of a clock in the room.

'Well Watty, if you can't tell us who killed your pals, or who might have it in for you, I guess we'll hold you here till the Drug Squad come to visit. The amount of heroin and fentanyl found in your house are enough to support a charge of possession with intent to supply. But that's not my department. Interview terminated at seventeen twenty-five.'

McManus went back to see Baillie while Edwards went off to find DC Fowler so they could get back to Dunfermline in the Inspector's car. The Drug Squad were sending two detectives to interview Watson, the Forensics and post mortem results on the two DBs were due the next day, and McManus was expecting a call back at Dunfermline. They had all had enough of Cowdenbeath by that time.

The call he had been dreading went better than he had hoped, the Super had calmed down a bit and McManus having called in the Drug Squad to deal with Watson placated him even more. They agreed to keep an open mind on McManus' venture off piste, at least until they got more information the following day. His team had all left for the evening when McManus switched off his office lights. Edwards had suggested he go back to her place, picking up a takeaway en route, at the same time mentioning that her flatmate would not be home till after ten. But he had politely declined, with a rain check agreed instead. There was just one more thing he wanted to do before he could forget about the MIT, the Super, and his misper case, at least for the night.

It was almost seven o'clock by the time he pulled up in front of the Bakhoum residence, two cars were parked in the driveway indicating hopefully that both the doctors were home from work. McManus walked wearily to the front door, trying hard to dredge up some enthusiasm to show the parents that the Police investigation into their son's disappearance was not over. He hoped his presence as a Detective Inspector on the case might reinforce that, and once inside, he explained that the case had been handed over to Cowdenbeath Police, based on the finding of their son's car in their area. He used the fact that no body had been found during the search of the flooded quarry as a positive, whilst trying not to give the parents any false hope.

Passing quickly over the facts, that there had been no calls received or made on Darius' cellphone since the night he disappeared, that there had been no bank activity during that same period, and that none of his friends or colleagues had received any contact from him, McManus tried to hold out hope that he might still be found. He asked to see Darius' bedroom, even though his team had already searched it, and also to have a general look round the house.

'Did my officers ask to see Darius' passport when they were here last?'

'I don't recall Inspector,' answered Mrs Bakhoum, 'is that important.' She shuffled on her feet, glancing at her husband, who instantly looked away.

'It was just a point on our check list for missing persons. It may have been an oversight, but that box on our form was left blank. Can you just show me his passport please? It's important to keep our paperwork in order. It's like searching under the beds when a child goes missing. We know they won't be there, but we have to check anyway. Can I see the passport, please?'

Mrs Bakhoum led the way back to the bedrooms, opening a door into a double bedroom at the rear of the house. 'This is Darius' room, he usually kept all his personal things in the bedside cabinet. I imagine his passport will be in here.' She pulled the top drawer open and rummaged about, apparently unsuccessfully, as she rammed it closed and opened the second drawer. 'It doesn't seem to be here, Inspector. Maybe he took it to Heather's house to be ready for their honeymoon.'

McManus wasn't satisfied however, and reached for the top drawer, pulling it fully out of the cabinet and dumping it upside down on the bed. Mrs Bakhoum looked horrified and moved to pull his arm away as he searched through the spilt contents. He shrugged her off and continued his sweep through the items. Doing the same with the second drawer he failed to find a passport, and began cramming all the things back into the two drawers, at the same time ignoring the mother's howls of indignation. 'This is outrageous, how dare you. I'm going to report you to your superiors.'

'That's ok, Mrs Bakhoum, at least I can complete the form now that we know the passport is missing.' Shoving the drawers back onto their runners he turned to face the angry woman. 'Are all your rooms as big as this one? It's a good size isn't it?' Without waiting for an invitation, McManus stepped out into the hallway and opened the next door along. The master bedroom was tidy, the bed was made, and the wardrobes and dressers were all closed. Mrs Bakhoum bustled into the room behind him, shouting angrily at him but McManus sidestepped her and went for the next door in the narrow corridor. This time the bedroom was occupied by a single hospital style bed, high sided with large wheels and a mechanism for adjusting the height and incline of the base. It was covered with pristine white sheets, a pale green woven blanket, and three large pillows at the head. A cabinet to the side held a large tray filled with bandages, tape, a box of latex gloves, and surgical masks. A strange smoky smell hung over the room despite the window being open into the evening air.

Mrs Bakhoum, evidently put out by this seeming intrusion, was quick to follow him into the room. 'A friend was living with us for a time while she recovered from an accident. The hospital said she was fit to go home, but she wasn't really. She came to stay with us till she got better, and I looked after her when I got home from work. She went back to her own house last week, didn't she Amun?' and she looked hopefully at her husband who stood ashen faced in the doorway.

'Yes, that's right. She made a great recovery and went home last week.'

McManus surveyed the room, but could see nothing to counter this explanation, nothing seemed out of place, but it would have been an excellent, and extremely private place to treat a burns victim. And where was that passport?

Chapter 31

The drive home was uneventful, taking only seven minutes at that time on a Thursday evening, and McManus considered stopping for a pint at the Adamson Hotel on the way past. It was only a short drive up the hill from there to his house and he felt he would be fine to drive after a single Guinness. He had stopped in there for almost as long as he had been in the Police and was impressed with what the new owners had done to the place when they took over some years before. He had stuff to do though and decided to give it a miss tonight.

He rued his decision moments later when he turned right into Knockhouse Road for the last uphill stretch to his home. Running along the pavement in the same direction was Joan Docherty, feet pounding the ground in designer running shoes. He noticed her backside first and found himself slowing down to stare as he drove past. The skin-tight black lycra running pants she wore left little to the imagination, and her breasts bounced only lightly in a tight pink sports bra top. She turned and caught him staring, a broad smile on her face, so he could only wave and drive on to hide his reddening face. He guessed she might take the short cut through the houses and get to his house before he did. That was the last thing he needed tonight, he thought, but she does look hot!

Sure enough, McManus had not even stepped out of the car onto his driveway when she jogged up towards him. 'I thought that was you, working late again?'

'This is relatively early for me, but things at work are a bit quiet. I've got a pile of stuff to get through tonight though. I didn't have you down for the running type, where's your dog tonight?'

'Is that going to be your opener from now on? Oh, I don´t need him anymore, he's at his real home, plus it's too dangerous for him to come running with me. I only decided to do this last week after my husband was sent down. After spending most of my life running after him and the kids, I thought I should do something for myself. And running just seemed the obvious choice. After you and me,…. well you know, last time we…….eh..met, I got to thinking about what I wanted from my life. So here I am, bought some running gear and decided to get back out into the world.'

'Good on you, Mrs Docherty. I have to say how well you look in your new gear, just don't overdo it will you?' Turning to close the car door, McManus felt her getting closer, could smell her sweat mixed with an expensive perfume, he could feel himself becoming aroused at the thought of inviting her in and peeling off her flimsy lycra layers. But he took a deep breath, adjusted his trousers, and turned to face her, finding her standing within touching distance, so that his elbow brushed her breasts as he stepped back from the car. 'I'm sorry Mrs Docherty, I'd love to invite you in for a cold drink, or something, but I really have a lot to do tonight.'

'Oh, come on Mark, you can call me Joan. Surely we know each other a bit better than using Mr and Mrs all the time. Anyway, I've something I want to show you.' And she reached to pluck her phone from the elastic strapping holding it to her upper arm. 'It's just an example of another thing I've decided to change in my life, something I've thought about ever since we first ….. em…, got together, so to speak.'

She swiped her phone screen several times and brought up a website, turning to stand beside McManus so they could both see. She rushed on breathlessly, the words tumbling out of her mouth as though she wanted to get all the words out before he could stop her. ¨You might think I'm being a bit naïve, or taking things too far too soon, but I found this website, and I'd really like to try some of the things that people seem to be doing on here, and my husband was never very adventurous, and I think it's time I explored some new things, and…. What do you think, would you maybe help me out to try some of this? I know I'd be safe with you.'

She pressed the screen one last time and brought up a personal profile of someone named '*Eager-Pupil'* on a website that he recognised immediately, Roughmeup.com.

'Maybe you'd like to come in after all, Joan'

Later that night he sat at the computer desk in his office, a neat and tidy space adapted from a spare bedroom at the back of the upper floor of his house. Several monitors were on at the same time but he concentrated mainly on the one open to Roughmeup.com. McManus had logged on using the ID and password he remembered from that last case in Pittenweem, and had already looked at profiles for *Spa-girl, Notverypc* and others he had visited during that case. *Spa-girl* had posted about having a very lucky night at the casino after running into an old friend. That one had made him chuckle. *Notverypc* was being regularly updated, and he read the posts with interest, noting the amount of activity in recent months. He looked forward to seeing the owner of that profile in the morning, but he would be sure not to let on that he had visited them online.

He had spent some time on the profile of Joan Docherty, carefully reading the content of *Eager-Pupil* to find out more about her sexual fantasies. She had been keen to experiment with some slave/master role plays when she agreed to have that cold drink he had offered, and he was eager to help with her exploration. To keep things simple he had re-enacted the scenario he had played out with Georgina Rutherford on the kitchen table the last time she had visited, complete with leather belt, sports socks, and fish slice. Joan had played the part of *Eager-Pupil* perfectly, and had stayed for almost two hours, before leaving much hotter and sweatier than she had been on arrival. She had stood naked in front of the hall mirror and examined the stripes on her buttocks with pride on her face, and McManus had assured her they would be gone by morning. This brought a small frown, but he changed that by pushing her to her knees in front of him, and opening his trousers once again he gave her a parting gift before sending her on her way.

Now he had work to do and he placed a call to Gregor Aitken after first checking his emails. 'How are you getting on with the checks on Hodges' bank account? Did you get a chance to check out his transactions after I phoned you last night?'

'I did, are you at your computer right now? I can email you some documents and we can talk through them; I think you'll find it very interesting.'

'Yes, I'm online, send them now and I'll have a look with you. Like I said last night, I saw him change a five-hundred-pound chip for what looked like ten thousand pounds in cash. It's unlikely he would deposit the cash in a bank, but I need to find something on him, find out where the money goes. Ok, I've got your email now, just opening the attachments.'

'Start on the first one, his bank statements for the last six months. You can see some basic things right there, his salary goes in every month, he pays his Council Tax monthly, there's the energy bill to Scottish Gas, his house insurance is on a monthly direct debit, as is the phone bill and the Sky TV contract. There are two payments each month to a life insurance company, and one to what looks like car insurance. Finally, every few months he makes a transfer of two or three thousand into a savings account with the same bank. That's document three that I sent you.

'I don't see anything unusual in any of that. What am I looking for?'

'That's the point, Mark. There is nothing unusual. But there are a lot of usual things that are missing as well. There are no debit card transactions, no payments to Asda or Tesco, no charges for petrol, nothing to any restaurants, DIY stores, no payments to credit cards, and no cash withdrawals at all. No cash from any ATM in six months is highly unlikely for most people.'

''So what are you saying, maybe his wife pays all those things on her account?'

'Not if you look at her statements, the second document I sent you. The only things on hers are a monthly subscription to a health club in Edinburgh, and a monthly transfer in of six hundred pounds from an investment company. You told me she likes the finer things, shopping, eating out, nice car, spa visits, holidays. Well, there is no sign of any payments to anything like that. You're the detective, work it out.'

'Ok, smartarse, I get it. The balance on his current account keeps going up every month when most people are the opposite. There's only one explanation then. It looks to me like they are living on cash, making cash payments for all the usual day to day stuff, petrol, groceries, shopping, eating out, all of that. But we know they are just back from a holiday in France and Spain. They must have booked ferry tickets or flights with a credit card, surely they couldn't pay things like that in cash?'

'Suppose it's possible if you book everything through a travel agent. They might be happy to accept cash payments.'

'Is it possible that they have other accounts with some other bank? Are there any withdrawals from the savings account? Don't they have a mortgage, like the rest of us?'

'No, the savings account gets deposits only, I've looked back for two years, and there are no withdrawals. The balance is standing at over forty-seven thousand pounds, so he must have been saving about a grand a month for the last four or five years. And we already know about the banks in France and Spain, but I can't find any other UK bank accounts. And no, there's no sign of a mortgage. I did a full credit check as well; they have no debts of any kind recorded anywhere.'

'I knew it. The bastard's bent. Taking backhanders from Paul Adams for information, must have been doing it for years to have that lifestyle with no obvious source of funds from the bank. Fuck! We slave away to make a decent living and that bastard just passes on confidential information and rakes in the cash.' McManus ran a hand through his hair in frustration at what he was hearing.

'There's more, Mark. You told me he drives a Jaguar SUV. Well I checked it out. It's a Jaguar F-Pace Sports, registered new in February this year, with no recorded credit against it. I don't know how, but it looks like he paid cash for it somehow. The showroom price on them is over fifty-seven thousand, and car dealers aren't supposed to accept that much in cash. But I guess he must have found a way.'

'I don't suppose you've anything we can actually use to nail this fucker?'

'Sorry, Mark. Maybe you can use the fact that he *doesn't* have all the usual transactions to show something is wrong. Other than that, you might just have to break into his house and find his cash in a wall safe behind a painting or something.'

'Aye right, Gregor, you've been watching too many movies. I'll have to think about all this, it's a lot to take in. Even if there is some evidence that would stand up, I've no idea who I would take it to.'

'That would be your problem then, I've done my bit. Give me a call if you need anything else.'

McManus did not sleep well that night. His mind was full of naked images of Joan Docherty, Georgina Rutherford, Gill Edwards, and Anne Morrison. As he fucked them one by one in his dreams, Detective Superintendent Nicholson stood there holding out a Police uniform on a hanger, and Chief Superintendent Hodges stood over them, playing with his Jaguar keyring and throwing hundred pound notes into the air. Hodges' wife Margaret watched on, from a sun lounger as the notes rained down on the naked writhing bodies, and when he looked up he saw Juan Kerr standing by the gate, swinging it to and fro causing it to squeak like a stuck pig. He woke up in a cold sweat, panting and with his shorts around his ankles. What did it all mean?

Screwing around and trying to nail Hodges was only going to lead him to a uniform job; he would be the stuck pig, minding a gate somewhere. In other words, he was totally fucked!

Chapter 32

A cup of tea and slice of toast had done little to energise McManus, and he pulled open the back door to Dunfermline Police Station with little enthusiasm. He was in a foul mood from lack of sleep, and his back hurt from his exertions at the kitchen table the night before, causing him to limp slightly along the corridor towards his office. Edwards arrived behind him and slowed her pace to match her boss, nodding a greeting in his direction.

'You ok, Mark, you don't look too well. Hurt your leg have you?' The sarcasm dripped from her voice, still hurting from being knocked back last night. She suspected he had been screwing someone else instead of her, and wasn't ready to overlook it just yet.

'Fuck off, Gill. Just get your arse in the squad room, tell the others we're meeting in five minutes.' and he stormed off to his office as fast as he could limp, leaving her staring at his back.

His whole team was gathered around the front of the room, sitting at their desks for those near the front of the room, or sitting on them with those who had stations towards the rear. 'This briefing is only in connection with the missing man, Darius Bakhoum, and the two suspicious deaths in Cowdenbeath yesterday. So I only need some of you, Liam, Ronnie, Bob, Gill, and Tom, you've all been involved at some stage, so the rest of you can get on with what you were doing.'

He waited while the team re-arranged themselves and then started again. 'We know that Darius went missing some time last Thursday night, after dropping his fiancée off at her flat about nine pm. His car was found in the flooded quarry on Sunday morning, but a search found no sign of a body. Darius is still missing. Anyone want to jump in here?'

Edwards was about to speak but thought better of it and sat back for a minute, thinking. McManus paced back and forth at the front of the room, his demeanour challenging anyone to argue. He hated repetition of case details every morning, but he was in a foul mood and determined to get to the bottom of the puzzles before him.

DS Robertson spoke up, 'Tom and I checked out his work and confirmed that he left there on Thursday evening with his fiancée, he's not been in contact since, and none of his colleagues have heard from him. I called there yesterday, and the answer is still the same. No sign of him. Ronnie was checking all his bank activity and phone records, what have you got for us, Ronnie?'

Gibson stood up and referred to his file, 'That's right, Liam. No cash withdrawals or credit card activity since he went missing last week. His last phone calls were on the day of his disappearance, lots of calls from his parents to that number, none were connected. Surprisingly, no calls were made to Darius' phone by his fiancée since that Thursday night.'

McManus knew what the answer would be, but he asked the question anyway. 'Why is that surprising Ronnie?'

'Well, her fiancé was missing, his car was found in a flooded quarry three days later, and she didn't pick up the phone to call him once during all that time. She has still not called his number since last Thursday. It's almost as if she knows where he is and doesn't need to call him. Even though his parents have been trying several times a day. But now even the calls from his parents have stopped.'

'Thanks Ronnie. Gill and I interviewed the fiancée and her friend, twice in fact, and they are still sticking to the story that they last saw him on the Thursday night, before they went to a party at the brother's house, for the whole weekend by the way!' McManus glared at Edwards, 'Anything to add, Gill?'

'We weren't convinced by their story, and think they are hiding something. They still had half full take-away cartons in the kitchen on the Monday when we saw them, the ones they ate on Thursday night, according to them. Why would they still have them in the house and not in the bin? We've no evidence but think that they know more than they are letting on. They seem scared of something, and that might be motivating them to lie to us. Now that Watson's two pals have been found dead they might be willing to tell us a bit more. I think it might be worthwhile going to speak to them again. I checked yesterday, and Rachel Taylor was back at her work, but Heather Watson is still off sick. Compassionate leave apparently.'

'I asked someone to visit the parents the other day, check on a few things, who did that?'

Fowler stuck his hand up, 'That was me, Boss. I went on Tuesday night on the way home. They are still distraught but have had no contact from Darius. I had a quick look in his room while I was there, everything looked very tidy, nothing out of place at all. I looked in the drawers in the bedside cabinet, checked through the papers that were there, mobile phone bill, a few odd credit card receipts for petrol, shopping, nothing out of the ordinary. I took a snap of the passport on my phone, to get all the details correctly, then put it back where I found it.'

'Good work Bob. Print out a copy for me so I can see the passport. What did you do after that?'

'SOP is to send details to the Border Agency: Gerry is the tech man for that kind of stuff, he did it the next morning and got email confirmation that the passport is on their watch list. Was that ok?'

'Sure Bob. The funny thing is though, I went to the parents' house last night to check a few things, and the passport was no longer in the bedside cabinet.' He looked out at the team but no-one spoke.

'Right, let's move on to the two DBs yesterday. I was the only one from our team who was allowed inside, and initially at least the ME is calling it an accidental overdose in each case. He will be doing both PMs this morning so we'll have to wait for the results before we can either proceed or stand down. Same for forensics, they only went in later in the afternoon. The house is leased by the council to Adam Watson, although he was not present at the scene until much later. The bodies were found by two teenagers who had been there the night before to buy drugs and then stayed to party a bit with the two deceased. They went back in the morning, apparently to collect some lost keys or something. Probably wanted to trade blowjobs for drugs again, but they found the two bodies instead. Gill and Bob interviewed the girls and found their story stacked up. They had nothing to do with the deaths, but I'm keeping an open mind for the moment. Gill and I then interviewed Watson. Tell us what you thought about that one, Gill.'

Edwards got to her feet and gave the team a summary of the interview. 'He's definitely dealing drugs from that house, but no-one had ever been able to pin anything on him. He's too small fry for the Drug Squad, but we called them in anyway. Hopefully with all the evidence collected by Forensics they'll be able to do him this time. But he was a bit flaky right from the off. He's scared of something, or someone, and he wouldn't tell us anything. Isn't that right, Boss?'

'That's fine, Gill. I have information that Watson has welched on a payment to his dealer in Edinburgh, that the dealer sent some boys round to frighten Watson, and that he went on a mad dash to try to sell some product. Probably why the two DBs were working on packing drug bags the night they died, getting a supply ready to sell, to get Watson out of the hole he was in with the Edinburgh gang. I can't prove any of this, but it could be that the dealers sent the heavies round again, and when the two pals couldn't give them the money, then they found themselves on the wrong end of a needle. Watson had been summoned to a meeting in Edinburgh by the dealer, maybe to be frightened a bit more to hear that his mates had been murdered. Anyway, that's all supposition till we get the PM reports and the forensics details.'

'Are you saying that this could be a double murder now?' piped up DS Robertson from his seat in the front row.

'Well, it could be, Liam, just like Darius Bakhoum could have been murdered as well. We just don't have any useful evidence.'

'But I thought the Super had binned our investigation, we spent all afternoon on Wednesday tidying up the misper file to hand over to Cowdenbeath.'

'You're right, Liam, we did hand it over, and the Super has told me to back off. But I still think there's more to this than a misper and a double OD.'

The briefing had not finished very satisfactorily and McManus sat in his office pondering his next steps. Only Edwards and him knew of the secret, illegal bug in the women's flat in Cowdenbeath. He knew it was still there, but he was unsure what to do next about it. Needing a breather, he decided to walk up to the Sheriff Court to try to catch the PF on her coffee break. He had found her in court on a case the last time he had tried, and he hoped for better luck this time.

Sitting across the desk from Michelle McAllister in the PF's office McManus enjoyed the hot coffee from the flask on the tray in front of him. 'I never know when court will break so I have my clerk put a flask out every morning, that way I have it ready whenever I get the chance of a quick cup,' the PF explained, 'and I never know when I might have to rush back again, of course.'

McManus nodded in agreement, wondering how to begin his enquiry. Jumping right in was best he thought. 'I have a case on my desk right now, where I think a woman was held captive by three men over a whole weekend, repeatedly beaten, raped and sodomized, but she denies that and won't co-operate with our investigation. Her friend was held along with her, but she was left alone. The victim refused to go to hospital, or to have a rape kit procedure, or to allow anyone to examine her injuries. Is there any way we can proceed with a case like this without a co-operating witness?'

'No.'

'No? is that it. That's your answer? Surely there's some way to move the case forward?'

'I'm afraid not Inspector. Without any supporting evidence there is no case to go forward with. You were here only a week or so ago, asking about the case of the rape of the University lecturer, remember. It was the same. The woman declined to give evidence, she was moving away to take up a new job, and the case was deserted as a result.'

'Yes, I remember it well. One of my detectives took it especially hard, she had put a lot of work into the case. So nothing we can do without the victim's support?'

'That's correct. It may not be right, or just, but that's the law. Now, is there anything else I can help you with, Inspector?'

'Please call me Mark, I'm sure we'll be visiting quite often now that the MIT has been moved to Dunfermline. I wanted to ask about the case you had in court on Wednesday, I stopped by for a few minutes and saw you presenting arguments to the Sheriff.'

'That one was quite interesting. It was about spousal privilege, particularly now that we have so many same sex marriages. But it was easy to deal with. The law used to say that one spouse could not be compelled to testify against the other spouse. The accused tried to claim this privilege when his husband was called to give evidence in an assault case. It was a nice try, but that law was changed over ten years ago in Scotland. The husband was called to give evidence and the accused was convicted. Job done!'

'Excellent, another one bites the dust, eh?'

'Exactly. My job is to prosecute within the law. It's a powerful weapon in the right hands.'

McManus thought of another kind of weapon that would be right at home in her hands and crossed his legs to hide his discomfort. "It looks like we might have some interesting discussions, if we had the time to sit and chat, Mrs McAllister. Maybe we could meet for a bite to eat after work one evening?'

That sounds interesting, Mark. Why don't you call me Michelle?' and she passed him her card with her phone numbers.

Chapter 33

Buoyed by his coffee with the PF, McManus detoured on the way back to the office, stopping in at Debenhams in the shopping centre. He usually bought his suits and shirts online, he had found two stores that sold exactly the right sizes for his tall slim frame, but he felt like treating himself today. He needed cheering up. In the men's department he wandered about the racks of suits, jackets, and trousers, pondering on something to lift his unusually dull mood. He spotted a mannequin wearing an open necked, button down lilac shirt under a navy suit, the shirt was in a soft luxurious fabric and cost twice as much as he would normally spend on a shirt. Looking around for an assistant to ask for help, he saw a man in his fifties busily tidying some shelves and McManus headed over in his direction. On the way he passed shelves of shirts, all neatly packaged and stacked in size order, and there were several shirts in the same style as that displayed on the mannequin. He picked the right sizes in two different colours, lilac, and a pale green, tucked them under his arm and headed for the fragrance sections at the front of the store. While browsing the displays of after shaves and colognes he could smell an amazing scent from nearby and traced it to a young woman working behind a nearby make up counter.

'That perfume you're wearing is absolutely fabulous, can you tell me what it is?'

She named the scent and pointed to a display on the counter next to hers, 'It's new, smells great doesn't it? Is it for someone special?'

Lost for words and dazzled by the brightness of the woman's smile he stuttered out a reply, 'Get a grip man', he thought to himself, 'she's barely out of school.' But he made a purchase of the new fragrance, found a new after shave for himself, paid for the shirts and left the store feeling like a new man. The backache was gone, and all thoughts of his terrible dreams the night before had vanished. The Super could stick his uniform up his arse, and the wee wanker better get some oil for his gate.

The duty roster showed that he was listed for dayshift again this weekend, even though his last weekend off had been ruined by a callout on the Sunday to the car in the quarry. He did the roster personally, so no one to blame but himself. So, no golf again, thought McManus, just as he was looking at the Scottish Golf Union website where it showed all the Gents Open competitions on that weekend. Scotscraig was on this Saturday, one of the oldest golf courses in the world, and one of his favourites, even though it was so close to St Andrews. A rap on his door brought him back to the present, and DS Robertson stuck his head round the door. 'Malcolm Brown was on the phone for you while you were out, can you call him back. It's about the two DBs from yesterday.'

The news from the Forensics Manager was not what he was hoping for. 'Definitely an overdose of heroin, from an examination of the syringe contents. Toxicology reports will be another few days, but it's pretty clear from my tests what was in the two syringes. I've got my forensics team´s most recent update as well, and I can confirm that the only fingerprints on the syringes belong to the two deceased men. One set on each syringe, just to be clear. It will have to be recorded as an accidental overdose, although technically I can't rule out suicide, but I think that's extremely unlikely. Neither man had any other injuries, there had been recent sexual activity, but I think you saw that for yourself, and I would say that neither had been a habitual heroin user, although there were some needle marks in various sites on both bodies.'

'So what you're really saying, Malcolm, is that this was not a murder, and although the circumstances could be considered suspicious, the evidence points to an accidental overdose in both cases. Is that what your report is going to say?'

'Exactly, Mark, I couldn't have put it more concisely myself. Just be happy that it's two less murders to record for you, and two more drug deaths for the First Minister to bleat on about, eh?'

'Fair enough, Malcolm. I still think there's more to it than that, but as the PF just said to me a couple of hours ago, we can't do anything without evidence. Is it ok if I contact the forensics lab direct, I've a few questions needing answers?'

'Sure Mark, go right ahead, as I said I don't have their full report here, just the summary I gave you. See you on the next one, hopefully not too soon.'

He made the call to the forensics lab in Dundee which handled all of his Divisions analysis, and he was put through to the appropriate evidence officer. The news was mixed, as he had anticipated. The scene had yielded numerous traces, with heroin, fentanyl, and traces of a Virtual Reality Drug, V251, being found on the coffee table, on the carpet, in the holdall under the table and in some of the kitchen cabinets. Fingerprints taken from the dead men matched many of those found at the scene, and some smaller fingerprints were believed to belong to the two teenage girls who had partied there on the Wednesday night. They would need to be matched up for elimination purposes. The dead men had been identified at the scene from driving licences and neither had a criminal record. Fingerprints from Adam Watson, who was in the criminal data base were also identified, but that was not significant given that he lived there. What was significant though, was that his prints were found on the bags of heroin and fentanyl found in the holdall, and in the kitchen. Total drugs haul from the scene was over two kilos of heroin and one kilo of fentanyl, the VRD collected weighed only six grams. Dozens of cans of baby milk formula were also found in the living room and kitchen. This was clear evidence that the house was being used to receive supplies of heroin, which was then cut with baby milk, and mixed with fentanyl before being bagged into smaller units then sold out again.

McManus was making hasty notes. 'I hope you're going to send me a copy of all of this.'

'Eh..., sorry Inspector, but Detective Superintendent Nicholson specifically said not to, the report's to go to Sgt Baillie at Cowdenbeath, with a copy to the Drug Squad at HQ. I understood it had been ruled accidental.'

'Fuck, surely you can email me a copy, no one will need to know. Come on, do me a favour here can't you?'

'Sorry sir, but it's more than my jobs worth, you know what your Super's like when he gets mad. He gave the instructions; you need to take it up with him I'm afraid.'

'So that's it, the drug dealing evidence goes to the Drug Squad, the forensics and PM report goes to uniform for an occurrence report on two sudden deaths, and I get nothing. Even though I suspect there's been a kidnapping, repeated rapes and beatings, at least one murder, possibly three, and I get fuck all!' McManus shouted down the phone at the poor LO.

'It's not my fault, don't fucking shout at me. And I haven't told you the best bit yet, it's in the report, but you didn't hear it from me, right?'

'Right, what is it, come on, spit it out man.'

'The fingerprints we took from the boot of the Audi recovered from the flooded quarry, well they're a match for the two dead men. Looks like it was your two DBs who pushed that car over the cliff.'

McManus burst out laughing. 'You might want to rephrase that before you put it in your report, or we'll be investigating some zombie apocalypse next.' and he slammed the phone down in unison with the crashing of his office door bursting inwards.

'I fucking told you to leave this case alone, it's Cowdenbeath's, not MIT. And while I'm on my way down here to speak to you about our little chat yesterday, I get a call in my car from Dundee telling me that you are on the phone chasing up PM and forensics reports for a case that isn't fucking yours.'

Detective Superintendent Nicholson slammed the door shut again as he rounded on McManus who sat stunned in his chair on the other side of the desk. He was not far enough away to avoid the spittle that flew from his boss's mouth as he continued his rant.

'You've been Inspector here for three months, the youngest ever to hold that job in any MIT in Scotland, ever. Yet here you are fucking around in something that doesn't belong to you. A case that you should never have been involved in, except as a favour to an overstretched uniform mob one weekend.'

McManus managed to stand up and lean over the desk, 'But Sir, it was you who asked me to do that, to look into this missing man. That led onto this drug dealer, then the two DBs, and now I find it's all connected……'

'I don't give a fuck, I told you to drop it so fucking drop it! Missing man…uniform job. Two overdosed druggies….. uniform job. Drug dealing…….Drug Squad job. Is there anywhere there that I mention MIT job, No!'

'But Sir, …..'

'Shut up and sit the fuck down before you get into more trouble, Inspector. Remember what I said yesterday, you are so close to being back in uniform, so close….. so sit down and listen up.'

McManus flopped back into his seat, there was nothing to be gained from arguing with the Super when he was in this kind of belligerent mood. There was no point, he had no proof of anything. He was damned sure he was not going back on the beat, he had come this far, and he would not go back. In this case it was better to run away and live to fight another day, so he sat back and said nothing about the fingerprints linking all the events together.

'Here's what you're going to do. Finish up whatever you have to do this afternoon, it's nearly four o'clock anyway, take the weekend off, in lieu of the one you missed out on last week, and report back on Monday morning. Hopefully, you can clear your head of all this nonsense by then, delegate what you have to DS Robertson, and go and enjoy your weekend. Am I clear? Don't make an enemy of me this early in your career, you won't get past me the same way you dealt with Rutherford. I'm not married and I'm not prone to falling down stairs, got it?'

'Yes Sir, I understand, Sir. Weekend off, sir. Clear head on Monday morning. I won't let you down, Sir.'

'Enough with the 'Sir' shit, Inspector, as long as we understand each other.' and with that the Super turned for the door and wrenched it open, marching along the corridor pointedly ignoring the heads which appeared from the adjacent MIT squad room.

Chapter 34

DC Edwards was the only one who dared approach the Inspector's door. She knocked lightly as she looked in and could see a hot flush spreading up her boss' neck and cheeks.

'Everything ok, Mark. Can I get you a cup of tea or something?'

'Oh sure, Gill. Everything's just peachy, and a cup of tea is exactly what I need right now…Not! I've just had my arse booted, again… not our investigation, turn it over to uniform, no evidence of a crime… What the fuck!'

'You didn't tell him about the bug, did you? No of course you didn't, you can't. But you and I both know that Watson and his two pals pushed Darius into the quarry, in his burning car. Then they imprisoned Heather and Rachel for a whole weekend while they raped and tortured Rachel, just to cover up what they had done to Darius. As to what happened to Bugsy and Gasser, we can both guess that one, it was Heather and Rachel, had to be. They had the motive didn't they. You surely don't think the dealer from Edinburgh sent some heavies over to kill them as warning to Watty? No, that doesn't add up.'

'Shut up for a minute Gill, will you? I need to think. I don´t need you to go over all the details again. I know you're just as frustrated as I am about this case, but give it a rest for a minute, will you?'

McManus took a deep breath, sat back in his chair, and linked his hands behind his head. 'It goes like this, I think. Watty and his mates set fire to Darius in his car and pushed him over the cliff into the quarry. Forensics told me today that they matched fingerprints from the boot lid to the two DBs in Watty's house. And we had it confirmed by Heather and Rachel on our bug. So that's the first *murder!* Then what you said about the girls held at Watty's house all weekend. That's kidnapping, rape and aggravated assault. We know Watty is dealing drugs, forensics have all the evidence now, and that all goes to the Drug Squad, so nothing for us there. But on Tuesday night I went round by the girls' flat and listened in on the bug. They were talking about paying back the bastards who killed Darius and raped Rachel. I heard them discussing it, maybe they followed through on that and stuck Bugsy and Gasser with the heroin OD.'

'But how would they know how to do that?'

'Really, Gill? Heather grew up in that house, she was around drugs all her life. All the stuff for shooting up was on the coffee table in the house. It would have been easy for them both to go there, flirt with the guys a bit, get them drunk, then stick them with their own drugs. Push the guys' hands onto the syringes to get their prints transferred. It would look accidental, which is exactly what the ME decided when he did the PM.'

'But how can we prove it, Mark?'

He sat forward again, hands open on the desk. 'I don't think we can, that's the frustrating bit. But here's the problem now. There's every chance Watty will be next. He murdered Darius just as sure as the two who pushed his car over the edge. But I don´t see what I can do about it. I've been told again to drop the case, and to take the weekend off.'

'That bastard deserves everything he gets if the two women go after him, fucking rapist. Leave them to it is what I say.'

'That's not the answer, Gill. But there's nothing more I can do, the case is now with Cowdenbeath, my job is on the line here, so I'm definitely taking the weekend off. If you decide you want to have an app on your phone that connects with an illegal listening device that's up to you. If you want to keep watch on Watty's house at night, then I can't stop you, can I? Now I need to step out for a minute, then I'm going to tidy up and go home.' McManus stood up and left the office leaving his mobile phone on the desk.

By the time he had left the office for the weekend, McManus had phoned Scotscraig Golf Club to get a cancellation entry into their Open the next day. He had also phoned Georgina Rutherford to explain that he had unexpectedly been given the weekend off, and arranged to take her out for dinner on Saturday night. He would pick her up in Leven and take her to the Lundin Links Hotel in the next village. He had even booked a room for the night, although more in hope than expectation. Feeling much better than he had a few hours ago, even though the bollocking from the Super had stung at the time, McManus found himself really looking forward to his days off. Deciding to start the weekend with a few beers, he drove straight home, left his car in the driveway, and walked down the shortcut to the Adamson Hotel. I wonder what route *Eager-Pupil* takes for her run, he thought to himself with a smile. But he pushed that aside, he had a lot more important things to think about, his entire future was at stake.

With a pint of Guinness in hand, he found a quiet corner in the back lounge and settled himself in. Where should he start? There were so many good things about his life and career, but so many things that he could change or improve, thoughts rushed through his head and he struggled for clarity. Remembering what his tutor at University always said, he went to the hotel reception in search of some blank paper, 'make a list of all the pluses, then all the minuses, add them up and make your decision.' Seated again at his corner table, he began with his job, quickly filling one side of his A4 sheet, plus points and minus points on either side of a dark line he had drawn down the centre. Without any further analysis he began on his private life, his women, his appearance, his home, and his finances, while his stout sat untouched on the table.

What was his purpose in life, in his career? Making more notes he was oblivious to the other drinkers at nearby tables, keeping his head down to ward off interruptions. He had to go back for more paper, before he could begin to write down some conclusions and action points, but he had reached some major decisions. His career was the most important thing in his life, after his family, but his father, mother and sister could not help him with his fundamental goal, catching crooks. Or more importantly, putting them away. He understood more than ever, from his recent encounters with his boss, that the Police service was a hierarchical organisation. Rank had its place, and while he did not agree with some of the structure, he knew he had to fit in, or get out. That was an easy decision, he could only make changes from within, so he had to fit in, shut up, accept orders, and do his job.

The pages for his finances and his home were quickly dealt with, without his father's support of a monthly allowance he could not afford the lifestyle he enjoyed, the nice house, the holidays, the golf trips. His relationship with his parents was ok but could be better. Having a millionaire for a father was a bonus that very few people had, so he resolved to make more of an effort with his parents, his sister, and his nephew and niece. His home was a great place but could do with a lick of paint here and there. One of the locals in the bar was a painter and decorator, that was an easy decision and could be enacted before he left the hotel tonight.

Only his appearance and his women were left now. He was not a vain person by nature, nor was he slovenly in his habits. He hated when detectives came to work in jeans and a t-shirt, and had elected from an early stage to wear a suit to work, or at least chinos and a jacket at worst. Ties were over-rated for police officers, so he wore one only when necessary for a big meeting, when his boss was expected, or for visits to HQ. Some of his suits were a bit past their best, so he would order some new ones when he got home. The two new shirts and the new after shave he had bought earlier were a good start to a new, smarter image. He tried to think of a role model for that but could only think of negatives like TV's Vera, and Columbo. He couldn't remember just how some of his father's favourites, Jim Taggart or Harry Bosch, dressed. He thought of the character DS Steve Arnott in Line Of Duty, he was always well turned out, suit, tie, shiny shoes, smart raincoat when required, and he was Scottish. If a DS could dress like that all the time, then surely he could as well. Maybe a waistcoat would be a nice touch, or was that fashion past its best?

That left his lifestyle, and women in particular. He had no plans for marriage, he believed that his job was too unpredictable to sustain a full-time relationship at this stage in his career. Besides, he like things just the way they were. Maybe he needed to re-asses the way he behaved with Gill Edwards. DC Edwards, Gill. DC Edwards or Gill; he weighed each name in his head. That was a difficult one, the workplace was a funny thing these days, harassment claims were never far away for inappropriate behaviour, but they shared secrets, and that bound them together. Ok, so she had to be kept close.

Georgie was an occasional thing, she lived forty minutes away, and they had lots of things in common. They both liked golf, she was married to a former DI so understood the demands of the job, they both enjoyed the same sexual experiences, she didn't want a regular relationship, even though she was in the process of divorcing her husband. He would keep up their friendship and sound her out about how she felt when they met for the dinner tomorrow night. The others, like Joan Docherty, and PC Morrison, well, they were new into his life, and could never come close to being called a relationship. Morrison was a one off, although she seemed friendly enough when he had seen her at the crime scene yesterday. Her husband was a plumber, often called out on emergencies, but she was much younger than the women he normally met up with. Maybe he could avoid getting tangled up there, especially when he was likely to visit her station from time to time. Yes, best left alone that one! But what about his recent encounters with *Spa-Girl*, Margaret Hodges, the wife of his ultimate boss. That could be dangerous in more ways than one. She obviously liked to play the same way McManus did, but would she be a help or a hindrance in his career. That left Mrs Docherty, she was keen, that was for sure, and had potential for a regular play date buddy. Her husband was in prison, that might not look so good if people at work found out about them, or his neighbours even. He'd have to play that one by ear. He had certainly enjoyed the few times they had got together, and she was hot!

McManus felt uplifted, enthused, and motivated, he would be a new man when he went back to work on Monday. Gathering his papers together he went to the bar to order another pint, and to ask the painter to pay him a visit.

Chapter 35

He had debated his choice of transport for the day, his golf clubs and trolley fit comfortably into either of his cars, but he had reasoned that Georgie might feel more comfortable in the Kuga. He expected she might be dressed up for their dinner out, and the higher seats in the Ford would be more elegant than sitting closer to the floor in the MX6. He was using the Mazda sports car less and less these days, the 1990's suspension was struggling more and more to cope with the increasing number of potholes in Scotland's roads. Was it still part of the new McManus that he had created last night, or should he make do with one car, something practical like his Ford SUV? He had been impressed by the Lexus that was involved in his last case, maybe it was time to trade up to a quality Hybrid SUV. Do his bit for the environment. Ford were about to launch a new model Kuga, with Hybrid options, and the main dealership was on his way to work, almost. Something to think about anyway. Then he could sell the Mazda, or not. Money was not a problem, he could buy whatever he wanted. A shiny new car, that might be another way to launch his new image on the world.

He pondered car choices all the way to Tayport, having driven up the M90 to Perth then along to Dundee before crossing back into Fife over the Tay Bridge. The short drive from the bridge, through Newport and along the high coastal road into Tayport afforded excellent views over the Tay Estuary and out to the North Sea. The car park at the golf club was busy, but he found a space and went into the clubhouse to check in for the competition, his tee time was one forty-seven pm, and he had ample time for a plate of soup and a bacon roll before he was due to start. He admired the plaque stating that Scotscraig was the 13th oldest golf club in the world before finding a seat in the lounge where he could watch the early starters coming up the 18th.

His game was a bit rusty and the scoring reflected that, he made it into the buffer zone after a fine finish but would not have to wait around for the prize presentations. No matter, he had enjoyed the walk, and was relatively pleased with his performance over the testing James Braid layout. He packed his clubs and trolley away in the car, picked up his sports bag and went to the locker rooms to shave, shower, and change for his dinner date. He had arranged to collect Georgie at her home at seven o'clock, it was about a forty-minute cross-country drive from Scotscraig, through the heart of Fife, and he had plenty of time to get spruced up. Driving down to Leven made him wish he had brought the Mazda, the roads were winding, with long sweeping curves, blind summits, and lots of low dips, and he would have enjoyed testing the car and himself on the challenging surfaces. But the Kuga sat much higher, allowing him to see across many of the bends that would have been blind to the MX6, and the comfort and road holding ability of the modern Ford suspension made the journey less tiring. As a result, when he pulled up at the house his trousers still held their crease, his shirt was not crumpled, and he was cool from the air conditioning. That clinched it for him, the Mazda had to go!

Georgina Rutherford was watching at the window, nervously looking for McManus to arrive, this would be the first time since she kicked her husband out that another man had come to pick her up. She was worried about the neighbours, what would they think? Would they tattle to her husband? She had only just started divorce proceedings, maybe she shouldn't be seeing other men just yet? 'Fuck it!' That prick had been cheating on her, lying to her, meeting gay men behind her back. She was well rid of him. He had lost his job, but she still had her bakery shop in town, that would give her enough to get by. They had no kids, no mortgage anymore, and she was damn sure she was not going to pay him a penny. She would fight for everything, the house, half his pension, half their investments, and she was bloody well going to enjoy herself tonight. McManus knew how to treat her, knew what she liked, and she secretly hoped he would take her away somewhere and fuck her till she couldn't walk. That would be good, if the neighbours saw her staggering in the door at three in the morning they would think she was only drunk! She saw him turn the corner into her street and draw up to the pavement at the foot of her drive. A quick look in the mirror at the door and she was ready.

McManus felt his pulse start to hammer when he saw her coming down the drive to meet him. Her blond shoulder length hair framed her face beautifully, and the large sunglasses shielded her eyes from the still bright sunshine. The long gypsy style multi coloured skirt billowed around her legs while the tight tank top fitted her perfectly, showing off a generous amount of cleavage. He was still staring when she pulled open the passenger door, hiked up her skirt and jumped up onto the seat. The yellow jacket and hand bag she had been carrying were casually tossed into the back, before she leaned over and kissed him full on the mouth. 'Fuck the neighbours, Mark, I'm just so pleased to see you again. I wasn't sure where we were going, I hope this is ok? she asked as she patted her skirt back into place.

Struggling to catch his breath, he stuck the car into gear, and as calmly as he could, got ready to drive away. 'You look great, Georgie, you always look great, and those sunglasses make you look twenty years younger.'

She didn't know quite how to take that, so slapped him on the thigh instead. 'Are you saying I look old?' and she burst out laughing, leaving her hand on his leg, squeezing gently. 'I'm only ten years older than you are, Mark, and you already know how much experience I've gathered in that time. But I feel like a new woman since Ian and I split up, and it has been a while since I've seen you.'

'I know Georgie, but that was all a bit messy back in May. It could have just as easily been *me* that lost my job, and Ian that kicked *you* out for fooling around. Are you sure you're doing the right thing; I could take you home again if you want?'

'No!, we're going out for dinner, two old friends together, we've a lot to catch up on, and I had my hair and nails done this afternoon. Not that you've noticed!'

'Sorry. Did I mention that you look great?'

'Hmmmm, you did, thanks. And did I say you smell good, is that a new after shave you're wearing?'

'Indeed it is, and I've got something nice for you too.' He handed her the gift-wrapped box, adjusted his seat belt and drove off.

The drive to Lundin Links was a short one and they turned into the Hotel entrance, taking a moment to find an empty space in the busy car park. Every time she went to play golf Georgie passed this Hotel, but she had not been inside it for years. It was one of those places that you drove past without thinking, because it was so close to her home. The fact that it was probably the closest bar or restaurant to her house never crossed her mind.

'I hope this is ok. It's possible that we might bump into some people we know, but I thought that would be better than going someplace in the middle of nowhere. Then it might look like we had something to hide.'

'It's perfectly fine, Mark. I've nothing to hide. I'm separated from Ian, and I have to start living my own life. Like I said before, I feel like a new woman, there's no reason I shouldn't be seen with a new man is there? Now, are we going to stand out in the car park all night, or are we going inside?'

The hostess showed them to a table in the window overlooking the magnificent links of Lundin Golf Club, with views further out to the Firth of Forth. There were more oil rigs to see than golfers at that time on a Saturday night. Their table had fresh flowers in the middle and the hostess lit a scented candle in a glass dish before leaving them with the menus. 'Trust you to get a table looking out over the links.' Georgie gazed out at the brown expanse of grass, burnt dry by the summer sun. The light was still good but shadows from the trees were lengthening as the sun dipped away to the west. She could smell his new aftershave and looked forward to experiencing it at close quarters. She played with her empty wine glass as she thought about the possibilities for later.

'Well, we're both golfers aren't we, and it gives us something to look at if we run out of things to say. I know things must be tough for you just now, you don't have to talk about it if you don't want to. We can enjoy a drink, a nice meal, and enjoy the view.'

'Thanks for being so thoughtful, Mark, but really, I'm over him now. Once I found out what he was up to, that was it. I know it must have been difficult for you to be the one that told me, but I made all those decisions for myself in the end. I told you, I feel much better for it now. I'm glad he's out of my life, I'm glad you told me. It would have been awful if everyone else knew except me, I couldn't stand that. You did me a huge favour, and I owe you big time. Especially for that night when he came charging round to your house in Elie.'

'You know he would have gone ballistic if he had found you that night, it's lucky it was only him that landed up in the hospital. And we all got something out of it. You got rid of a cheating husband, I got a promotion, and as for Ian, well, that was the beginning of his downfall, so to speak.'

The frown turned into a big grin as Georgie burst out laughing at that. 'Yes, you could say he got plastered and lost his job. Oh shit, I've spilled my wine, now. That's your fault for making me laugh so much. Can we change the subject now, please?'

McManus obliged by starting to describe his round that afternoon, hole by hole, shot by shot, but a sharp kick on his ankle stopped him mid-sentence. She laughed out loud again, pointing a finger across the table. 'That's not what I meant you arsehole! '

They enjoyed a delicious dinner, and the conversation flowed effortlessly, with laughs galore as they remembered their times together, all the way back to when they had first met. 'I had an economics essay to work on after the golf lessons, but you insisted on teaching me anatomy and biology instead, remember. I was young and innocent, and you made me fuck you all afternoon. I was just a boy; twenty I was then and you took advantage of me'

'It was only because of what I taught you that you were able to fuck me all afternoon, of course I took advantage of you. I was thirty, hardly ever saw my husband, you were young, and fit too, and available, and I have never regretted it for a single moment since. And I have to say, you've made good progress since.'

McManus saw his opening to change the tone of the conversation, 'Me neither, Georgie, not a single regret. But where do we go from here, what do you want from this, from what we are doing?'

'I don't know, Mark, I haven't thought that far ahead.' She looked out at the darkness beyond the window, trying hard to ignore his handsome profile reflected in the window. The candle wafted its scent over their table as other diners vacated their tables. 'I don't know what I want really. I've just got rid of one cheating bastard; I don't know that I want to have another man in my life on a permanent basis so soon. I mean, I enjoy what we do, the sex is brilliant, you know the games I like to play, I want to do everything I can to please you when we're together, but I want it for me too.' She ran out of words and just looked at McManus across the table, hoping he understood.

He didn't know what to say, he had hoped she would want to continue to see him, maybe on a more regular basis, but he had a job with irregular hours, she ran a business, they were both busy people, they lived nearly an hour apart. He laid his hand on the table, hoping she would respond, give him some clue what to do next. His mind mentally checked that he had a fresh box of condoms stored in the secret hollow under the floor mat on the floor of his car. Yes, check! He watched as she placed her hand in his, then looked into her eyes, 'I've booked a room upstairs, I didn't think you would want me coming back to your place.'

'You cheeky bastard, booked a room upstairs did you? Well you can stuff that idea.' She got up from the table, threw her wine over him, picked up her jacket and bag and stormed off towards the front door.

Taken aback, and wiping his face, McManus threw some notes on the table, apologised to the hostess as he nearly knocked her over, and ran after Georgie. He found her in the car park by his car, standing facing the front, laughing her head off. She reached under her full skirt and pulled her knickers down, waving them at him with a flourish. She leaned over towards the bonnet, pulled her skirt to her waist exposing her bare cheeks and turned her head to him. 'I'll tell you what I want from this. You can fuck me here, in this car park, or you can drive us down to the beach, somewhere a bit more private, and fuck me there. That's what I want from this.'

'I've a better idea, let's do both!'

Chapter 36

DC Edwards was also out late this Saturday night, but she was on her own. She had shared the app from McManus's phone the day before, and as she had done last night, she was parked in Muir Place, Cowdenbeath, listening in to the conversation between Heather Watson and Rachel Taylor. The listening bug attached to the table was still sending signals strongly, and she was able to park her Citroen C3 among the other cars on the street, but not too close to the house she was monitoring. No-one from the office knew she was here, but she was determined to find out what had happened to Darius, as well as Bugsy and Gasser. She didn't buy the accidental overdose findings any more than McManus had, she just hadn't made a song and dance about it. Instead she sat and listened, she made no notes, any kind of record could prove dangerous if the illegal surveillance ever came to light.

On the Friday night the two women had come home drunk, and began arguing about telling the Police that Watty had killed Darius. They had talked openly about Bugsy and Gasser overdosing, and considered doing the same thing to Watty. Edwards had paid more attention then. Were they seriously confessing to having killed the two druggies, it sure sounded like it, but all went quiet in the flat. The next thing she heard was the two women getting ready for bed, promising that they would never tell a soul what they had done. It sounded like the two women were becoming very close, intimate even, judging from the sounds that came from the phone speaker. She had been embarrassed listening to the couple and left once it was obvious they had fallen asleep.

Now tonight she fought the desperate need to sleep, and listened again as the two women were preparing to leave.

'It's two o'clock, time to go. Have you got the book?'

'Yes, I've got the book. Have you got the wire and the clippers from Watty´s shed?'

'They're in the bag with the gloves and the syringes. Stop worrying, it's all here. I got it all the other night. Now sort your hair, tie it up under your hat. We need to go; he should be fast asleep by now. We'll make sure that bastard will never rape another woman. After what he did to me, I'm looking forward to seeing the look in his eye as he goes over the edge.'

'Me too, Rachel. Darius would be proud of us.'

Edwards sat stunned in the front seat of her car, unable to believe what she had just heard. Were they seriously planning to kill Watson? She was unsure what to do, but her mind was made up when the two women appeared from the lane leading to their flat, got into Rachel's car and drove away. Turning her Citroen to follow them, she was shaking, she had not slept for eighteen hours, and struggled to steer her car in a straight line. Eventually the car in front of her pulled up and parked in the street one over from Watty's house. Edwards parked some way behind them and watched as they got out, each carrying one bag. They were dressed from head to foot in black, tracksuits most likely, she thought as she watched from a distance. The two black shapes walked calmly into the back court of a block of flats, vandals had broken most of the street lights and the area was dark. Edwards got out of her car once the shapes were out of sight, carefully looking around for signs of anyone else awake in any of the flats. A few lights shone from behind curtains, but no-one looked out.

The two women had effectively disappeared, blending closely with the darkness, but she saw a black shape passing across the outline of a white door, and realised they had reached Watson's back door. One shape bent over at the lock and the door was opened without hesitation; Heather must have kept a set of keys from when she had lived there, and both shapes entered the darkened kitchen. Edwards watched from her position at the rear of the flats as a dim light escaped from the window opposite, the living room light must have gone on, it was too dim to be the kitchen one. But there was nothing else to see. She stood unable to move, unsure what to do. Should she call it in? She couldn't, she was only there because of illegally obtained information. She wasn't even supposed to be on duty. McManus would suspend her at best, transfer her maybe, fire her more likely. She could claim it was his idea. No, that wouldn't work either, he was officially on a weekend off. She owed him. She had to follow this through. But what were they doing in there? She tried to move closer but a low fence was in the way. There must be a gap, the other two had gone straight through here. She waited, just a bit longer she told herself.

Edwards had no idea how much time had passed until she heard a car engine starting in the next street. It could have been any car, certainly not the one that Heather and Rachel had arrived in, it was behind her. Feeling her way along the fence she found the gap and walked into Watson's back garden, carefully passing the back door and around the end of the terraced house. She stopped at the front corner, her back to the wall, and listened again.

She heard a shuffling sound from the front of the house, to her left, and peered around the corner to see Heather half carrying and half dragging Watson down the garden path towards the street. He was unable to hold himself up, and Rachel came in the gate to help Heather manoeuvre him out onto the pavement and into the back seat of his Astra. That must have been the engine she heard starting, Watson's beat up old Astra, and she watched as Rachel got into the front and drove slowly and quietly away from the house.

She was in it right up to her neck now, she thought, as she ran back to the next street towards her own car. She couldn't afford to lose them now, not after what she had heard the night before. Several thoughts vied for her attention as she drove to the end of the street hoping to pick up the trail of the Astra. Had he OD'd and they were taking him to hospital? No, they would have called an ambulance, or just left him to die even. Had they drugged him and were taking him somewhere else to kill him? That was it, they would be going to the quarry. She rounded a corner and saw tail lights turning at a junction ahead. It could only be the Astra, she had seen no other cars about at that time of the morning and she speeded up, trying to close the gap. The car approached the track leading into the old quarry and stopped at the closed gate. She saw Heather get out and push the barrier aside, allowing Rachel to drive through, but she did not close it again before jumping back into the rear seat. The car drove on down the track as Edwards pondered her next move.

It was a classic case of good and evil perched on her shoulders, one said save him, the other said let the bastard die. Either way she shouldn't be here and the turmoil in her mind would not stop. Adam Watson was a rapist, a murderer, a kidnapper, a blackmailer, a drug dealer, and if he had done something like that to her she would have killed him herself. She remembered the last case in Pittenweem. He had been a rapist, a wife beater, a people smuggler, and a drug dealer, and he had deserved to die. This one was no different. She remembered the pain she had suffered, not being able to tell anyone what had happened to her. Rachel must be feeling the same. Rachel deserved her revenge, so Edwards reached her decision. It wasn´t easy and went against all her Police training. It was yet another decision she would have to live with for the rest of her life, but she took it anyway. She turned her car around and drove away.

Rachel pulled the Astra to a halt a few yards from the quarry's edge and turned to Heather in the back, 'Ready? This is it then and she stepped out of the car leaving the engine running.'

Heather also got out and together they pulled Watson from the rear seat and shoved him in behind the steering wheel. Rachel reached into the back and pulled out the black holdall they had brought with them. She took out the roll of wire and the old wire cutters they had remembered from the garden shed, the syringes, the spoon and lighter, the bags of heroin, fentanyl and VRD, and placed everything on the car bonnet. Heather prepared the VRD ready for injection and wrapped a rubber strap around Watson's upper arm, before injecting him with the drug. Watson's head immediately began to roll from side to side as he stared wide eyed at his surroundings.

'You killed my fiancé only weeks before his wedding. You left me without a husband. You destroyed two lives and you can't just walk away from that.

Watson was fully under the influence of the hallucinatory drug and as he looked around he could see nothing that made any sense to him. He was in a car, he could see that, but why was he here? Where exactly was he? He could see a face looking down at him. It was a woman's face. She was beautiful, her long hair fell over her black top. It was his sister. What was happening to him? What was she going to do? He couldn't speak, but his mouth gaped, and drool spilled from his mouth and over his shirt.

Rachel was preparing the wire and had walked some distance away to a sign supported by a steel pole cemented into the ground. The wire was wrapped around the pole, and she walked back to the car where she opened the rear window and threaded the wire through. Sitting in the back seat she looped the wire in a noose around his neck from behind, making sure there was enough slack in a short coil. It took three attempts with the ancient wire cutters to snip through the wire, as rust flaked from the old handles, but she finally cut through then took the excess and coiled it around her arm. Taking the cutters, she wiped the grips and metal handles before pressing them into position in Watson's own willing hands. Sure that his prints had been transferred as best as possible, she brushed more rust onto his hands. She carefully removed them from the car and took the cutters and wire coil back to the warning sign, where she dumped both bits of evidence in the long grass. She then went back to the car, and made up a heroin and fentanyl mixture which she melted on the spoon before drawing it up into the syringe. Finally she wiped the syringe clean with a cloth and passed it to Heather.

With her gloved hands Heather held the syringe out to Watson and stuck it into his arm once more, the plunger ready. Reaching over him she released the parking brake, pushed his left leg down onto the clutch pedal and made sure the gear lever was in first. The car jumped forward a foot and the engine stalled, Watson's head jerked down before he looked back up at his sister.

She adjusted his grip on the syringe and withdrew from the car, standing by the open driver's door. With a sharp tug she removed the head restraint from the driving seat and dropped it into the back footwell. A last look confirmed all the details. The keys were in the ignition, the parking brake was off, the gear lever was in first, the engine was stalled, the syringe was in his arm, his thumb was on the plunger, the headrest was off, the drugs bags, spoon, and lighter were now on the passenger seat. Perfect.

Rachel gave the signal. 'NOW!' Heather leaned over Watson and depressed his thumb on the plunger, watching coldly as his body jerked, his eyes rolled up into his head, and he died.

Rachel and Heather moved to the back of the car, showed each other their gloved hands, placed them on the boot lid and pushed as hard as they could. Rachel grunted in pain as she leaned over, but together they generated enough momentum to overcome the car´s gearbox and get the car over the edge.

The car rolled slowly, ever more slowly, towards the edge, and they watched as gravity complied to complete the final part of Watty's glorious suicide. They gave one final push to seal Watty´s fate. The car plunged into the inky blackness at the base of the cliff, almost disappearing under the dirty water before it came to rest with only the rear bumper in view. The women turned to each other and hugged, then turned to look at the car below. 'Guess he won´t be coming back from that anytime soon.'

They stuffed their black vinyl gloves into the holdall and strolled hand in hand towards the quarry entrance, remembering to close the gate on their way past. They walked all the way home like that, pausing only to drop the evidence into separate rubbish bins along the way. They could collect Rachel's car in the morning.

Chapter 37

The vibrations of the cellphone echoed against the worktop in the kitchen, making a barely audible rattling sound. It lasted for thirty seconds before it stopped. Ten seconds later it emitted a double rattle and fell silent. This happened three more times at one-minute intervals, before the intervals changed to five minutes, then stopped altogether as the phone fell from the worktop to crash onto the vinyl flooring beneath.
The sun flooded through the partly closed blinds and a shaft of light crept towards his eyes as the sun moved gradually in the sky. The light in his eye and the crash from the kitchen were enough of a combination of stimuli to wake McManus from his slumbers. He was enjoying his best sleep for weeks and was reluctant to open his eyes, but something had disturbed him. Throwing the covers back he slowly sat up, then pivoted to roll his legs over the edge of the bed, his feet searching for his rubber sandals he used instead of slippers. The clock showed it was already the afternoon as he stood up in his shorts and went in search of the noise.
He had dropped Georgie off at her house in the early hours of the morning, and had only got to his place and into bed about four. They had gone to the beach as she had demanded, and they had done everything she asked, until they both collapsed exhausted in the long grass of the sand dunes. They had talked as well, for hours it seemed, and had

made some decisions about the future of their friendship. They struggled to find a word to describe what they had together, relationship seemed too permanent, fuckbuddies too vulgar, friends with benefits too temporary. They finally agreed that there was no word suitable, so friends would have to suffice for now. They had arranged to meet again during the week for dinner, a picnic really, at a remote picnic spot in the hills outside Kennoway. Georgie was to bring the food from her bakery, McManus would supply the Irn Bru. They would need the extra energy.

The buzzing sound began again as he approached the kitchen door, and he watched the phone spinning and vibrating on the vinyl like a demented upturned cockroach. He picked it up and looked at the screen before deciding not to answer. The figures showed several missed calls and a number of voicemails. 'It's my fucking weekend off, can't you leave me alone?' he said to the phone, and he placed it back on the worktop and switched on the kettle. Clicking the remote for the small TV at the end of the breakfast bar, he searched the sports channels for any golf coverage while he waited for the water to boil for his tea. Feeling cool now, he ran back upstairs to find some clothes before he had his tea, but the phone buzzed again downstairs. He grabbed his discarded shirt from the night before, threw it on, and ran back into the kitchen in time to hear the final buzz before silence reigned again.

Most of the missed calls and voicemails were from DC Edwards, essentially asking him to call her as soon as possible, there was one missed call from Georgie, he would call her back later, but one of the calls and messages were from Superintendent Nicholson, asking him to call back immediately he got the message. 'He knows it's my weekend off, he fucking told me to take the time off.' It was an easy decision, he called Edwards first, forewarned is forearmed he thought.

'Thank God you've called, Mark. The shit's really hit the fan here, you need to get going right away.' She rambled on for a while before he interrupted.

'Gill, take a breath will you. Just calm down a minute. Start again. What the fuck's all the excitement about? It's my weekend off, you know that don't you? Now, slowly, what's all the fuss about?'

'It's Watty. They've found his car nose down in the same quarry. Two boys walking their dog again, this morning. Cowdenbeath uniforms are on it, but Liz Baillie phoned MIT out of courtesy once they checked the vehicle records. It's a white Astra, registered to Adam Watson. She thought we would want to know.'

'Why the panic, Gill? It's not our case anymore, the Super took us off it, remember. I've a missed call from him as well, is this what his call is about?'

'I don't know, Mark, but someone has to go out to the scene, and I need to speak to you before you do anything else, even before you phone the Super.'

'This better be good, Gill. I'm sitting here drinking my tea, I was out late last night and I'm just up. You better give me the story.'

'Not on the phone, Mark. We need to meet someplace, not the office. You have to trust me on this, it has to stay between us.'

It was thirty minutes before McManus pulled his Ford up next to Edward's Citroen in the Glen Bridge Car Park.

What kept you, I've been waiting for ages. I'm shitting bricks here waiting while you get all cleaned up and pretty.'

'Steady Gill, it's my weekend off, you got me out of bed, I took a shower, now I'm here. What's the problem?'

She told him.

'Oh fuck!'

The instruction from Superintendent Nicholson was simple. Go to the quarry in Cowdenbeath and assist Sgt Baillie with her investigation. This was not an MIT case, but a show of support for the uniforms, only because the car in the quarry belonged to a person connected to the recent disappearance of Darius Bakhoum, and the accidental deaths of the two men a few days earlier. 'Assistance, and advice only, Inspector. I want updates every two hours, I don't want you going off all cowboy on this. Am I clear?'

McManus had muttered his understanding and ended the call. He didn't feel like having the same argument with the Superintendent all over again. Turning to Edwards he asked, 'Does anyone else in the team know about this?'

'No, I was the only one in the room when Sgt Baillie phoned. Liam is out on enquiries with Tom, the rest were in the canteen on a break. I phoned you right away. What do you want me to do?'

'Drop your car at your flat, I'll follow you round and we'll drive out to the quarry in my car. I'll phone Liam and put him in the picture, he needs to know where you are, but it'll be better if it's just you and me that go out there. We can talk a bit more about this on the way.'

During the short drive to the quarry McManus kept his cool, he didn't shout and rant at Edwards although he really wanted to. She kept her head facing away from him, staring out the window, her body language made it clear she was not up for talking. He took several deep breaths, turned on the radio and concentrated on his driving. He would have to look like a man in control when he arrived to assist Sgt Baillie, she had no idea just what she was dealing with. There was every chance a dead body would be found in the car this time.

The entrance to the quarry was blocked by a Police patrol car, McManus did not recognise the officer at the wheel, but stepped up to the window and flashed his ID. His entry to the scene noted on the familiar clipboard, the officer reversed his car away to allow McManus to pass. He had half expected to see Kerr and Morrison there again this Sunday, but that would have been déjà vu all over again!

Sgt Baillie had heard their arrival, the gravel flying up from the Kuga wheels gave them away, and she approached the car as McManus and Edwards got out. 'Well Inspector, you seem to have developed a fondness for Cowdenbeath, we're seeing rather a lot of you and your team this week.'

'Happy to oblige, Sergeant, assistance is at hand as requested. So what have you got?'

'Why don't you come over and have a look for yourself?'

Looking over the edge of the quarry he could see the bumper of a white car just breaking through the surface of the water, but there was nothing on view to indicate the make or model. 'That's impossible, it's in exactly the same place as the one last weekend. There must be a rock or something sticking out, stopping it going right under. I know you've run the plate, what else have you done so far.'

'We've had time to do lots of things, Inspector. A car's been sent round to the registered address, you know it's Adam Watson's car I presume.' With a short nod he encouraged her to continue. 'There was no one home, one of my officers found the door unlocked and went in, found the house empty and has stood guard there since. Also, I've called out a tow truck, a crane and the dive team. We'll need the divers to go down and attach a tow line, the Health and Safety form is in my car if you want to see it.'

'No, we're only here to offer assistance, it's your show. Any other evidence, car tracks, footprints, CCTV cameras, witnesses?'

'The gravel at the edge is all disturbed, and even our prints are not clear. There are so many tyre tracks here it's hard to tell which set is which. The nearest camera is about a half mile away, and the only witnesses so far are the two young boys who spotted the car in the water while they were walking their dog. Seems like it's a regular thing for them on a Sunday now. Walk the dog, find a car in the quarry, get a lift home in a Police car.'

"Thanks Liz, I guess all we can do now is wait for the tow truck and the divers.'

The dive team had arrived, the tow truck had arrived, the crane had arrived and McManus was bored. There was nothing else to do, and the other officers present were waiting by the cliff edge to see the car being dragged up onto dry land. He mooched about around the quarry site, kicking rocks, and checking his phone, strolling in ever widening circles. DC Edwards paced at his side as they discussed the events of the night before. 'But what I don't understand Gill, is after you saw Rachel and Heather get Watty into the car, and drive up here, why did you turn around and drive away?' Why would you do that? You must have at least suspected that they were going to do something to him?'

'I had no idea what they were going to do to him.'

'But you said you were listening in to them all night, you heard them talking about getting revenge.'

'I'm not really sure what I heard now. They were upset, sure, angry even, but it could have been all talk. They could have brought him up here just to frighten the shit out of him. I knew the bug was illegal, we have no evidence about what happened to Rachel or Heather, how would I explain it if I came across them up here. I wasn't even supposed to be on duty. Not at that time in the morning. How was I going to explain that?'

McManus continued kicking stones, giving her a sharp look, 'Let's hope it never comes to anything that needs to be explained. I need to get that bug back though.' He stopped suddenly as his foot caught on something in the grass near the danger warning sign. Bending down to part the stems, he saw a loose coil of wire lying in a heap and a set of wire cutters next to it. He looked up again just as Sgt Baillie waved from the edge of the cliff, beckoning them over.

Edwards saw her too, 'Looks like they're ready to pull the car up.'

'Yeah, and I think I know what we're going to find.'

The crane driver worked the electric motor on the winch once the diver had given him the signal that its cable was hooked up to the car thirty feet below. They all stood back and watched as the white car slowly appeared from the water, first the boot lid came into view, then the roof, the front windscreen and finally the bonnet was partly out before the diver let out a loud cry. 'Stop! There's a body in there.'

The car hung suspended on the cable, still dangling its front end in the water. The Dive Team Sergeant shouted at the diver below to stay away from the car in case the cable broke, and he swam away to a safe distance.

Baillie and McManus conferred with the Dive Sergeant and the crane driver, and finally agreed it would be easier to recover the body if they brought the car to the top of the cliff, onto the flat surface where they huddled. The instruction given, the car was brought up the cliff face and deposited on its wheels on the flat gravel, well away from the cliff edge.

'It's your show Sergeant,' McManus said motioning Baillie forwards to the car, 'you can do the honours.'

She opened the driver's door allowing water to pour out onto the gravel, forming a large puddle at their feet. Some plastic bags, and bits of paper flowed out on the stream, coming to rest floating in the dirty water. Baillie seemed rooted to the spot as the headless corpse fell out of the open door, knocking into her and sending her flying to land on her arse in the puddle. She shrieked and pushed the body off her while she struggled to her feet, wiping her hands on her trousers. "Not my show any more Inspector, looks like there's been a murder!'

Chapter 38

The severed head had been found in the passenger footwell behind the driver's seat when McManus had wrenched open the back door. He knew what he would find and he fought hard to keep his face neutral. Sure enough, the front head restraint had been removed from the seat and dropped in the back, the rear window on that side was open and there was some thick blood spatter on the roof lining. McManus left the door open and stepped back, nearly tripping over Edwards, who was peering ashen faced over his shoulder.

'Never seen a headless body before, Gill? It's ok, it's a first time for me too. Come on, stop gawping. We've things to do.'

McManus wasted no time in getting his investigation underway, six hours had passed since the boys found the car in the quarry, but the patrol car at the foot of the track kept nosy parkers well back, and the scene remained relatively undisturbed. The forensics team had arrived within an hour, and had already been at work for thirty minutes now. A second team had been dispatched to Watson's home, and the ME was expected soon. DS Robertson had been called and tasked with searching and securing the house in Parkside Crescent, accompanied by DC Fraser, and the team back at the office were examining Watson's phone records. McManus also wanted them to obtain the records for Heather Watson and Rachel Taylor as soon as possible but did not explain why. Local ANPR cameras were also to be trawled for any sightings of Watson's car; based on what he had heard from Edwards there was no need but he wanted his team to collect all of the information that they would expect in a murder enquiry. The last thing remaining at that time was to notify the victim's sister, but he decided to wait. He wanted to do that himself, and to see her reaction at first hand, he would take Gill along for corroboration in case she blurted out a confession. Fat chance of that he thought, given the events related by Gill earlier.

Edwards had finally managed to get McManus away from the others and spoke in frightened whispers. 'How did you know?'

'Know what Gill?'

'The headless body, the head in the back, you knew before they even pulled the car out, didn't you? How?'

'I could tell you………….but it will be easier if I show you. You'll have to wait till we're finished here. I think the answer will be in Watty's house.'

'Come on, Mark, you're not going to go all 'Death in Paradise' on me are you. We both know who did this, I just want to know how you knew.'

'Patience, Gwasshopper.' he said in his best Mr Myagi accent.

'I'd say he's been dead about twelve hours, give or take. I can give you a more accurate TOD once I've conducted the PM, that's going to be tomorrow morning at the earliest. As for cause of death, did someone get a bit enthusiastic with the resuscitation? Looks like someone blew his head off!'

'Come on Doc, you can do better than that. What about drowning, did he get in over his head?' added McManus chuckling along with the ME. 'Can you give me anything here?' Once again, McManus knew what had happened but was playing along. 'Was the head removed here, or somewhere else? Are we looking for a particular type of weapon maybe? What can you tell from the syringe in his arm?'

'Whoa, Mark, one at a time please. I don't know, I don't know, and I don't know. Ask me again after the PM tomorrow.'

'I have to phone the Super, he's going to ask me all of that, I need to tell him something.'

'Rather you than me.' The ME shrugged and turned back to his examination of the corpse.

'I thought I told you to call me in two hours, what the fuck's going on with you, Inspector?' the Superintendent had yelled down the phone when McManus had finally made the call. McManus had explained the need to get the dive team in, to do Health and Safety checks, to get a crane and a tow truck, passing the blame as best he could. Then he had got to the bit about the headless corpse.

'It's definitely Adam Watson, Sir, the body was in the front seat, the head in the back, a needle sticking out of his left arm, and some drug evidence floating about inside the car. I would have to call it suspicious, Sir.'

The Super had exploded down the phone, '*Suspicious*, you have to call it *suspicious*, Inspector. What the fuck else could it be man? Your judgement this week is way off somehow. First you told me that the missing Egyptian had been murdered, but there was no body. Then you told me that the two DBs were murdered, even though the best Medical Examiner in the country ruled it an accidental overdose. Now you're telling me this headless corpse looks *suspicious.* Damn right it looks suspicious, it sounds like a murder maybe, not a fucking shaving accident, Inspector. Now get your team deployed on a full-scale homicide investigation and call me with an update every two hours.'

It was hard to get the effect of slamming the phone down with a cell phone, but McManus got the message. His ears rung and he was surprised at the latest outburst from his boss. He knew the investigation was already well under way, he had put all the correct steps into place earlier, but he couldn't get a word in to let his boss know that. He sometimes wondered if his boss really knew what he was doing. McManus thought he was the only one who had a handle on the situation. He was thoroughly pissed off and looked around for something to take it out on, but everyone looked to be hard at work. He lobbed a rock at the warning sign anyway, missing it by miles. But he remembered to tell the forensics team leader about the evidence in the long grass. Watty the Drug Dealer in the Quarry with the Wire Noose.

While the teams continued with their evidence gathering McManus went in search of food, he hadn't eaten since dinner the night before, and he had used up more than that intake in calories already today. He approached everyone at the scene with the same unsuccessful question, 'Got anything to eat?' until he spied the crane driver retching over a growing puddle of vomit at the side of his cab. He tried his luck again and the driver pointed to the interior where McManus found a full sandwich box, complete with chocolate biscuits and two bags of crisps. Holding a partly eaten sandwich towards the driver, McManus thanked him, spitting crumbs everywhere, but the driver was too busy counting his carrots.

It was after seven when the forensic team started to pack up their gear, and McManus approached Baillie who was sitting in a nearby patrol car. 'Looks like we're off now. I don't see any need to protect the scene any further, so you can relieve your officer at the gate. The forensics boys are ready to load the car onto their trailer, the body is on its way to the mortuary, the ME has gone, the crane and tow truck can go now as well, and I think that's us. Funny how things turn out, I only came out here to assist *you*, but it seems it all connects together into a case for MIT. The missing man, the car in the water here last weekend, the two DBs in Parkside Crescent, and now this. I thought Cowdenbeath was a nice quiet place?'

McManus and Edwards drew up outside the victim's house, where crime scene tape and a clipboard wielding officer blocked their entry. ID in hand, they completed the formalities and approached the front door, where a number of stepping plates showed the pathway into the house. A forensics technician was busy in the living room, photographing and bagging drugs evidence, while another was searching the upper floor. Almost every hard surface in the living room and kitchen was covered in black dust from the last visit earlier in the week. The technician looked up at McManus and Edwards, holding out an evidence bag. 'I was here for the other two, and none of this stuff was here that day. We cleared everything out on the last visit, so all this drug stuff, the bags, the powder, syringes, beer cans, they're all new.'

'Well that was only on Thursday, if you cleared it all out then, where's all this new stuff come from.'

'Jim's doing the kitchen, and he thought the sink seemed choked up, so he checked the u-bend and the pipes out to the back garden. They were full of water, nothing else, until he lifted the inspection cover out back. The space under it had been dug out to three times the normal size and was jammed full of plastic bags, full of drugs, syringes, and the smaller empty plastic bags. The scales were in there, and a bag of cash as well.'

'Ok, so why didn't you find all this on Thursday, clever clogs.'

'The ME said accidental OD, so the team leader said a simple run round the living room and kitchen would be enough. That's all we did. It's all in the report from Thursday.'

Leaving the technician to squirm, McManus scanned the room, knowing that what he was looking for would not be hard to find. He drew Edwards attention to the shelf under the coffee table. 'See that book there? That's the piece of evidence that will close this case for us. You'll notice the complete absence of fingerprint powder.'

She looked closer; he was right. No black powder. From the cover she could tell it was a crime novel, by some author she had never heard of, but the significance was lost on her.

'It's ok, I'll explain later once we've interviewed Heather and Rachel. Get an evidence bag for that book and bring it with you.'

'But won't the tech need to log it first?'

'We can worry about that later. I don't think this case will get to the stage where we need to present evidence anyway. Come on, we've one more visit to make tonight before we're done. I can phone the boss on the way.'

McManus pulled the car to a stop at the kerb in Muir Place, and looked up at the windows of number 6. There was light on even though it was still daylight outside, although there was no sign of any movement. Pressing the app on his phone, McManus listened in to the bug transmission from the flat above. All he could hear was the sound of a television playing, at least that was an indication that someone was at home. 'That sounded like a car outside, have a look will you?' Heather's voice came clearly through the phone speakers, and Edwards looked up from the passenger seat in time to see a figure at the flat window. The speakers came to life again.

'It's those two detectives again, Rachel. What are we going to do?'

'Calm down, girl. They've got nothing. Our clothes from last night were all washed this morning, even the undies and trainers went in the machine. Everything is dried and put away again. They won't find anything here, just keep calm and answer their questions. Don't say anything unless they ask a question, don't volunteer anything else, don't look at them, look at the TV instead.'

McManus looked at Edwards with a smug grin. 'They don't know what we know, do they? Officially we are just here to notify Heather of the death of her brother, nothing more. We have to be careful or we're both in the shit. As far as they are concerned we are treating it as a murder investigation and we expect to get more information tomorrow that will guide our enquiries. Keep a close eye on her reaction, she might just crack up and give the game away herself. And we have to get that bug back somehow.'

The two detectives sat on the chairs at the dining table by the window while the two women occupied the sofa opposite. Heather had burst into tears when she received the news about her brother's body being found in the quarry, and Rachel had immediately reached out to comfort her. There were the usual questions between the sobs, how?, who?, why?, but McManus had deflected them with the ongoing enquiries platitude.

Edwards sat on the chair, silently resolved not to be the one who made the tea for the grieving sister. She was amazed at the act being put on by both women. Deciding to keep quiet, she left the rest to McManus.

'This is not a good time, I know, but we have to ask you a few questions before we can go. When was the last time you saw your brother?'

'I've not seen him since last weekend, he dropped us off here on the Saturday morning. I didn't go to work this week after you found Darius' car in the quarry.'

Rachel pulled Heather closer to her, 'Do you really have to do this now detective? Her fiancée has disappeared, and now her brother is dead. I think she's been through enough for just now.'

'The first few hours of an investigation like this are vital. If there is anything you can tell us that might help, then we need to know it now. Was someone threatening your brother? Was he in some kind of trouble? Is this connected to the other two deaths, his two pals? Is there anything you can tell us about any of this?'

Heather continued to sob and cling to Rachel on the sofa. 'Just leave us alone. We don't know anything that can help you. He was up to his ears in drugs. It was only a matter of time before he killed himself, or someone else did it for him. Neither of us wanted anything to do with him and his two pals. Now can you please leave?'

McManus moved to put his notebook and pen into his jacket pocket but missed, and his pen tumbled to the floor under the dining table. Kneeling down with his back to the sofa he smoothly stroked the table, palming the bug from its hiding place on the way to picking up the pen, before slowly getting to his feet. 'Just one last question?' and he reached for the evidence bag still held by Edwards. 'Do either of you recognise this book?'

The two women looked at each other before Rachel replied. 'That's mine. I lent it to Watty when we went to the party last week. I got it from a charity shop. I knew he liked detective stories, and I was finished with it, so I took it round for him. Why?'

'I was just curious. We'll leave it at that for now, but we'll probably have to speak to you again. One more thing…..where were you last night, say, from ten o'clock onwards.'

'We were here, Detective, together all night. We didn't go out.'

'What are we going to do, and when are you going to tell me about this book?' Edwards asked as they drove back towards Dunfermline.

'Give me a chance to think about it a bit more,' and he pulled over to park outside the chip shop in Halbeath. Without a word he got out of the car and went round to the boot, rummaged about, and came back to the passenger side. Edwards let the window down as he approached, handing her a pair of latex gloves. 'I really need something to eat, what would you like?, and while I'm in there I suggest you read the first chapter in that book.'

When he returned with their orders, a haggis and chips for him and a fish supper for Edwards, he found her staring straight ahead out of the windscreen, the book open on her lap, mouth agape. 'That's how I knew. Now, is your flatmate likely to be home?'

'What? No, she's not home till after ten. But I don't think this is the right time to collect on your rain check do you?'

'No! that's not what I meant. We've a lot to talk about before the PM and forensics results come in tomorrow, preferably in private, and we might as well do it somewhere comfortable. Besides, we need to eat.'

They sat at the small table in the kitchen of Edwards' shared flat, the empty chip wrappers were in the bin, but the smell of vinegar still hung in the air. The sound of the key in the door made them realise they had sat there for over an hour discussing the case and their next steps. They had limited options; it would all depend on the ME and the findings of his post mortem examination. Of course, it would be up to McManus to run the details past the Superintendent, but he was confident of an acceptable outcome in the case. The door closed and PC Susan Rogers walked into the kitchen, still in her black uniform but with a civvy jacket on top. Edwards made the introductions and Rogers smiled and stuck out her hand for a shake. McManus stood, shook the offered hand, and went towards the door. He was sure he had seen a profile pic that could have been Rogers on a website just recently, but he was tired and wanted to get home. He was about to say goodnight when she beat him to it.

'You don't have to leave on my account Inspector. It usually takes me a while to wind down after my shift, we wouldn't want to see you rushing off like that for no reason, would we Gill?' Edwards smiled awkwardly and nodded at Rogers.

'Why don't you stay, Mark? I think you might find you and Susan have a lot in common.'

Rogers stood in the doorway watching McManus' reaction, hoping he would stay a while, but he looked from one woman to the other, then back again. 'Rain check?'

Chapter 39

First thing the next morning McManus had called his boss to bring him up to speed on the investigation, but with the PM and forensics reports not in yet, there was little new to add. He was pleased to hear that his boss seemed in a better mood. That would be important for the conversation he expected to have with him later in the day.

Now he stood at the whiteboard at the front of the MIT squad room and reviewed this on again off again case that had plagued them all for a week now. He had asked the civilian assistant Lynn to sit in and make careful notes to allow her to make an outline summary for him by lunchtime. He covered the main points as he ticked them off on the board.

'Darius Bakhoum is still missing. So, apparently, is his passport. Strange! His parents haven't pestered us for information since Monday at least. Anyone else heard from them at all? No-one spoke.' Also strange. They were climbing all over us at the quarry last Sunday when we found his car, now they are ignoring us. The behaviour of the fiancée seems a bit odd, no phone calls to Darius' phone since the weekend, no texts, no WhatsApp messages. Even more strange. It almost seems as if they know where he is. Anyone else have any opinions?' Again, no-one spoke.

'Forensics don't have much from his car; it was set alight, an accelerant was used, but the only sign of him was his shoe in the front footwell. All the main players were at a party at the fiancée's brother's house from Thursday night until Saturday afternoon. A neighbour heard noises, a woman screaming, loud music, banging, but all consistent with a loud party. Nothing much more to go on there. The Super instructed us to pass the misper case to Cowdenbeath. Case closed'

'Next, we have two dead bodies found in that same house on Thursday morning, lots of drugs, two teenage girls, a bit of a party, and two drugs overdoses. ME says accidental death, Super says he agrees. NFA by MIT he says, so we take no further action. Feel free to join in anytime here.' Silence.

They knew he wasn't happy and were determined to stay out of the firing line, literally. They had all heard, or heard about, the Super's rant at their boss in the office next door.

'So there we are, minding our own MIT business when lo and behold, another white car takes a nose dive into the quarry. Now I don't know much about Cowdenbeath, I know they still have stock car racing at Central Park on a weekend, but those cars usually have numbers on the side! What the fuck's going on out there. Anyone?' More silence. 'Lynn, make sure you write that down, no-one had anything else to add!'

He turned and waved again at the board, then back to his team. 'Gill and I get to the scene, a re-run of last week, tow truck, crane, dive team, health and safety assessments, no tea urn this time though. Uniforms at the gate, big Liz Baillie stomping around kicking up dust in her size twelves. God, that woman's got big feet! Anyhow, they pulled the car out of the water, Liz opens the door and the headless body lunges out at her, knocking her onto her arse in a puddle.' McManus paused for laughter, none.

'Lynn, make a note, at least I thought it was funny. I suppose you had to have been there!'

He continued to list the evidence recovered from the scene and taken away, either by him and Edwards or by the forensics team, deliberately avoiding any mention of the paperback book found at Watson's house. He had dropped it in his desk drawer when he got into the office that morning. He had picked up his own copy from his own collection and brought it into the office in a separate bag.

'Cause of death and time of death are unknown, at least until the PM results are in, but I suspect the severed head might have had something to do with it. Until then, we are treating this as a murder case and will take the appropriate actions. Any non-urgent current cases are to be set aside until further notice, and your assignments today are on here.' He lifted the cover sheet off the flipchart to reveal a list of names and tasks.

'Ronnie, you take Bob and Brian, go out to the quarry, and work back from there to Watson´s place in Parkside Crescent, house to house. See if anyone saw anything, anything at all on the Saturday night, especially this white Astra registered to Adam Watson. See if there was anyone, or any cars on the streets late on Saturday night or early Sunday morning. Whoever did this might have travelled to the quarry in the Astra, but they had to get back some other way. Find out who was out and about that night.'

'Liam, you and Tom speak to the neighbour in the house next door, Barry Jackson, he's a military man, he's been helpful before, he might have seen something. '

'Steve and Gerry, you're on the tech stuff, ANPR cameras, phone tracking, and calls between the victim and his sister or her pal, check them out. I know I asked you about this yesterday, but you've not had much time. Stick on it.'

'Gill, you stay in the office with me for now, depending on the PM report we might need to interview Rachel and Heather again. Right, get to it everybody, from now on briefings at nine and four every day till the case is closed. Lynn, can you get me those notes as soon as possible, please.'

Edwards followed him into his office after the briefing, 'What have I done now? Why am I stuck here in the office?' she huffed. He could see fatigue in her face but her eyes blazed in a warning.

He kept his voice low, almost a whisper. 'You know what you've done. Do I have to spell it out for you? You fucked up Gill. You had a fair idea what those two women were going to do to Watson, you'd been listening to them all night, getting themselves worked up to it. You followed them out to the quarry, then you walked away and let them get on with it! They murdered him, while you were standing at the gate! At least the two others, Bugsy, and Gasser, have been ruled accidental. Although I have my suspicions.'

'So what if Rachel and Heather pushed the plunger on those two, you said last night we've no *evidence*. He was a fucking rapist, they all were, Mark, they deserve everything they got.' She was getting mad now. 'What were the chances they would be charged on any of the things we both know happened at that party, over that whole weekend? None.'

' That's the whole point though Gill. We know what happened, but we can't tell anyone, we can't prove any of it. We've no *evidence*! But that didn´t mean you could just let them drag him off to the quarry and cut his fucking head off!'

'He fucking deserved to die! They all did! Filthy bastards, what good would it have done even if we did have evidence, if we did charge them and they went to court. Rachel was never going to stand up in the box and say what they did to her. They would get away with it. Another rapist beats the system. Just like the one who raped the lecturer. He walked didn't he? And what about the fat bastard who raped me, well,….he got exactly what he deserved. And I'd do it again without hesitation'. She stood there, exhausted, and out of breath, tears streaming down her mottled cheeks.

He stood up from the desk and leaned over towards her, a flush rising up his neck into his cheeks. 'I'm trying to protect you, you stupid woman. There's every chance this will all go away. But there's one other thing I didn't ask you last night, but I need to know now.'

She folded her arms over her chest and he knew he could not trust her answer as she looked past him out of the window. 'Where were you on Wednesday night, from eleven o'clock onwards.'

'What the fuck is this Mark? Are you serious? Do you really think I killed Bugsy and Gasser? Now you think *I'm* a murderer?'

'Just answer the question Gill.'

She collapsed into the visitor chair, hung her head and began to weep, 'I thought you were my friend, you were going to look out for me after Pittenweem, now you're asking me this. You know everything about me now Mark, you know my story, I confided in you. I trusted you.'

'So trust me now Gill. I can still make this right, but I need to know. Where were you on Wednesday night? Tell me the truth and this can all go away.'

'I was in bed with Susan, she came home off the backshift about ten thirty, we had a bottle of wine then went to bed.' She slumped even lower in the chair.

'And she'll confirm this will she?'

'I think so, … yes, I'm sure she will if *you* ask her, but it has to be you, please, Mark. I couldn't go anywhere; she had tied me to the headboard and I was still like that when we woke up in the morning.' She hid her face in her hands, trying to melt into the chair.

He tried hard to hide his amazement, but just as her blushes could not be overlooked, his open mouth gave him away.

Chapter 40

The morning dragged on as McManus tried to keep busy while he waited to hear from the ME. He could have gone to the PM in Dundee, but with the centralisation of forensics and medical services on the new campus there less and less officers were attending. Instead a dedicated technician from the forensics department handled the evidence requirements, from the point of the corpse's arrival at the facility until the time it was released to the family, keeping the chain of custody intact. Instead he checked reports and updates from his team on the minor cases they were handling on behalf on an overwhelmed Dunfermline CID. There was always one of them on holiday at some point. The parents of one of the DCs had a house in Spain and McManus was always trying to wangle an invitation. That might be just what he needed after this case. The summer was halfway through, and he had not even thought about a holiday yet. Would Georgie fancy a break somewhere warm, he wondered. Probably not, still too early after her marriage breakup. He made a mental note to call her later once her shop closed for the day.

He had called Superintendent Nicholson to tell him the actions he had taken at the morning briefing, somewhat surprised by the Super's better mood on the phone. He had promised to call again when the PM report was in. Meantime he wandered the corridors, thinking about the mess he and Edwards were in, trying to figure a way out. It was simple really, he just had to wait for the PM report, then convince the ME to change his mind.

Calls started to come in from his team out on the investigation in Cowdenbeath. DS Gibson and his two DCs had found nothing, no-one had seen Watson's car driving towards the quarry on the Saturday night or Sunday morning. Before returning to the office they were planning on widening their visits to households by going one street over in each direction away from Parkside Crescent. McManus considered this for a moment, 'No witnesses so far, Ronnie? Seems like a waste of time to continue then. Did you get an answer at every house?'

'Nearly all, it's a crap area, most people are unemployed or on the sick. I can come back later to catch up with the empties. I think Liam is still at the victim's house, I'll go down there, see if he needs any help.'

McManus had agreed, then gone back to this reports. When he next looked at his watch he was surprised to find it was after twelve, and he wandered along to the canteen for more coffee. He passed the time speaking to one of the traffic patrol teams who used Dunfermline for their meal breaks. 'You know I drive the metallic grey Kuga. The one up in the car park, right now, you know the one I mean don't you?'

'Yes, Inspector, we know the one. That's the one with the two bald tyres and the broken taillight?' The two traffic cops played their poker faces, but cracked quickly, sharing a grin.

'Aye, right, very funny. I just wanted to make sure you knew which was my car.'

'And you've still got the MX6 I hear, that's a great car. I bet it's pretty nippy on the motorway.'

'Not really, it always seems to top out at seventy!'

He turned at the sound of his name, as Lynn came over to tell him that Malcolm had phoned. He was going to video call again in five minutes.

Malcolm Brown´s face filled the laptop screen as he logged in from his office, his official title was Forensic Science Team Manager but as a qualified MD he handled a lot of cases and knew his stuff. McManus had only worked one case with him before, but he was beginning to like him. No-one else from his side sat in on the call, but off-screen Edwards sat in the corner opposite McManus, under threat of dire consequences to keep quiet. Malcolm began with his conclusion before giving more details from the PM report.

'Murder is the conclusion we draw from this, Mark. Someone cut the victim´s head off immediately prior to death, probably with a garotte and considerable force. The blood on the head lining inside the car shows he was still alive when he was beheaded. The syringe in the arm was used to deliver a substantial dose of a mix of heroin and fentanyl, we´ve tested that in the lab this morning, other toxicology results will be in here tomorrow. The drugs themselves would have been enough to kill him, but that was only contributory to the cause of death. I put the time of death as somewhere around three in the morning, give or take an hour or so, and the body had been in the water for twelve hours or so.'

'It must have taken someone really strong and determined to sever the head like that with a garotte. Did you examine the length of wire we found at the scene?'

'We did, and I can confirm that there were traces of the victim´s blood on the wire, specifically on the loop that probably was used like a noose around the neck. The wire cutters were a little more difficult due to the rust on the handles, but we did find a partial print there that matched the victim. Also, rust particles found in his clenched fist are likely to have come from the cutters, but tests are still to be done on that.'

'What about any prints from inside the car, on the handles, on the mirror, on the outside door handles?'

'No, sorry, the car had been submerged for too long, and no prints were recoverable from the vehicle. The drugs paraphernalia found in the car will likely prove to be consistent with the syringe contents and the drugs we might find in the body once the tox results are back. There were no usable prints on the syringe either before you ask.'

'Any other evidence from the car?'

'We did find that the keys were in the ignition, the ignition was on, the gear lever was in first, the brake was off, and find it likely that the driver had either stalled it or was sitting idling with a foot on the clutch and the brake pedal.'

'Can you think of any reason to support either of those conclusions?'

'Sorry, Inspector, but that's your job, you're the detective.'

'Well, I can think of one scenario that would fit with all of your evidence, Malcolm. What about suicide?'

'Highly unlikely, Mark.' Malcolm said on screen. 'What makes you think that?'

'He was under severe threats from a major gang lord in Edinburgh, he owed a substantial amount of money to him and had no way of paying it back in the time allowed. His two pals, his main drug salesmen, both died from an overdose during the week, he was being investigated by our Drug Squad for his dealing activities and was facing a lengthy jail sentence.'

'But there's no evidence to support that. It's clearly a homicide, Mark.'

'Don't take my word for it. I'm going to send you something, it's the first chapter of a book. I have a copy at home, I´d read it some time ago, but this case made me remember it. The same book was on the coffee table in the victim´s house when we searched it with your team yesterday.' McManus held up the book inside the evidence bag towards the camera. 'I've copied the relevant pages from my own book, and I'm going to email it to you now, read it and call me back in ten minutes. I think you might enjoy it!'

Once the call ended Edwards spoke up. 'He can't possibly think it's a murder once he reads that chapter.' She was calmer now, knowing that there was little more she could do.

'Let's hope so,' replied McManus as he leaned back in his chair now that the video call was over.

'I notice you made no mention of seeing the book in Heather and Rachel´s flat first.'

'Best not to go there yet. I told you I had your back, be patient.'

Fifteen minutes had elapsed and Malcolm Brown had not called back. McManus stared out of the window while Edwards picked at a ragged nail. He had no admissible evidence that would tie the women to any of the deaths in this case. Anyway, the two druggies had been dealt with, accidental overdose, and he wanted to leave that case untouched. He was fairly certain Heather and Rachel were responsible for that, but he had no proof. They certainly had motive, and opportunity, but he had no proof of either their motive, or their guilt. The listening device only transmitted in real time, and there was no recording of any of it. Not that he could use it if there were. He continued to watch the cars approach the roundabout on the road outside. The big question in his mind right now was Lexus or Jaguar. They both made great SUVs, and both could take his golf clubs and trolley.

The incoming call tone sounded from the laptop and McManus sat down again and pressed the cursor on the answer symbol. Malcom's face came into view as he settled himself in front of his camera.

'That is one catchy opening to a book, Mark. I could see how the ME in the story would have missed it. It certainly is not something I've ever come across before.'

'I'm glad you liked it, but have you found anything in the evidence in this case that might fit with my suicide theory.' McManus held his breath while he waited for the scientist's reply. He looked over at Edwards, who sat with her face in her hands, her fingers crossed as she rocked back and forward in her chair.

'There are many interesting similarities, that's true. The wire noose found in the long grass, especially noting that the other end was secured to the pole. Also the wire cutters were lying in the grass in the same spot. One might be led to believe that the victim, intent on killing himself, prepared the noose, tied the wire round the pole, cut off the excess, and had done all that while the car was parked next to the pole. Hence the evidence being left where we found it. But how did the noose cut off the head, then end up back at the pole again?'

'Well, the wire would stretch a bit as the car went over the cliff edge, then the tension in it would make it spring back in the direction of its fixed point.' suggested McManus trying to remain calm. 'That's why the head restraint was taken off the driver seat, to allow the head to be pulled backwards and severed without the wire getting tangled up in the restraint on the top of the seat. The rear driver side window would be left open for the same reason. To give the wire a straighter line of tension from the pole to the driver´s neck than would be possible if the wire was passed through the driver's window.'

'Yes, that fits with the evidence found at the scene. The rear window was down, while the driver window was closed. The blood spatter on the roof lining would have come about as soon as the neck arteries were severed. Any blood reaching the windscreen or dashboard would have been washed away while the car lay in the water. The severed head would have fallen backwards into the rear foot well as the wire sprung back out of the window. Hence the blood traces on the wire noose. The wire sprung back like an elastic band and finished in the grass behind the pole. I can see how it could all have been done. But it is all rather elaborate, isn't it?'

'Not if you´ve read that book and know that it might at first sight be ruled a murder. Maybe he wanted to throw suspicion on someone, like the gang lord who had threatened him. We knew about that from a confidential source, and Watson knew that I knew.'

'So, you're trying to establish that the victim did all that with the wire noose, then injected himself with the massive dose of drugs, while at the same time driving the car over the cliff to his death. Without anyone else being involved?'

'Sounds about right, Malcolm. It's exactly like the case in that book, identical even. You have to agree that it would be bloody difficult for someone else to cut off that head with a wire noose, with a cut as clean as the one I saw, with no obvious knife or saw marks. And no signs of a struggle, even though we agree he was alive at the time.'

'I'm leaning that way, but I want to speak to the ME and have another look at the body before we reach a final decision. It´s after three just now, I´ve another PM report call to make on another case, so give me until five and I´ll call you back. The call was ended and the screen went back to a picture of the 17th hole at TPC Sawgrass. McManus called his boss with an update and promised to call him back as soon as he had any more information. Edwards still sat in the corner with her fingers crossed.

DS Robertson and DS Gibson both called the office to speak to McManus that afternoon, both with nothing to report, no witnesses had seen anything useful in the area around the times relevant to Watson´s death. He recalled them and their teams to the office for a briefing to start around five. He had given them no instructions about witnesses in the vicinity of Muir Place around the same times, and none of them thought to mention it.

The two women's movements on Saturday night went unnoticed, except for DC Edwards, who had been observing them closely, up to a point. The neighbour at Number 8 had seen Edwards though, sitting in her Citroen on the quiet street for several hours. He had also seen his two neighbours drive off in their car, with the Citroen falling in behind them early on the Sunday morning. But he had taken two paracetamol and gone back to his bed, where he sweated out his flu bug for the next four days. By the time he had recovered he had forgotten what day it was, and had no recollection of the Citroen, or his neighbours early morning drive.

An elderly couple who lived in the flats behind Watson´s house in Parkside Crescent were enjoying a cup of tea in their kitchen, overlooking their back court. They had been amused for days by the comings and goings at the house across the back. They could see the next street through a gap between the houses opposite and had watched Police cars, Police vans, a black wagon and some white vans stopping. There had been men in white paper suits searching the back garden, digging in the drains, and poking in the garden shed, but that had been Wednesday, or was it Friday. They weren't sure. Every day was the same to them, except for the TV schedule.

'Should we call the Police and tell them about the two burglars we saw on Saturday night?' asked the old man.

'Don´t be daft, they weren´t burglars. Probably more druggies coming to buy stuff from that dealer that lives there,' said his wife.

'But they were all dressed in black and had a big black bag with them. They parked their car on our street then sneaked through the gardens to the back of that house. They must have been burglars.'

'There's nothing worth stealing round here. It´s what I said. Druggies. Now get the dishes done, Tipping Point´s on in a minute.'

No witnesses came forward to tell about the events of Saturday night into Sunday morning, and although Edwards knew most of the story, Rachel and Heather knew the full thing, and they had no plans to tell it any time soon. They were going about their business as best they could. Rachel had gone to work like a normal Monday morning, while Heather had stayed at home. She had called her work to let them know her brother had died the day before, and she would have to take more time off. Her manager had sounded sympathetic, but she knew he was bound to be a bit fed up with her absence. She couldn´t make a start to any funeral arrangements until the police released his body, which might be days yet. At least she could use some of the money she had liberated from Watty´s secret hiding place. The thousands of pounds in dirty notes were stuffed in an old bag of grass seed in the shed, next to the rusty wire cutters and the coils of old wire that he used to mend the fence from time to time. There should be enough left over to buy their flights after paying for the funeral.

Chapter 41

The video call from Forensics came in at ten to five as McManus sat looking at car websites. He closed his office door before answering the call, Malcolm Brown´s face appearing on his screen for the third time that afternoon.

Without preamble he launched into his findings. 'A second look at the body has made me think about this extremely hard. The flesh around the neck area, both on the body and on the head, is not what you would typically find in a severed head case. It would be quite an arduous, if not to say, gruesome, task to even contemplate cutting someone´s head off. Particularly while they were still alive. It would take someone with amazing fortitude to achieve this in the manner evident in this case. I say this because normally a saw or large knife would have to be used, or a power tool even, but we can rule out a power tool due to the locus. It is quite clear the victim died in the car, most likely at the scene, as it does appear that the body was naturally positioned in the driving seat. By that I mean not having been forced there by another person.

In addition, in most cases like this, a few tentative cuts would be visible, trial runs if you like, often because of the murderer being unsure, nervous, or inexperienced. However, in this case there is only one single cut, the cut made by the wire noose. Evidence supports this, the wire noose severed the head, no question. That leads us to consider the other evidence, of which there is truly little, all of which I described to you earlier. The huge overdose of drugs, we got a fast track tox screen result for heroin and fentanyl that confirms the dosage in his blood, and the noose secured to the pole would have combined to kill him. It's possible that he had enough awareness to release the clutch and apply the accelerator of the car sufficiently to drive it over the cliff before the effects of the drugs overtook him. The tightening wire as the car plunged into the water would certainly have had enough tension to sever the head cleanly, as the ME and I have seen on re-examination.'

McManus sat still in front of his screen, waiting for the hammer to drop. 'But……?'

'There are no buts, Mark. Having read your chapter of fiction, and taking into account the position of the head, the head restraint in the back seat, and the cleanliness of the cut, I am inclined to agree with you that this is indeed a suicide. It´s an unusual and very elaborate one, but a suicide nonetheless. But, before I write up my report, is there anything you want to add. You can relax, this call is not being recorded.'

'Nothing really, Malcolm. As soon as I saw the scene, then found that book in the victim's house, that's when I knew. We had no stand out suspects, we could have run around trying to pin this on drugs, you know, a fight over territory, or money, or supplies, but the most obvious answer is often the right one.'

'I agree, and I´ll write my official report accordingly. But first I need to get something straight. Last Sunday my team came down to your patch for a car in the water in a quarry, but no body, no murder, just a missing person. Then on Thursday we had two bodies, less than a mile away from the quarry, but ruled accidental overdose, not murder. Now we've had another body in a car in the same quarry, but ruled a suicide, again, not a murder. What exactly does your MIT do?'

'Very funny, Malcolm. It´s not you who has to explain all this to the Super, all the man hours and resources spent on three of *Cowdenbeath´s* DBs. Their budget must be well underspent, thanks to us!

'Not my problem, Mark. Thank goodness. Just one last thing, be sure to send that book up to us for fingerprinting, we don't want any loose ends now, do we?' and he ended the call.

The afternoon briefing began only a few minutes late, and the team gathered in their usual spots. The whiteboard showed details of the drug overdose cases from mid-week, and the notes from the Watson headless corpse case. McManus walked up to the board and faced his team.

'Good work this last week, everyone. I've just been on a call with Forensics, and we have a result.'

 He turned to the board, grabbed the dry duster, and wiped the board completely clean to the amazement of the stunned detectives. 'It's official. Watson was a suicide, nothing more for us to do. On my watch we've had one murder so far and we're one for one. This case is closed and we're still undefeated, so file all your notes with Lynn and take the rest of the day off.'

There were only a few grumbles as people looked at their watches, confirming it was already after five. 'Thanks Boss,' was the only comment he chose to hear.

'Gill, I have to phone the Super, then when I´m clear I need you to come and see me in my office.'

McManus took a moment to compose himself, he straightened his shirt and tucked it tighter into his trousers then picked his jacket from the hanger on the back of the door and put it on. He had an especially important call to make, his career depended on it, and Edwards´ career now depended on him having a future in the MIT.

'Malcolm Brown has just given me his findings on the case of the headless corpse in the quarry, he´ll give us his full written report some time tomorrow, but I know you would want to hear it today.' He steeled himself, ready to withstand the Super's icy comments, and stood straighter beside his desk. He had read somewhere once that making important phone calls was better done while standing, something to do with adrenaline, and the way the voice projected. He wasn't sure but he did it anyway. Looking at his notes from Lynn, and the conversation with Malcolm, he started with his main bullet points, building towards the conclusion. The super did not interrupt him once, which only made him worry and start to talk faster. When he got to the end, he paused for breath, still no sound from the other end of the call.

'Sir, sir, are you still there. Hello!'

'It´s ok, Mark. I´m still here, just thinking, that's all.'

Encouraged by the use of his first name, McManus jumped into the silence. 'I know it's a lot to take in, Sir, but it fits all the facts. All the evidence we have leans in that direction.'

'Right, let me get this straight. We agree about the missing person, the man whose car was found in the quarry last week. You handed that back to Cowdenbeath, right?'

'Yes sir, I took the file over there personally on Wednesday.'

'Then the two men found dead in the house the next day, Malcolm is writing that one up as an accidental overdose in each case, correct?

'That´s correct, Sir.' McManus was tempted to add some extra information but stopped himself. It looked like things were going his way so far. He stood rigid beside the desk, trying not to shake, feeling the powerful flow of adrenaline rushing through his body as he waited for the Superintendent to confirm his agreement.

'Then we come to the case of the headless corpse found in the submerged car yesterday, with the dive team, the crane, the tow truck and your team of detectives leading the investigation. You're telling me he cut off his own head then drove over the cliff.'

'Er.....not quite like that, sir. But yes that seems the most likely explanation, and Forensics agree. The official medical ruling is suicide.'

'Yes, I got that bit, Mark. That only leaves us with one problem.'

'I don't understand, Sir. I thought we were closing the case.'

'Yes, Mark, and well done on seeing it through. As far as MIT is concerned the case is closed. The only thing left to do now is figure out how to get Inspector Philp at Cowdenbeath to accept the contra charge for MIT assistance. I'm damned sure it's not going in our budget!'

Edwards had approached McManus´ door twice already, retreating once when she heard his conversation with the Superintendent was still going on, and the second time because she was so nervous she had to run to the toilet. By the third time it was almost six o'clock, so she decided to get two cups of coffee from the canteen and take them with her. He opened the door to the sound of the mugs clinking against it and she went in.

'Gill, we've only known each other for a few months but already it feels like we're holding hands and diving over a cliff, with no bottom. If we told anyone else the things we know about each other we would both lose our jobs, and probably go to prison.'

She said nothing, and drank her coffee, avoiding his gaze, waiting for him to continue.

'The Super bought our story and the evidence supports it; the case is closed. But that's not the end of it for us. What is it they say? 'Joined at the hip.' Well, that's us for so many reasons that I don't want to get into right now, but let's get a few things on the table.'

She spluttered her coffee, and blushed. They had shared some memorable moments *on the table.*

'No, that didn´t sound right, sorry. You know what I mean, we have to talk. I'm only thirty-four and a Detective Inspector after ten years in the job, my career is on the up. You´re thirty-nine and only recently made it to DC, after fourteen years out in the sticks, the last eight on a bike in Pittenweem.'

'That´s not fair. So maybe I'm a slow starter!' she bristled and leaned forward to bang her mug on the desk, splashing coffee over the surface.

He ignored the reaction. 'That's not what I mean. You're intelligent, motivated, and a woman in what is still a man's world. Now don't get shitty, it's not my fault it's like that. But if we stick together, keep our secrets, and look out for each other then we can both move up the ladder, together.'

'What, like, you scratch my back, I'll scratch yours. Is that it? I already come to yours every week for a Saturday night fuck. Don't get me wrong. I quite enjoy our little get togethers, but you're not making me into your own personal sex slave to keep me quiet. This is a two-way street, Mark.'

'It's not like that Gill. We have an arrangement; I think it works ok. I'm just saying we have to watch our backs, make sure we don't let anything slip about our last case, or these ones either.'

'Ok, I get it. I'm not complaining about anything, I like our Saturdays, I don´t need any complications in my life. I've left Pittenweem behind, Gregor was just a distraction, and I had no privacy in a little fishing village. Everyone knew everything about everyone else. I've still got to think about selling my flat there, but I'll wait a bit to see how I settle in Dunfermline.'

'It seems like you've settled in ok with PC Rogers.' He smiled knowingly, 'I'm still holding a rain check from the two of you, remember. Let me know when you've got a night free, one when you're not tied up.'

They both burst out laughing, the atmosphere changing instantly.

'Right, on that happy note, let's get out of here. The case is closed and we have to celebrate in our traditional manner.' He rose from his chair and moved towards the door.

'Wait a minute, the last time you fucked me on that picnic bench I had splinters in my arse for weeks. It's too far to drive up to Crail, Susan's working till ten, you can come to mine.'

Chapter 42 -- 5 weeks later

He sat still behind the wheel, looking out at the red Mazda MX6 sports coupe, wondering if he had made a mistake. PC Collins climbed out of the Mazda pulling his lunch bag from the passenger seat, and turned away towards the stairs down to the locker rooms. Collins' fractured jaw had healed well and he had gone back to work after four weeks off. He had thoroughly enjoyed kicking the shit out of that solicitor, and that had helped his recovery, but unfortunately his marriage remained broken. The purchase of the MX6 from McManus had been a sign to the world of his freedom after throwing his cheating wife out of their rented house. It looked as though he would take good care of the car, it´s bodywork shone like new, and the alloy wheels were spotless.

McManus sat for a few more minutes, savouring the smell of new leather, admiring the well-appointed interior of the Lexus NX F Sport with its ten-inch digital display screen. He had found the decision easy to make, especially after meeting an old golfing buddy of his father, who worked for Lexus in Edinburgh. Andy had put a great deal together for him, and he had gladly handed over the keys for his dull grey Kuga before driving away in his new bright Mesa Red SUV. Now, as he climbed reluctantly out of the car he spied DC Edwards waving to him from the staff door at the end of the top corridor.

Pulling his new suit jacket from the rear seat, he adjusted his tie, rubbed his hand over his new beard, ran his fingers over his fresh haircut, polished his shoes on the back of his trouser legs, and closed the doors. He was looking forward to his date with Georgie that night, they had agreed to meet once a fortnight to see how things went, and he was hoping she would like to try out his new car. Yes, he felt like a new man and he was ready for anything.

Edwards was excited about something and ushered him along the corridor towards the MIT squad room. 'You're never going to believe it. I couldn´t believe it myself when I heard, and especially on the same day. It can't be a coincidence.'

'What are you talking about Gill? I've just arrived and you're bending my ear already. What's going on?'

'That's what I'm trying to tell you. Gerry had an email in his inbox when he logged on this morning. Remember you told him to notify the Border Agency about Darius Bakhoum´s passport? He heard nothing back, so he had set an automatic follow up email to go out last week. They emailed back. Darius left the country two weeks after he was reported missing.'

'What? That doesn't make sense. Where could he have been for that time? Ah, wait a minute, his mum was a doctor wasn't she.'

'Right, right, but that's not the best bit. He boarded a package holiday flight to Egypt, and according to the BA he never came back into the country.'

'Ok, so his parents probably knew all along, which is why they never pestered us about finding him. He would have had some burns from the fire, his mum must have been treating him in their back bedroom, then got him out of the country. So what´s that got to do with us? He´s not missing anymore, but we passed it over to Cowdenbeath, remember.'

'That´s not the best bit. You've got visitors waiting in the public reception.'

They walked together down the main stairs and along the glass corridor towards the door to the public entrance. The lock on the door allowed access from their side only and was locked against anyone trying to enter from the public side. Pushing open the door, McManus led the way into the carpeted waiting area, where he immediately saw Heather Watson and Rachel Taylor sitting on the hard plastic chairs. They were holding hands and stood up as he and Edwards approached. McManus immediately noticed the nervous way the women were rubbing the shiny diamond rings on their wedding fingers. He also found it odd that they both wore white trouser suits.
'Well this is nice. Come to ask us to be bridesmaids or something?'
The two women looked at each other, unsure who would take the lead, until Rachel spoke up. 'We're here to let you know we're leaving. We're starting over, after everything we've been through we just had to get away. In an hour we´ll be married at the Registrar's Office, by tea time we'll be in Egypt with Darius.'
' What? You two are getting married?'
'Yeah, no more men for us, they…..' Heather gave Rachel a dig in the ribs, and took over.
'What she means is we are getting married. Then when we get to Egypt we'll meet up with Darius. His uncle is going to look after us, he´s loaded. We won´t ever have to work again. Darius is going to study to be a doctor. It´s going to be a whole new life for us. There´s nothing to keep us here anymore'
McManus rapped his knuckles on the window separating the reception from the control room, 'We´re done here, let us through!'

He waited till he heard the click of the lock being released, then hand on the door he turned to the two women, 'You're wasting your money getting married, that one doesn't work anymore. But then I don´t really give a fuck. It´s not my case!'

Thank You

Thank you for reading Not Very Lucky, the second book in the Mark McManus Murder Mystery Series. I hope you enjoyed it!

Posting a review will help other readers find my books. I appreciate every review, whether positive or negative, and if you have a second to spare a review will be genuinely appreciated. Please leave a review at the online store where you purchased this book.

About the Author

Alan Craig is retired and now spends most of his time in Spain, playing golf and reading and writing crime fiction. Born and raised in Fife, he spent some time as a Police Officer in the very area where this novel is set.

Connect with Alan Craig

On Twitter @AlanCraigAuthor

www.alancraigauthor.com

Other Books by Alan Craig

The Mark McManus Murder Mystery Series

Not Very PC

Short Stories from the Mark McManus Case Files

The Brazil Shirt
She was only twelve
The Shaky Lamp Post

Printed in Great Britain
by Amazon